Salem Mean Girls

SYLVIA PRINCE

Salem Mean Girls
© 2017 by Sylvia Prince
First edition

ISBN-13: 978-1548694715

ISBN-10: 1548694711

Visit the author's website at www.sylviaprincebooks.com.

This is a work of fiction. The characters, organizations, and events portrayed in this novel are either products of the author's imagination or are used fictionally. For more, see the Author's Note.

Cover design by BubbaShop

CONTENTS

ONE

Salem Village
Massachusetts Bay Colony

December, 1691

We moved to Salem Village because my parents wanted me to have a "normal teenage experience."

But Salem was anything but normal.

The first frost had already coated the fields in white when my family arrived on a ship from Virginia. Our wagon wheels squeaked and shuddered as we turned away from Salem Town and headed into the woods. Salem Town looked like an actual place—I grew up in London, so it wasn't quite a city to my eyes, but at least their buildings had more than one story.

The road that led away from the harbor was empty. It felt like we were slowly rolling away from civilization.

My dad insisted we'd love Salem Village. "It's great for farming!"

Note: he clearly doesn't know how to win over a teenage girl.

Why the Village? I kept asking my parents why we couldn't live in town.

The Village had a bad reputation, after all. The other passengers on the boat stopped talking when they learned we were moving to Salem Village. When my dad mentioned the Village, our ship's captain just blinked and changed the subject. Once we reached Salem Town, the carter who sold us the wagon chuckled when he heard we were going to the Village. "Watch out or you'll get sued!" he laughed.

I wasn't the only one who thought it was crazy to move to the Village.

Salem Village was apparently famous for its quarrels and petty disputes. My dad thought it was hilarious. As I shifted on the hard wagon seat, Dad told us about some fight over a minister. Apparently ministers were a big deal in the Village. The minister's enemies stopped paying him, and when the minister complained, they had him arrested.

Is that how my dad wanted me to deal with conflicts? I don't think so.

The road trailed on through a dense forest. I ignored my dad's sunny commentary about the strong wood and healthy venison. As if he knew anything about hunting. Finally, the wagon slowed to a stop in front of a house, its walls still bright and fresh from cutting. I had to admit that it looked nicer than I expected. A wide porch stood in front, and there was even a row of windows above the ground floor. I guess there were two story buildings in the Village after all.

And the house was at least a quarter mile from the nearest neighbor.

Maybe I could avoid the crazy Villagers.

"Isn't this perfect?" my father asked, staring up at the house. "And look at those fields." His gaze swept over the long, dead grass surrounding the house. Apparently no one had farmed here in a number of years. "I can't wait to get started."

"Wait. *You're* going to farm?" The words blurted out. Sure, my dad had been talking about farming since he uprooted us—*again*—to live in Salem. But he was a scholar, not a farmer. When we first moved to the English Colonies from London, he said it was to learn about the way of life and the people. He claimed to be writing a book about living in the colonies.

Why else would anyone leave the greatest city in the British Empire for this backwater?

I looked at the grass and hoped that he didn't expect me to help clear it out.

Dad didn't pick up on my mood. With a grin, he hopped from the wagon and started moving our various trunks and provisions onto the porch. "What can I say? I want to experience life like a colonist."

"And as your daughter, how should I *experience life like a colonist?*" If my dad had an entire philosophy designed around living like a native, I better figure out where I fit in his plan.

"Well, you'll attend the local school, of course," he said authoritatively. "It will be good for you. You haven't attended a regular school since we left London two years ago."

I slouched on the wagon seat. Everything in London was better than the Colonies, except the girls' preparatory academy that I attended back in England. It hadn't been the worst experience of my life, but it had been close. I shivered just remembering the vapid debates about marriage prospects and formal dances. The only preparation those girls undertook was for married life. And they acted like my interest in history and poetry was strange. While I buried my nose in books, they just wanted to study themselves in the mirror and dream about their future husbands.

When we moved to Virginia, my parents home schooled me. My dad had a degree from King's College, and my mom had read practically every book ever printed.

And I never had to talk to *them* about my future husband.

Mom had been quiet on the wagon ride from Salem Town, but now she reached out to touch my arm. "Let's try to fit in here. All of us have to make the adjustment together."

My stomach still rolled at the thought of attending school in Salem Village, but I nodded and jumped down from the wagon. I knew there was no point arguing with my parents. They had made up their minds, and I was along for the ride.

And maybe the girls in Salem would be different.

~ ~ ~

I was comfortably tucked in bed early the next morning when the silence was shattered by a deafening—and clearly animal—sound. I pulled the blankets over my head, but the racket continued. During a pause in the rooster's vocal warmups, I could hear my dad's excited voice through the wall. "We're really in the country now!"

Living in Salem Village was already getting old. And it was only our second day.

My dad's new obsession with nature was baffling. All three of us were more used to cities than the countryside, though back in London we did have a country house that we visited several times a year. It was idyllic. And there were no roosters.

I groaned and wondered again why my parents had chosen this backwater village. We had money. We could have lived in Boston or New York, or anywhere in Europe. I screwed my eyes shut and pictured Paris, the Seine, the bakeries.

But the rooster interrupted my fantasy, and I was rudely pulled back to Salem Village.

Maybe my parents were torturing me.

I heard a knock at my door and the creaking sound as it opened. "Are you awake, Cavie?"

Oh, I should probably explain my name. My parents are big fans of Margaret Cavendish, both her poetry and her philosophical works. They claimed a distant family relation as well, third cousins or some nonsense. So they named me after her, literally. Margaret Cavendish Lucas. They call me Cavie.

I know, it's not the greatest nickname.

"I'm awake," I told my mom as I swung my legs over the edge of the bed. A chill was drifting through the walls and it was still early December. I wondered how much worse things would get by February.

"Are you excited for your first day at the schoolhouse?" Mom asked. "It should be fun to meet some new friends."

My mom, the perpetual optimist. "Sure, I'm excited," I said, just to end the conversation. "But I need to get ready if I'm going to leave on time."

Mom nodded. "Come down when you're ready for breakfast." She pulled the door closed behind her.

I reached for my outfit—if you could call it that. Apparently black was all the rage in Salem Village. And aprons. When did aprons become popular? I awkwardly tied the white apron behind my back. I looked more like a baker than a student.

I sank back onto the bed and wished I could climb back in and pull the covers over my head. I missed my beautiful clothes from London. They came in colors besides black and white. But Dad said that it was important to fit in, particularly since we weren't Puritans.

I think he was hoping no one would notice.

But the clothes didn't transform me into a proper Puritan girl. I looked completely out of place in the ill-fitting black dress and crooked white apron.

I felt like a child playing dress up in someone else's clothes.

But I couldn't hide in my room forever.

When I walked down the narrow staircase, my dad clapped his hands together. "You look perfect," he said, gesturing that I should spin around. I ignored his signals. "But what about your hair?"

"My hair?" It was pinned back at my neck but the burnt auburn color was on full display. It was the only bit of color in my entire outfit.

"Girls here cover their heads," my father said, handing me a white bonnet. My eyes widened. "You want to fit in, right?"

My stomach clenched as I imagined walking into the schoolhouse where everyone had known each other since they were babies. I was tired of being the new kid. Making friends might come easy to some people, but not to me.

"I guess." I took a deep breath before I pulled the bonnet over my hair. At least you could still see some color peeking out the sides.

I really did want to fit in. I'd felt like an outsider my entire life. London was great, but I stood out like a sore thumb at the academy. In Paris and Virginia, I spent most of my time with my parents. I'd never had close friends, outside of the pages of a book. And those ones don't really count.

I tugged at the edge of the bonnet. I probably wouldn't make friends in Salem Village, either.

My nerves covered up a truth I'd rather keep hidden: I *wanted* to make friends. I didn't want to be miserable in Salem Village. So I'd wear a bonnet. And I would try to fit in.

After a breakfast of gruel—my dad was maybe trying *too* hard to fit in—I set off on the mile-long walk to the Salem Village school. I ignored the butterflies in my stomach and tried to enjoy the sights.

The trees had already dropped their leaves and the woods seemed to press in on the road from all sides. But as I drew closer to the Village, houses became more common than woods. I saw goodwives already putting out the laundry or tending to the animals. The women nodded to me as I passed and I nodded back. I also saw men hard at work chopping wood, tending to the fields, and in one case, repairing his roof.

I guess they weren't joking about the "idle hands" thing.

And I saw boys, too young yet for school, running and chasing each other. They were miniature versions of their fathers, down to the flat brimmed hats they wore. But something wasn't right. It took me a few minutes to realize what was strange about the boys. Even in their exuberance, the children were mostly silent.

I quickened my pace with a shiver.

Finally I saw the school. It didn't look much bigger than our house, but it somehow held all the Village's students.

There were two doors on the side of the building. The first led to a room for the younger students. I stepped toward the second door and tried to peek through the window. My dad said the upper room included everyone between thirteen and seventeen. Most of the students would be girls. By that age, Salem's boys had already joined their fathers to work on their farms, or if they were lucky they'd gone off to Salem Town or even Boston for an apprenticeship.

When I walked in the door, the low chatter of the students stopped and twenty pairs of eyes turned on me. They looked like perfect little Puritans, their spines stiff and their bonnets on straight, sitting in even rows.

I swallowed hard and looked for the teacher.

"You must be the new student," the school master said. I jumped at the nearness of his voice. He was standing at the front of the room, right next to me.

"Uh, yes," I responded, dipping my head slightly. Did Puritans bow? How did they treat teachers? I felt unsteady. I didn't want to make a bad first impression.

"Margaret Cavendish Lucas, is that right?" he said with a glance down at his desk. My dad must have sent a letter before our arrival to inform the school master of his new student.

"Yes, sir."

The room was silent. A shiver snaked up my back. My hands gripped the hem of my apron, even as I told myself to loosen them. I couldn't stop thinking about all those eyes watching me.

"My name is Mr. Green," the school master said. He paused, as if he expected a reply. My words caught in my throat, and when I said nothing, he continued. "You're sixteen, is that right?"

I nodded.

"Why don't you sit next to Joy Titus. She can show you how we do things here in Salem Village."

A tittering came from the back of the classroom at the name Joy Titus. I turned toward the sound and saw a row of girls in the back of the room. They sat next to the few older boys in class. One of the girls was leaning into the boy next to her, whispering something. Another gave me a withering look and shook her head.

It wasn't hard to figure out who they were. Every school had them. The girls everyone else wanted to be.

I bit my lip and nodded to Mr. Green. Had I already made a fool of myself in front of the popular girls? I lowered my head and followed Mr. Green's outstretched finger to the desk where Joy Titus sat.

Joy was wearing a black bonnet—the only one I saw in the classroom—and she sat alone on a two-person bench.

Why had the girls in the back row giggled at Joy? Did she have a bad reputation? She didn't look like a model Puritan based on her choice of bonnet. Then again, I didn't look like a model Puritan either.

"Hey," Joy whispered as I sat down. "Welcome to hell."

~ ~ ~

The day was filled with grammar, history, and arithmetic. I did pretty well, considering it was my first day. Mr. Green called on me three times, and I answered correctly each time. I guess the years of home schooling had served me well.

Next to me, Joy barely paid attention to Mr. Green's lessons. Instead, she kept tilting her head toward the back of the room at the popular girls. Joy would eavesdrop, and then shake her head while rolling her eyes. Her restless shifting made me sit even straighter on my side of the bench. It was like sitting next to a spooked horse. And Joy didn't even try to conceal her disgust. I clenched my jaw, waiting for Mr. Green to reprimand her, but he didn't say anything.

That's how my first week in Salem Village went. I walked back and forth to the schoolhouse alone. At school, I didn't talk to anyone except Mr. Green when he called on me. I stayed at my desk during lunch time, while the students filed out of the building to socialize.

I kept my bonnet tilted down so I didn't make eye contact with anyone.

And Joy ignored me—and our lessons—while she gave her full attention to the girls in the back row.

I had just started to wonder if I had turned invisible when, on Friday, Joy finally acknowledged my existence.

Out of nowhere, when class stopped for lunch, Joy grabbed my arm and led me a few steps away from everyone else. "I wish we could have tobacco at school," she said in a low voice.

I tripped over my tongue. My mouth was dry from so many days without talking. "Oh, I don't—" I started, and she cut me off.

"Of course you don't. No one in the Village is interesting." She rolled her eyes. I had quickly learned that was her favorite expression.

"Well, I'm new . . . as you know . . ." I trailed off, my neck tingling with embarrassment. Obviously she knew I'd just moved to Salem Village. What a dumb thing to say. I didn't want Joy to go back to ignoring me—she was the first person in the Village to speak to me. "So tell me about this place." My face felt hot. Clearly I was terrible at small talk.

Joy looked me over with an appreciating eye. I wondered what she saw. Could she tell how uncomfortable I felt in my Puritan costume? "Where did you move from, anyway?"

"Virginia Colony. And before that, London. And for six months, I lived in Paris."

She narrowed her eyes. I couldn't tell if my answer intrigued her or annoyed her. "I grew up in the Massachusetts Bay Colony. You're so lucky. I wish I could live someplace cool."

"Well I'm stuck here now, just like you." This was clearly the right answer. Her demeanor softened, and she put her arm through mine to lead me outside, where our classmates were eating lunch.

"Sorry I didn't talk to you sooner," Joy said. "We don't get a lot of new people here in the Village." We sat on a bench next to the schoolhouse. It was one of those rare days in December when the temperature outside was tolerable.

"That's okay."

But she wasn't listening. Her gaze had jumped to the popular girls, who were sitting on a low hill across the road from our bench. I was dying to ask why she paid so much attention to them, but I didn't want to upset her. Joy was my only friend in the Village. If I could even call her a friend.

I didn't want to go back to being invisible.

"Joy is such an interesting name—" I began.

"I hate it," she interrupted. "There's nothing *joyful* about Salem Village, and there's nothing joyful about me."

"Oh."

"I didn't mean to snap at you," she said with a sigh.

We fell silent for a minute. I searched for topics of conversation, but nothing came to me. Then Joy nudged my shoulder. Her mood had changed again.

"You're new, so I'll tell you what you need to know about this school," she said. "Those are the young kids." She pointed to a group of children playing what looked like some variation of hop scotch. "They go to the other room. You don't want to be seen with them. And over here are the military types—you know, hunting, trapping, shooting. Love their guns."

Those kids looked like miniature militiamen. As I watched, one hoisted a huge musket on his shoulder. They were allowed to bring *muskets* to school? I gulped.

"The nerds," she pointed behind us, through the window of the schoolhouse. "They only hang in the classroom because they aren't allowed to take books outside. Not after Prudence dropped one in a mud puddle. She ruined a copy of Tacitus."

My heart stopped at the thought of a destroyed book, but I kept my face blank.

"And there are the godly kids. You know, always praying, always judging?" They were sitting on the grass in what looked like a prayer circle. Yep, it was a prayer circle. "Don't talk to them unless you can quote every verse in the Bible, or they'll declare you a heathen."

I quickly shook my head. I already knew I wanted to avoid those kids. In just one week of living in Salem Village, I'd already overheard enough Bible quotes to fill, well, a Bible. The Villagers took the whole "City on a Hill" thing very seriously.

"And there—" Joy said, pointing to the popular girls over on the hill, "—those are the Glass Girls. You know, cold, expensive, fragile. And out of *our* reach. The cool clique. Everyone loves them. Everyone's afraid of them." Her voice dropped to a mutter. "They always know when the adults are around so they can act like good Puritans, but as soon as no one's looking, they break all the rules."

I tilted my head as I studied the Glass Girls. The three of them were laughing and looking at the boys standing a few feet away. Somehow, their black dresses fit better than everyone else's. Their bonnets were pure white, like fresh snow in the sunlight. I could practically see their teeth sparkling.

For a flash, I wondered how much I really wanted to fit in.

Joy's voice snapped me back. "That one there, the blonde staring at the grass? That's Mercy Lewis. She's one of the dumbest girls in the Village. Last year she interrupted the minister in the middle of a sermon to ask why her copy of the Bible didn't have the 'Middle Testament.' But no one says anything because her parents were killed by Indians."

I gasped, my hand flying to my mouth. I hadn't expected that kind of turn.

"And the brunette is Abigail Williams. Her uncle is the minister, and she makes sure everyone knows it. Abigail hears all the gossip in the Village. That's why her bonnet's so big. It's filled with secrets."

Joy's lip curled back as she pointed at the blonde sitting between Mercy and Abigail. "And the worst, the most evil girl in Salem—" I could hear the venom dripping from her voice. "Don't be fooled by her good Puritan act. She's the most conniving, devious girl you'll ever meet. That's Ann Putnam. Her dad owns a bunch of land and thinks she walks on water. Ann's the queen bee, the leader of the Glass Girls."

Joy clenched her jaw and shot daggers at Ann with her eyes. It was a pretty intense reaction. I almost expected Ann to flinch.

But she was too busy whispering something to Abigail.

"Do you . . . have some kind of history with them?" I was dying to know.

Joy snorted loudly. "You could say that. I used to be friends with Ann Putnam. But not anymore. Mercy and Abigail trail behind Ann now, as if she shits gold."

I couldn't imagine Joy being friends with the Glass Girls. I studied Ann. She laughed at something and shook her head, her cheeks rose-pink in the winter air. Then she pulled off her bonnet, unleashing a long blonde mane, even though good Puritan girls never took off their bonnets.

She was stunning. And clearly, she knew it.

She also had a sixth sense about when adults were around. In a flash, Ann tucked her hair under her bonnet right before Mr. Green walked out of the school to announce that lunch was over.

The Glass Girls stood and walked right toward us, Mercy and Abigail half a step behind Ann.

As they passed, Abigail stopped. She turned toward our bench and tilted her head to the side like a bird. She completely ignored Joy, but gave me a curious look, as though she had just noticed me.

"What was your name?" she asked.

"Um, I'm called Cavie," I replied. "Short for Cavendish?" My cheeks grew hot. Why did I turn into an imbecile whenever someone asked me a question?

"I'm Abigail. Abigail Williams." She was shorter than Ann, with a button nose, and her bonnet didn't quite hide her dark brown curls. "I'm sure you've heard of my uncle. Minister Parris?"

I shook my head. My father had said something about the minister, but under Abigail's icy gaze my mind went blank.

"Well, he's kind of a big deal," Abigail responded. "Anyway, you should eat lunch with us tomorrow. You can sit with us."

"Maybe."

Abigail frowned as if she smelled a rotting elk corpse. Apparently no one said 'maybe' to the Glass Girls. She made a noise that I could only describe as a huff and walked into the schoolhouse.

Next to me, Joy stifled a laugh behind her hand. "I can't believe you said 'maybe' to Abigail," she whispered. "And I can't believe they invited you to sit with them!"

But Mr. Green interrupted her revelry, pointing us back to our seats.

That afternoon, I sat at my desk wondering about the Glass Girls. What made them so popular? Why hadn't I accepted Abigail's offer?

If I really wanted to fit in, shouldn't I sit with the Glass Girls?

When school was out for the day Joy pulled my arm and led me away from the other students. "Did you see Abigail's face? She was about to spit nails!"

"Was it really that bad?" We walked away from the school, down the winding dirt road that led toward my family's house.

"They're the *Glass Girls*. The most popular girls in Salem. Everyone acts like they're famous." Joy laughed, a short cackling noise. "But you talked to Abigail like she didn't matter at all." It was the first time I'd seen Joy Titus smile. And then she grew even more animated, waving her arms around. "Wait. WAIT. I have an idea." She grabbed my arm and pulled me off the road, glancing over her shoulder. Before I could ask where she was taking me, we reached a small glen in the woods, only a hundred yards down the road from the schoolhouse. "You never know when people are watching," Joy explained.

"You think people are watching us?" The skin between my shoulder blades itched at the thought. I glanced around the empty glade. Was someone hiding in the trees? A squirrel bound out of the underbrush and I jumped.

"Puritans are the nosiest people in the world," she said, rolling her eyes. "Now listen. You should sit with the Glass Girls tomorrow."

I bit the inside of my lip. "Why?"

Joy grinned, her eyes sparkling. "Because. We can totally mess with Ann Putnam's life. We can find out all her secrets and use them against her."

I hesitated. I didn't care about the Glass Girls. I didn't even know them. Then again, Joy was my only friend so far in Salem Village. I didn't want to let her down.

Maybe it wouldn't hurt to have lunch with the Glass Girls.

"What do I have to do?"

"Let's start small. On Monday, just sit with the Glass Girls at lunch and try to act cool."

I plucked a piece of grass from the ground and spun it around my fingers. "What kinds of things do they think are cool?" For the last two years, I'd been home schooled. I spent more time with my parents than with other teenagers. And while Mom and Dad said I was a fantastic kid, that didn't make me cool. I had no idea how to impress the Glass Girls.

"You're new, you're mysterious," Joy blurted out. "You're *already* cool!"

I raised an eyebrow. If that was true, why was everyone in Salem Village except Joy ignoring me? "Okay, I'll try my best," I promised.

"And pay attention to what they talk about. Especially anything that might be embarrassing or a secret. We can meet here after school on Monday and you can tell me what they said." In spite of the chill in the air, Joy flung her body back into the grass and laughed. "This is going to be hilarious."

The frost from that morning had melted. I found myself

smiling, too.

I was about to become one of the cool girls in Salem Village.

TWO

I pushed open the heavy wooden door of our new house and found my mom knitting socks in front of the fire. Dad was probably out in the fields somewhere, playing the farmer. I wasn't sure he even knew how to farm. Wasn't it too late in the season to plant? Each night, frost made the grass sparkle as if it were coated in crystals.

But what did I know? I grew up in London, where we didn't grow our food, we bought it.

I rolled my eyes, imitating Joy's favorite gesture. It felt good. And it perfectly captured my mood. I probably knew as much about farming as my dad. He also grew up in a city, after all. Good thing the Lucas family had a fairly large estate to support us if the farming plan didn't work out.

"How was school today?" my mother asked, looking up from the socks.

"It was okay." My parents hadn't spent much time in the Village yet. And I didn't know how to explain the uncomfortable itching between my shoulder blades when I walked through the Village Square. I could practically feel the eyes following me, like I was on display.

With only six hundred Villagers, I couldn't exactly blend in. But I also couldn't say that to my mother.

"Did you learn anything new?" she asked, her knitting needled clicking together in the silence before I answered.

"Not really." I walked toward the stairs.

"Did you make any new friends?"

I stopped, my foot hovering over the bottom step. My mom was making an effort. But my limbs felt heavy. I didn't want to have a long chat about my day, I just wanted to change out of my weird Puritan clothes and pull the blankets over my head. Still . . . Mom was alone here, just like me.

"I might have made a friend." Was Joy my friend? She talked to me, and she didn't act like I had two heads. But she also seemed to hate Ann Putnam more than she cared about anything else.

Was I just a new weapon in her war against the Glass Girls?

"Well that's nice," my mom said, as she finished up one of the socks. "Change into your work clothes and you can help your father with the chores before supper."

I sighed. My glamorous life in Salem Village was off to a great start.

~ ~ ~

The next Monday was almost an exact replica of the previous one: I woke to cold air wafting through the walls (didn't anyone in the Village understand insulation?) and the loud crowing of our enthusiastic neighbor, the rooster. My mother's knock came only moments after the cursed rooster call. I struggled to swallow a bowl of flavorless gruel, and then set off on my long, lonely walk to school.

But everything changed once I reached the schoolhouse.

Instead of an awkward conversation with Mr. Green while all the upper level students stared at me, I quickly walked to my desk but stopped before I sat. Something pushed me past Joy, all the way to the back row, where Abigail sat by herself.

"Hey," I said.

Her face barely tilted up, a tight smile on her lips. "Oh." She looked toward the door and then back to her book.

I could feel my cheeks burning. Abigail had just invited me to lunch a few days earlier. Had I ruined everything already? I slid into my seat next to Joy, ready to bury my nose in a book about the Punic Wars.

I tried not to think about the Glass Girls but I found myself sneaking glances at them. They barely paid attention to Mr. Green's lesson. He didn't seem to notice.

Finally, it was lunch time. Joy stared at me with a raised eyebrow. I knew she wanted me to go sit with the Glass Girls, but Abigail's coldness left my stomach tied in knots. Instead of walking to the grassy hill, I turned back into the schoolhouse and ate at my desk.

All afternoon, Joy shot angry looks at me. When school ended, she cornered me and wouldn't let up until I promised to sit with the Glass Girls the next day. I hurried home alone, afraid I had already lost my only friend.

On Tuesday, I steeled myself to talk to the Glass Girls. But when Mr. Green dismissed us for lunch, I froze in the doorway of the schoolhouse. Abigail, Ann, and Mercy were already sitting on their hill, pulling things out of their lunch pails.

I took a deep breath and forced myself forward.

"Hello," I said, trying to sound friendly and cool at the same time, and probably failing miserably.

Ann narrowed her green eyes at me. "Oh, you're the new girl, right? Cady?"

"It's Cavie," I said. "And yeah, I just moved here."

"Where did you move from?" Mercy asked, twirling a lock of loose hair around her finger.

"I'm from London, but we lived in Virginia for two years before we came here."

"Oooh, Virginia," Mercy said. "Did you see any lions?"

Before I could come up with a response, Ann broke in. "Don't be stupid, Mercy. Tell us about London, Cavie. Was it fabulous?"

"Um, I guess so. Have you been?"

Abigail broke in, her chirpy voice like a bird's. "No, Ann's never been to London. I mean, none of us has. It's just a long way, you know? We all grew up here in the colony."

"I'm planning to go to London," Ann said, her eyes flashing at Abigail. "My father said I can go after I get married. And maybe I'll take Cavie with me."

Abigail's chin trembled.

I burrowed my hands under my apron awkwardly. "I would love to go back to London."

Ann looked me over. "Come sit next to me, Cavie. We can talk about London." She patted the grass next to her and waved at Abigail to scoot over. For a moment, Abigail sat frozen in place, her eyes wide. And then she moved.

I sat. Ann started peppering me with questions about London, what people wore, if I'd ever seen Queen Mary. Mercy broke in every once in a while to ask about Virginia, which she clearly had confused with someplace more interesting. I hadn't liked living there—it was a swampy backwoods town with no interesting people, although after living in Salem Village, Virginia didn't look so bad.

"Wait." Ann raised her eyebrows until they practically brushed the top of her bonnet. "So you've never been in a schoolhouse before?"

Was that weird? "No. I went to a preparatory academy in

London for a few years, and in Virginia my parents home schooled me."

"Then you've never been to a *real* school," Ann exclaimed.

"I guess not?" I shifted my weight.

Abigail gave me a withering smile. "It's not that difficult," she said in her clipped voice. "I'm sure you'll fit in." Abigail had been grinding her teeth and shooting glances at Ann ever since I took her spot.

"I just can't believe you haven't been to a real school," Ann repeated for the third time. "And you're so comely!"

My mouth fell open before I could stop myself. "Thanks?" I didn't mean it to come out like a question.

"So you agree. That you're pretty."

I blinked and bit my lip. Before I could figure out how to respond, Ann changed the subject.

"I'm sure you'll fit in fine here, Cavie."

I shrugged my shoulders. "I figure if I just pay attention and keep up with the reading I should be okay."

"Oh, Cavie." Ann shook her head. "School's not about the reading." Her tone said she was teaching me a valuable lesson. "School is the most important place in the Village to make your reputation, to see people and be seen. To establish your credentials."

I had a sudden flashback to the girls at the London preparatory academy who only cared about their future husbands. Had I found their duplicates in a backwoods Puritan village?

Ann looked over my clothes and shook her head. "Speaking of appearances, you really should go shopping. It's obvious that your dress doesn't fit."

My eyes widened as I looked down at my dress. It was exactly the same as what every other girl wore. Maybe it was a little baggy? Was the white apron crooked? I glanced back at

Ann. She somehow did look better than everyone else, even in her identical Puritan uniform.

"You can come shopping with us after school tomorrow," Ann declared. "My father said we could take the wagon to Salem Town. The Town has all the best shops."

Mercy clapped her hands together with excitement and practically squealed.

Abigail leaned across me and whispered to Ann. "But I thought you were going to help me buy a new dress."

"Abigail, we need to make Cavie feel welcome," Ann scolded. Abigail frowned and dropped her eyes to the ground. Ann turned her attention back to me. "Cavie, I love your bracelet."

I looked down at my wrist. It was just a simple leather band, nothing special. My dad had given it to me when we moved to the colonies. "Thanks."

Lunch was nearly over, but before we went back inside Mercy turned to me. "On Wednesdays we wear pink bonnets," she said with a glassy grin. And then they vanished into the schoolhouse.

My knees felt weak, as if I'd come down with smallpox. Pink bonnets? I had no idea what Mercy was talking about. And Ann was nothing like Joy had described. She'd asked me to sit next to her, after all, and complimented my bracelet. Hadn't she said we should go to London together? Joy had never even invited me to do anything outside of school.

Maybe Joy was wrong about Ann Putnam.

I trailed after the Glass Girls. Before I reached the doorway, Ann popped out and raised one of her perfectly manicured eyebrows.

"Oh, Cavie. Watch out for Joy," she whispered. "She's, like, totally psycho."

THREE

I was supposed to meet Joy in the glen after school, but I had no idea what to tell her.

I'd barely passed the line of trees bordering the grass when Joy burst out, "So what happened? What did they say? Did they mention me?"

I stared at the ground. "They didn't mention you," I lied.

"Really? Those bitches," Joy said. She rolled her eyes. "I'm not surprised."

"And they invited me to go shopping tomorrow in the Town."

"This is too perfect. That's, like, Glass Girls *church.* They shop all the time. I don't even know how they afford it since no one in Salem Village is rich." Joy scrunched up her nose. "You totally have to go."

"I told Ann I'd go. After all, I really could use some clothes." I smoothed my skirt under my hands. I'd never liked the baggy black dress, but lately I cringed whenever I thought about it. "Mercy also said something about pink bonnets?"

Joy snorted. "They're so weird. They call them pink bonnets, but it's really just a white bonnet that they soak with something red. It's barely pink at all."

"Um, do you have one I could borrow?"

Joy gave me a withering stare. "You think I wear pink?"

"Oh. I'll figure something out."

Joy waved off my words. "I bet Ann's going to spill all her secrets when you go shopping."

"What kind of secrets?"

"Who knows? Maybe she steals cream from her neighbors. Or she slaps babies for fun." Joy's eyes practically twinkled in anticipation.

"What happened between you and Ann, anyway?" I deserved to know. Why did Ann call Joy psycho? They'd been friends once. But somehow things had gone sour. I was no expert on friendship, but it struck me as odd.

"Ugh. I don't want to talk about it."

Curiosity roiled under my skin, but I held my tongue.

Joy was happy to change the subject. "I should warn you about Salem Town. You should avoid the harbor, if you care about your reputation. Plus it smells terrible. The main row of shops is up on the hill—you know, butcher, baker, candlestick maker. And a few different tailors. There's this mercantile with a big bucket of candy. Ann always stops because she says sweets make her look plump and healthy."

I raised an eyebrow. Ann probably didn't want anyone to think she was too thin—she had to prove her family could afford expensive foods.

Joy laughed. "I know, right? As if you can see anything in these outfits." She pulled out her skirt, revealing enough fabric to make a second dress. "I saw her smack a candy out of Abigail's hand one day and gobble it up. The look on Abigail's face was priceless." Joy's grin vanished, replaced by a serious expression. In an instant, she was all business. "I'm sure you'll visit the fanciest tailors. Ann's family is the richest in Salem, and she doesn't want anyone to forget it. I don't know how Mercy can afford any of that stuff. She's an orphan."

"I probably can't afford it, either." My nerves boiled up again. I'd saved a few coins, but I didn't want to spend them on a plain black dress.

"Don't worry about that. You don't *have* to buy anything." Joy gave me a very serious look. "Just watch your back around Ann Putnam. She's a total bitch."

~ ~ ~

I walked to school the next morning wearing a clammy, loose bonnet that wasn't pink at all.

I'd boiled water over the small fire in our hearth and then tossed in a bonnet and a pair of red stockings. Instead of a pink bonnet, I'd gotten a dense white blob of cloth that still hadn't dried out the next morning. Somehow the soaking had loosened the fabric, and it hung on my head like a dead jellyfish.

I felt ridiculous.

Joy raised an eyebrow at me but didn't say anything when I slid into the seat next to her. "It'll dry by this afternoon," I whispered.

But the damp Village air was no help, so after school I approached Abigail and Mercy looking like a Puritan who supported adult baptism. Abigail narrowed her eyes at me but kept her mouth closed. Mercy stared at my head, and asked, "Is it raining?"

At least their bonnets didn't look pink, either.

Then a wagon pulled up outside the schoolhouse. Ann was already sitting in the front next to the driver, who looked too young to be her father.

"Get in, wenches, we're going shopping!" Ann called.

I ducked my head at Ann's language. Even though I hadn't

been raised in the Village, I knew we weren't supposed to talk like sailors. No one cursed in Salem, but somehow Ann never got in trouble.

Ann shook her head at me and laughed. "Don't be such a baby," she chided. She turned to the driver, her voice jumping an octave higher. "William would never say anything, right, William?"

He shook his head. I couldn't tell if William was afraid of Ann or attracted to her.

As we climbed in, Mercy leaned over and whispered, "He's one of the Putnam servants. William would never cross Ann."

Somehow that didn't reassure me.

"Let's go, already," Ann ordered. William lifted the reins and the horses pulled forward. As we slowly passed the other students walking away from the schoolhouse, I caught Joy's eye. She smirked as she gave me a nod. I pulled a hand in front of my face to hide my smile.

It wasn't a fast ride by any means, but it was better than walking. We joined the main road toward the Town—I'd been here only ten days earlier, when I arrived in Salem Village with my parents, but it already felt like a lifetime ago.

Ann turned around, her golden hair, loosened from its bonnet, already whipping in the breeze. "I can't wait to get out of here," she said. "Mr. Green is so boring. As if I care about Roman emperors and their silly wars."

I bit my tongue. Defending Mr. Green and the poor, maligned Roman emperors wouldn't improve my standing with the Glass Girls.

"Yeah," Mercy added. "Like I even know what a *Caligula* is." She laughed.

Abigail rolled her eyes at Mercy. William sat silently, not commenting on our conversation. The Glass Girls really could get away with a lot.

I shrugged my shoulders. "I kind of like history." I watched Ann to see how she would react.

She shrieked and turned back again toward us. "No. Way. I should have known. You look like a book worm."

"I guess it just makes sense to me," I stammered. "Understanding the past and where we came from."

"I didn't come from a Roman emperor," Mercy stated flatly.

"But maybe you're the descendant of a Roman patrician," I said.

Mercy's eyes lit up. "I do look good in a toga."

I flinched. How did Mercy know how she looked in a toga? I tried to hide my surprise, but inside my stomach swirled. I'd expected the Glass Girls to be Puritans, even if they were "cool" Puritans. But so far, they weren't acting like Puritans at all.

Ann glared at Mercy. "History is just a bunch of boring old dead people," she declared. "And school is just something we have to endure until we can finally get married."

Abigail sighed. "We're already sixteen. Are we ever going to find husbands?"

In a flash, they sounded like Puritans again. I'd heard that Puritan girls felt called to marry and have children, although Joy didn't fit that mold at all. I also didn't feel any desire to marry. I could barely handle the responsibilities of being a teenager.

"I heard Samuel Cheever is buying his own farm," Mercy said. "So he'll probably want a wife soon."

"Ewww Samuel Cheever?!" Ann cried. "I can't believe you even said that. Gross. Have you seen his acne?"

"He's so tall," Mercy said, a dreamy quality in her voice.

"He's so *gross*," Ann retorted.

"I want to marry a Putnam," Abigail said, her eyes trained on Ann's back.

"You could do a lot worse," Ann snorted. "I do have a ton of eligible cousins."

Abigail's grin stretched across her face. "And then *we* would be cousins," she blurted out.

Ann sighed, but she didn't turn around.

Abigail shrank back in her seat. The wagon was quiet until Ann started gossiping about other girls in our class. That topic kept them occupied until we rolled down the main street in Salem Town.

Ann shrieked excitedly and pointed at a tailor shop with bales of cloth displayed in the windows. "Look, new fabrics! Let's start there."

We piled out of the wagon. Ann grabbed Abigail's arm as they raced into the store.

"Look at these colors," Ann sighed. "And the quality is so much better than the rough spun cotton the poor girls in the village have to wear." She rubbed the cloth between her fingers.

To me, it looked exactly like the scratchy dress I was already wearing.

"And look at the bonnets," Abigail called from another part of the store. Mercy rushed over and oohed. "So many new designs!"

Mercy rubbed one against her cheek. "This one is so fine you could practically see your hair through it." She pranced in front of us wearing the bonnet.

I smiled uneasily and shifted my weight from one foot to the other. Everything looked the same to me. Then again, I was wearing a dead jellyfish on my head, so clearly my fashion sense was not to be trusted.

"And look at the embroidery on this one," Abigail said. "This one would totally cover up the weird shape of my ears." She turned to me. "I totally hate my ears."

"I hate my nose," Mercy said, "Is there a bonnet to cover that?"

I laughed, but cut short when Mercy scowled at me. I guess

she wasn't joking.

"I hate my ankles," Ann said as she walked over.

I'd never been shopping with other girls. My mom usually brought home a bolt of fabric and made my dresses. I chewed on my lip as the other girls stared at me, waiting. Ann's hands were on her hips, as if daring me to join in.

"I, uh . . ." I tried to think of something. "My feet sometimes smell?"

"Ew," Ann replied, ending the conversation. She turned her back on us to look at more fabric.

They spent an hour rifling through everything in the shop, from pre-made dresses and bonnets to heavy rolls of cloth. Then Ann started asking the tailor questions about customizing different pieces. Finally, she and Abigail placed orders and we left. I didn't buy anything.

Next we went to a shop that sold gloves, and another that carried other types of hats, and then one that sold leather belts.

The sun was already dipping in the sky when Ann finally led us back to the wagon. But before we could climb in, Ann pulled us aside, away from the adults crowding the street in Salem Town. "So, I was thinking. Next Friday night." She raised one eyebrow and the corner of her mouth curled up into a grin.

"Ooooh I'm scared," Mercy said. "Are you sure you want to do it again?"

"Well, I'm not afraid," Abigail chirped. "I mean, it's not *that* scary."

"You almost peed yourself last time," Mercy said.

"Mercy!" Abigail blushed.

I waited for someone to explain. But they were ignoring me. "What are you talking about?"

Ann's grin made me shiver. "You'll just have to come next Friday night and see." She paused. "We'll meet two hours after sunset in the woods behind the Old Cleary Farm. Mercy can show you the way," she said to me as an afterthought.

What had I signed up for? I didn't want to run around the woods at night with Ann Putnam. Still, Joy would be thrilled. She'd say it was the perfect chance to find out Ann's secrets.

But it also sounded dangerous.

They climbed into the wagon. Ann looked at me, frozen on the sidewalk. "Aren't you coming?"

I ignored the nagging doubts in my stomach and nodded. "I'll be there."

FOUR

Joy grabbed my arm as I rounded the corner of the schoolhouse the next morning. She raised her eyebrows expectantly. "What happened?" she whispered. "I need the full shopping report."

The schoolyard was empty, but I still led her around the corner of the building before I answered. "Nothing really happened. We went shopping. Ann bought some new gloves. They complained about stuff." I paused. "Oh, and they invited me to some *thing* in the woods next Friday."

"No. Way." Joy intoned this solemnly. "They really invited you? Already?"

I opened my mouth, but nothing came out. Did Joy already know what the Glass Girls did in the woods? I had laid awake the night before imagining all kinds of things. I hadn't slept well. "Do they hang out in the woods a lot?"

Joy lowered her voice and leaned closer. I could smell bitter tea on her breath. "There are rumors, but no one really knows what they do. I heard they take off their clothes and dance under the full moon. And a few weeks ago they must have started a fire because there were all these weird singe marks in the woods."

I swallowed, hard. "So Ann never took you out to the woods back when you were friends?"

Joy snorted. "No, she hadn't fully perfected her devious act back then. The most exciting thing we ever did was braid each other's hair and jump off the hay pile in the fall." She locked eyes with me. "You *have* to go."

I wanted to say no. My skin crawled when I imagined running around the woods at night with the Glass Girls. But Joy's voice carried a whisper of desperation. I didn't want to let her down.

And I was curious. What made Ann and her friends so popular? And why did they want to spend time with me? The entire time we lived in Virginia, I didn't have any friends. Maybe because the colony was totally overrun with men, so my parents mainly tried to keep me at home. But here in Salem Village I'd already made an entire group of friends—Ann, Abigail, and Mercy, and of course Joy. I didn't want to lose them—any of them.

And there was something intoxicating about the Glass Girls—not that I'd ever been drunk. But like a moth circling a candle, I was drawn to them. Ann left me off-balance, and I didn't trust her, but I still wanted her to like me.

I couldn't explain the power she had over people.

Joy was staring at me. I sighed. "Fine, I'll go."

My voice might have sounded certain, but my stomach still fluttered nervously.

~ ~ ~

As the day drew closer, my sense of dread about Friday

didn't fade. Instead, my worries constantly churned in my thoughts, even when I sat with the Glass Girls for lunch. Abigail and Mercy would chatter on about some boy, and my thoughts would wander to the woods. Ann would shoot me an irritated look. I'd try to join in their conversations, but my mind kept running back to the forest.

And suddenly it was Friday.

Joy pulled me aside after school. "Ready for tonight?" she whispered.

I nodded and tried to stop my voice from shaking. "I guess so."

"Don't be scared," Joy chided. "Come on, they're just teenage girls!" She shook her head at me in mock seriousness and gave my hand a squeeze. And then she made me promise to tell her everything.

I stood outside the schoolhouse after Joy left. Wind whistled through the bare trees, a mournful winter cry. The first winter snow of the year had already melted, but I could feel more on the air. Then I turned home, too. My feet dragged. When my house came into view, I saw my mom standing at the door waiting for me. She waved ferociously. I couldn't help but smile.

"Have you already forgotten what day it is?" she called.

It was late December, but I couldn't remember the date. The days all ran together in Salem Village.

When I reached the porch, Mom held out a small box. "It's a little late. Christmas was on Tuesday. And I know the Puritans don't celebrate Christmas, but we still can in our house," she said. "You've been working so hard, Cavie. I thought you could use a little gift. Here, open it."

I reached inside the box and found a delicate silver locket nestled inside, just like the ones that girls wore in London. "It's beautiful," I breathed, watching it sparkle in the weak New England sun. "Thank you."

"Your dad bought it from a merchant in Salem Town when we arrived. He thought you might like it. Here, I'll help you put it around your neck." In one smooth move she fastened the hook latch at the nape of my neck. "But remember, Puritan girls don't usually wear jewelry. You should probably keep it inside your dress."

I nodded and tucked the locket under my collar, where I could feel the cold metal brushing my skin. "Thank you," I said again. I gave her a tight hug.

After dinner, I got ready for bed as usual. But instead of pulling off my dress, I climbed into bed still wearing my clothes. I tugged the blankets up high so my parents wouldn't notice.

I lay stiff as a board in my bed with my eyes closed, but sleep was the furthest thing from my mind. I counted down the minutes until I was certain that at least two hours had passed.

Slowly, I eased a foot out of bed, cursing the squeaky floorboards. I crept across the room and silently slid the door open. I froze, listening for sounds from my parents' room, but the house was still.

I floated down the stairs and out the front door.

My heart raced as I hurried up the road. I felt a little thrill course through my body—this was the first time I'd ever snuck out of my house. I felt like a character in a novel. And then a crow's caw broke the silence. I nearly leapt out of my skin.

My pulse was still pounding when I saw a dark figure on the road ahead of me. I almost yelped before I realized it was Mercy. She was waving her arms and calling out, "Cavie! Cavie!"

"Shhh!"

"It's okay, everyone goes to bed at sunset," Mercy sniffed,

"This is the most boring place in the world." She grabbed my arm and pulled me off the road onto a smaller path that led into the woods. I'd never noticed it, even though I walked past it every day on my way to school.

Twigs cracked under our steps and our legs ruffled the dark undergrowth as we pushed deeper into the woods. My breath was shallow. "How often do you guys . . . do this?"

"Oh, like fortnightly?" Mercy replied absentmindedly.

Ahead of us several dots of light shattered the night. My heart pounded in my chest. As we drew closer, I saw that the lights were arranged in a ring. I wondered for a moment if Ann had carted out the candles and arranged them in the woods just to impress me.

"Here they are," Mercy said, pointing ahead of us.

The hazy figures moving within the circle of light solidified into Abigail and Ann. They weren't wearing bonnets. Seeing Ann's long blond hair and Abigail's tight, dark curls made them look like different people.

Ann clutched a heavy leather-bound book in her arms.

"Hi guys," Mercy said. "Sorry we're late."

"It's fine," Ann said in a brusque voice. "Let's get down to business." She pulled open the thick volume.

"What's that?" I asked, leaning closer.

Ann glared at me over the top of the thick binding. She adopted a tone like I was an idiot. "It's our Burning Book. You know, a book of spells."

A burning book?

Ann was so matter-of-fact that I didn't know how to respond. Spells? Magic? That had to be completely forbidden in Godly Salem Village.

Where had Ann found it?

And what would happen if someone caught us with the book?

"We read spells from it," Mercy added unhelpfully.

"It's really cool," Abigail concluded. "It's, like, contraband."

So that's what they did in the woods at night. Magic. I gave a shaky smile. At least we wouldn't have to get naked.

Or, I hoped not.

"Now unless you have more questions—" Ann said, scowling at me. I kept my mouth shut. "Then let's get started. Who should we curse tonight?"

My voice shot out. "You're going to *curse* someone?" In truth, I wasn't sure if I believed in magic. But I didn't want to cast spells on people. Just in case.

Ann shook her head at me. "Cavie, the Burning Book isn't a joke. You should have seen what we did a few months ago to Jemma Doyle."

"Who's Jemma Doyle?"

Abigail took over the story. "She was this crazy old lady who lived on the edge of town. A total nut. Probably a witch. So we put a curse on her."

The candles flickered in the wind, casting eerie shadows in the trees.

"What kind of curse?"

Mercy leaned closer. "We used this spell to make men reject her. It's our best spell. And the day after we cast the curse, John Putnam pushed her into a puddle."

They broke into laughter, their voices echoing in the deserted woods.

I frowned. It didn't sound funny to me. It also didn't sound like magic. Everyone in the Village knew that John Putnam was kind of a jerk, even me.

"You look a little pale. You aren't afraid of magic, are you, Cavie?" Ann said. Suddenly her voice turned from sharp to sweet. "Don't they have magic in London?"

"I'm not against magic or anything," I said quickly. "I just think we're too old for spells. Back in London only kids believed in curses. It's kind of childish, don't you think?" My entire body was tense, from my jaw down to my toes.

"We do other things with the Burning Book too," Abigail insisted. "Not just curses."

"The book has some charms and stuff, like love spells," Mercy said.

"And we also record stuff about people in the school," Abigail added. "Like if they're ugly, or stupid, or whatever."

"Shut up," Ann said to Abigail. She turned her green eyes on me, sizing me up like a hawk targeting a mouse. I shivered. "It's *our* Burning Book. And maybe we invited you too soon." She clutched the book to her chest.

I didn't want to put spells on anyone. But all the muscles in my body went tight under Ann's gaze. I wanted her to like me. I wanted all of them to like me.

And if I left before they even opened the Burning Book, Joy would be furious.

"Sorry," I mumbled. "I guess I didn't understand the book."

Ann stared at me for a long, drawn out moment. The air crackled with tension. Abigail and Mercy watched Ann, waiting for their orders.

"Okay," Ann finally said. "Fine."

Somehow, the tightness in my shoulders didn't vanish.

But Mercy clapped her hands together. "This is going to be fun!"

Ann was still eyeing me, so I plastered a false smile on my

face. After another glare, she flipped open the book and turned to one the pages in the back. "We should probably start by warning you about the freaks in our class, Cavie. Janice Smith, you know her? The one with buck teeth and acne? Well she's a *total slut.*"

Mercy raised her eyebrows. "She took Jacob Porter out to the woods and *had sex with him.*"

"Eww."

"And Prudence Whitacre? She prays all the time. She also drinks milk from other people's cows when she thinks no one is looking." Ann reported this salacious detail authoritatively.

"That's . . . weird," I said.

Abigail nodded. "Poor Prudence, she tries so hard to look like her family has enough money for butter. She'll never be pretty."

"And Joy Titus." Ann paused for effect. "I don't want to scare you, Cavie, since you sit next to her . . . but she's a total follower of Sappho if you know what I mean."

A follower of Sappho? Was she talking about the Greek woman who wrote poetry?

Oh.

"You mean she's attracted to other women?"

"Exactly." Ann sighed and tossed her hair over her shoulder. "Just watch out for her, because she'll probably fall in love with you or something. We used to be friends a few years ago. I know, I can't believe it either. And then Benjamin Cuthbert started courting me. It didn't mean anything, we were like, thirteen. So I let him take me on walks after school and escort me to church. Joy got super jealous and angry, like she was *in love* with me. She didn't want me to pay any attention to Benjamin. Obviously she's a follower of Sappho."

I opened my mouth, but no sound came out. That's why Ann and Joy stopped being friends? I'd expected something much worse. After all, if my friend ditched me for a guy, I'd be hurt, too.

"That's not all. One time I was organizing a trip to the swimming hole for all the girls. You know. Swimming? In swim garments?" Ann looked at me expectantly.

I had an idea what women in London and Virginia wore to go swimming: full-body costumes that covered everything. I'm sure the swimming clothes in a Puritan village were even less revealing.

Ann's mouth tightened. "I told her she wasn't invited. She would have seen us all in our swimming clothes. I couldn't invite a follower of *Sappho*." Her eyes widened at the scandalous idea. "It wouldn't be fair to the other girls."

At that moment a twig snapped in the woods. My heart jumped into my throat, and all our heads jerked in the direction of the sound. Someone was walking through the woods, headed right toward us.

My blood ran cold. Mercy opened her mouth but Ann quickly shushed her. "Whoever it is can already see us," she said quietly, nodding to the candles.

A second later, a shape emerged from the woods.

"Tituba," Abigail sighed. "You scared us half to death!" The woman's mahogany skin gleamed in the candlelight. Her dark hair hung nearly to her waist. She was wrapped in thick shawls even though the chill from the last week had finally lightened.

"Miss Abigail, you really shouldn't be out here in the woods," Tituba warned.

Mercy leaned over and whispered, "That's the Parris family's slave. She's from Barbados or Atlantis or something."

I opened my mouth to correct Mercy, but Abigail interrupted me.

"You really have to stop following me, Tituba," she complained. "I'm not a little kid anymore. I can take care of myself."

I pictured Abigail stamping her foot like a child. It was all too easy to imagine. But I let the thought evaporate from my mind before I started laughing.

"If Minister Parris finds out that you've been wandering around the woods at night, up to all kinds of things, he will be furious," Tituba insisted. "It's time to go home."

At that moment, her eyes turned to the book in Ann's hands. Tituba shifted her gaze onto us, one by one. She lingered on my face for a second longer than anyone else. Then she glanced at the candles. "Oh, I see." She turned back to Ann. "You think you can learn magic from a book."

Mercy opened her mouth to deny the accusation, but Ann stepped in quickly. "What would you know of magic?" she asked haughtily.

Tituba chuckled to herself. The sound sent a shiver up my spine. "More than you might know. If you want to see *real* magic, meet me here in a fortnight. I'll show you the true power of magic."

Ann frowned and bit her lip. I had never seen her confident mask slip. But in an instant the uncertainty vanished, replaced with her normal arrogant posture. "Fine," she said breezily.

I shuffled my feet in the dense leaves that coated the ground. Some part of me was curious, too, but fear still coursed through my body. I hadn't wanted to play at magic with the Glass Girls, and Tituba was promising something darker.

Plus, I didn't want to spend *every* Friday in the woods.

"Then meet back here in two weeks," Tituba said. "And now, Abigail, it is time for us to go home."

Abigail sighed, mouthed "Sorry" to Ann, and walked off with Tituba.

Ann spun around toward me and Mercy, her hands on her hips. "You can put away the candles. I'm going home." She stalked off in the opposite direction, leaving us to clean up after the night's events.

Mercy sighed and began collecting the candles. She started telling me about her pet goat and her younger brother, but I didn't respond. My stomach was churning. I couldn't keep up with Mercy's chatter.

She blew out the last candle and for a moment we were plunged into darkness.

Thankfully, our eyes adjusted to the light from the nearly full moon. Mercy piled up the candles and hid them in a waxed cloth bag concealed under a fallen stump. She offered to walk me home, but I waved her off. I wasn't confident that I could find my way back to the road, but I didn't want company.

After a few wrong turns, I finally made it home. I lay in bed for hours, my eyes open, wondering what would happen in the woods next week.

FIVE

I finally fell into a restless sleep and woke to the rooster's crow. Memories from the previous night seeped in like light through a poorly caulked log cabin, and I groaned.

The Glass Girls weren't what I'd expected.

I pulled myself from bed and forced myself into the fields, where icy turf had to be tilled by hand. The labor kept me from thinking about Ann Putnam and her Burning Book.

As the sun carved a low crescent across the sky, I stopped and brushed the sweat off my brow. Something on the road caught my eye. I watched as Joy approached our farm.

My respite from the Glass Girls was over.

The corner of Joy's mouth pulled back as she examined my farming work. She didn't look impressed. "I couldn't wait until Monday for the full report," Joy explained. "I have to know what happened last night."

I dropped my spade and sank onto a tree stump. "It was strange." I halted, mentally sorting through the events of the evening.

Joy could barely contain her eagerness. She was practically

standing on the tips of her feet. "Strange?"

"They set up this circle of candles in the woods. Ann had a book of spells, and they were planning to put magical curses on people."

"What?" Joy exclaimed. "No. Way."

"Yeah. It wasn't what I expected, either."

"So they've been sneaking out into the woods to do spells?" Joy dissolved into laughter, and my eyes darted to the house to make sure my parents weren't watching.

"Ann said they put a curse on Jemma Doyle. Abigail called her crazy."

"Goody Doyle? She isn't some batty old lady. She lives with her son. She's just very private."

"Well, the Glass Girls put a curse on her, and then John Putnam pushed her into a puddle."

"I remember that," Joy said. "But that's not how it happened at all. Her son did some work on Putnam's farm and Ann's dad refused to pay his wages. Goody Doyle told her son to take the case to the magistrate, but he was scared because of what happened to George Burroughs."

The blank look on my face made it clear to Joy that I'd never heard of George Burroughs.

"Oh, sorry. Sometimes I forget that you don't know anything about Salem Village. George Burroughs was the minister when I was a kid. It's a complicated story. The Village is officially under the authority of Salem Town. But the Village wants to be self-governing. We pay taxes to the Town, but we're barely represented on their councils. You probably noticed that the Town has a lot more rich people than the Village."

I nodded, thinking back to the well-dressed men in the Town's shopping district.

"The Village is full of farmers and the Town is full of merchants. And it's not just the taxes. We have to send people to serve in the Salem Town night watch, even though we don't even have a night watch in the Village. And it's a long ride at night. Anyway, for a long time the Village wasn't allowed to have a minister. Which is a big deal to Puritans. And even now, our minister—you know, Abigail's uncle—can't give communion. We have to bring in the Salem Town minister for that. But the Town won't grant the Village independence."

"Why?"

"I have no idea. Taxes? Or maybe they don't want to give up the land? But anyway, the fight between the Town and Village causes all kinds of problems. Like, it's not even clear if the Village is allowed to settle our own disputes. Giles Corey—have you seen him? Super old, super cranky?"

I lowered an eyebrow. "Is he the one who's always arguing in the Village Square?"

"Yeah, that's him. He keeps suing people but he refuses to go to court in the Town. It's a mess. No one knows how to resolve the lawsuits." She leaned back on her heels and paused. "But a lot of Villagers don't mind the fighting with Salem Town. Like the Porters, they have tons of business connections in the Town. Have you met any of them?"

"I don't think so. But my dad might have mentioned them."

"I'm not surprised, your father being an important Londoner and all. I'm sure the Porters will be at your door sucking up before the week is over."

I laughed at the mental image of a well-dressed Villager approaching my farmer dad, expecting some English Lord.

"The Porters are rich. Israel Porter keeps getting elected to the Salem Town Council, even though he lives in the Village. So the Porters don't want independence. The Putnams on the other hand . . ."

I nodded. The divisions in the Village were starting to make sense. "Ann's family is also rich, and they want more power in the Village."

"Exactly." Joy punctuated the word with a pointed finger.

"So . . . George Burroughs?"

"Yeah, George Burroughs. That's right. He was the minister back in the 1680s, and he pissed off the Putnams. To be fair, it's pretty easy to piss off the Putnams. The apple doesn't fall far from the tree if you know what I mean," she said, raising an eyebrow. "And so they stopped paying his salary."

"Just completely stopped?"

"Yep. He got pretty mad. He tried to contact the magistrate, but the Putnams have a lot of sway in the Village even if no one likes them in the Town. So somehow Minister Burroughs ended up getting arrested."

My eyebrows shot up. "He was arrested for . . . not getting paid?" That was insane.

"I don't know how the Putnams managed it, but they drove Minister Burroughs out of town. I heard he moved all the way to Maine." Joy shook her head. "And that's why Goody Doyle's son was afraid to complain to the magistrate when the Putnams didn't pay him."

"That's . . . I don't even know what to say."

"The whole Village is crazy, Cavie. I tried to warn you."

I was starting to agree with Joy. "And then John Putnam pushed Goody Doyle into a puddle?"

"No one saw exactly what happened," Joy admitted. "But that's the rumor. And if Ann said it happened . . . well John Putnam is her uncle so she's probably right. It wouldn't surprise me."

Suddenly everything happening in Salem Village took on a different cast for me. I had stumbled into the middle of a major conflict. And it sounded like the Putnams weren't above dirty tactics to take down their rivals. Ann's dad might intimidate his enemies using the magistrate, but his daughter had jumped straight to spells.

And somehow, I had become friends with Ann Putnam.

"So enough about that," Joy said, waving away the issue. "What else happened last night?"

I took a deep breath. "I tried to convince the Glass Girls that spells were stupid."

"You did?" Joy shrieked. "I would have killed to see Ann's reaction."

I couldn't hold back a grin. "She wanted to bite my face off."

Joy tilted her head back and laughed. "I can't believe Ann would be stupid enough to do magic. Puritans have no sense of humor when it comes to the dark arts. Have you read Cotton Mather's new book? Minister Parris has a copy. He talks about it all the time. Cotton Mather is like his hero or something."

I had heard of Cotton Mather—he was the boisterous son of Increase Mather, and he led a church in Boston. But I'd never heard of the book. "What's the book about?"

"It's about witches and bewitchment and all that. A few years back, Boston executed a poor Irish washerwoman for being a witch. It was totally ridiculous. These girls said the washerwoman had bewitched them." Joy rolled her eyes. "It was just an excuse for them to yell out dirty words during church service and drink wine without getting in trouble."

"Wait, seriously?" I couldn't picture good Puritan children swearing during sermons.

"Really. And the Puritans, especially Cotton Mather, were obsessed. Those girls became celebrities. And then Mather made them even more famous when he wrote a book about it."

I chewed the inside of my cheek before I built up the courage to ask Joy a question. "Aren't you a Puritan?"

"What?"

"You keep talking about 'the Puritans.' But I thought you were a Puritan?"

Joy's face contorted. Had I said something wrong?

"I was born into a Puritan family, but I don't consider myself a Puritan."

"You can do that?" I squeaked. I'd assumed that everyone in the Village was a Puritan. Didn't they drive out non-Puritans? Wasn't that why I had to dress up in this ridiculous bonnet and apron?

Joy stuck out her jaw. "Who's going to stop me?"

I threw up my hands. "Not me! I'm not a Puritan, either."

"It's a match made in heaven," she said with a grin.

I returned her smile and let out a breath. "If Minister Parris hates witches, it can't be good that his niece is running around the woods putting curses on people."

"It's too perfect." Joy clapped her hands together and almost shook with happiness.

"But it's pretty bad for the Glass Girls to have a Burning Book of spells and magic."

"Bad? No, it's great! We'll finally show everyone that the Glass Girls are hypocrites. I mean, don't get me wrong. I'm not a Puritan, so I don't care, but they love to flaunt the rules. They'll be in so much trouble if anyone catches them with a book of spells." She chewed on one of her nails, deep in thought. Then her eyes leapt to mine. "Is it obvious that the book belongs to them?"

"They've written a bunch of stuff in the back about people they don't like. Just mean stuff like so and so has acne, so and so is ugly."

Joy reached out and grabbed my sleeve. "Did they say anything about me?"

My breath caught in my throat. I wasn't going to tell Joy that Ann said she was a friend of Sappho. "No. They didn't."

"Bitches," Joy spat out. "But whatever. When their spell book gets out, everyone will know who wrote it."

I looked down at the patch of turf near my feet. My mouth had gone dry. "Couldn't they get into big trouble?" I was on board with taking Ann down a peg, but I didn't want her to actually get hurt. She was mean, but she didn't seem *evil.*

"They'll probably have to go to church every day for a year or something. But nothing worse than that."

"Okay." The sense of unease in my stomach hadn't vanished, but I felt a little better.

Joy shook her head. Her next words were low, almost to herself. "I can't believe they would be so stupid!"

"I should probably get back to work."

"Oh, okay. My mom is probably wondering where I am, too."

"Then I'll see you in school?"

"See you Monday."

Joy gave me a little wave as she walked away. I picked up the spade and put the Glass Girls out of my mind.

~ ~ ~

But I couldn't ignore them for long. On Monday, I arrived at school before the Glass Girls. When Ann and Abigail walked in together, they went straight to the back row. But Ann kept shooting me looks all morning. Every time I glanced over my shoulder, she was watching, her eyebrows raised.

I finally walked over to her during lunch break. "What's going on?"

She grabbed my arm and pulled me aside. "Oh my God, can you believe last Friday?" Before I could respond, she looked over her shoulder and led me out the door. Abigail watched us, her shoulders slumped. Instead of following us, she headed in the opposite direction with Mercy.

Ann raised an eyebrow at me, expectantly.

"It was pretty . . . wild," I said. Was that what she wanted to hear? Ann seemed to love all the secrets. It was the first time I'd been involved in anything like that. I already knew I didn't like it very much. I felt guilty for lying to my family, and scared that we would all get caught. Or worse, what if someone murdered us and left our bodies in the woods?

I mean, it could happen.

"Wild doesn't even *start* to describe it," she whispered. I followed her to the hill where we ate lunch. Ann settled in her usual spot, and patted the ground next to her, where Abigail always sat. Ann gave me a sideways look. "Did you see Abigail's face when Tituba showed up? She looked so terrified, I thought she was going to pee her petticoats—*again*." She laughed loudly, even though Mercy and Abigail were heading over to join us.

Ann hadn't even tried to lower her voice.

"What are you guys talking about?" Abigail asked, her eyebrows wrinkling.

"Oh, nothing," Ann said in a sing-song voice. "We'll talk more later," Ann said to me, loud enough that Mercy and Abigail heard.

Abigail frowned at me. I shifted my weight. I wanted to jump up and offer Abigail my seat, but Ann grabbed my arm before I could move. Abigail awkwardly sat on Ann's other side.

A faint smile flickered across Ann's face.

I knew Ann was using me to punish Abigail—for what, I had no idea. I knew she wanted us to compete for her attention.

But why was I participating?

And why did it feel so good that I was winning?

"Did you guys see what Dorothy Marsh was wearing today?" Ann said once we were all sitting.

Dorothy Marsh was a quiet girl, a few years younger than us. Like everyone in the schoolhouse, she worshipped the ground Ann walked on. You couldn't miss the girls who whispered in Ann's wake, telling tales about Ann's greatness. And just that morning, Ann had stopped by Dorothy's desk to compliment her new bonnet, where everyone could hear. Dorothy's grin had stretched from ear to ear.

Before I could say anything, Ann continued. "She looked *so bad*. That hideous bonnet makes her look like a total pumpkin head."

Abigail and Mercy burst into giggles at Ann's description. My stomach turned. With a sinking feeling, I remembered the first day we spoke. She had complimented my bracelet. I tucked the leather band under my sleeve.

What did Ann say about me when I wasn't around?

"Dorothy probably thinks she's a trend setter," Abigail added, looking to Ann for approval.

"I don't want to look like a pumpkin," Mercy said.

"*As if* we'd ever wear something that ugly. Maybe her family is too poor to afford a mirror." Ann shook her head in mock concern as Abigail and Mercy dissolved into laughter.

Ann turned on me with a frown. "Don't tell me you liked her bonnet."

There was no mistaking it for a question. I stumbled over my words. "Oh, sorry. I guess I don't know anything about bonnet fashions?" My voice rose to a squeak, and my cheeks burned.

"That's pretty obvious," Ann replied curtly, eyeing the bonnet on my head. Mercy laughed and the corner of Abigail's mouth inched upward.

I reached up to touch my plain white bonnet. I should have bought one of the expensive, fashionable bonnets in Salem Town.

My cheeks were still burning. I turned away from Ann. Hopefully she wouldn't read the insecurity written all over my face.

And at just that moment, the most gorgeous guy in the world walked past the hill where we sat. He was tall, with broad shoulders that made it look like he knew his way around an axe. As I watched, he ran a hand through his sandy hair. And then he looked right at me, and even though I was red in the face and still touching my bonnet, he smiled at me. My lips parted slightly and I stared at him as though bewitched.

How had I not seen him in the Village before? He was like a Greek God brought to life, Emperor Augustus in the flesh.

"Uh, embarrassing," Ann interjected, breaking me out of my dream world. "Edmund Hale was totally just staring at me."

I barely registered Ann's words. Mercy leaned toward me and said, "That's Ann's old beau."

My stomach sank. Of course.

Abigail shook her head. "She's totally out of his league. Like a Putnam would marry a Hale. It's ridiculous."

"I know," Ann said, her face tilted up toward the weak winter sun. "He totally wanted to marry me, but I can do better."

I frowned and squinted my eyes. Ann's words made no sense to me. How could anyone be more perfect than Edmund Hale?

But he was Ann's ex.

But he smiled at me.

"Does he go to school here?" I asked.

"No, he stopped last year. He had to start working on his family's farm," Abigail explained.

"Why are you so curious?" Ann asked, her eyes narrowing. "Oh no. *Oh no.* Don't tell me you have a crush on Edmund Hale."

My mouth opened, and then I shut it. Was I that obvious? I could feel my face flushing again.

"I don't care if you like him." Ann said. "Edmund and I are completely done. We were practically engaged, but you should go for it. I mean, if you don't mind that he's just a poor farmer."

I knew that Ann was insulting me. Edmund Hale wasn't good enough for her, but he was good enough for me. But on some level I just didn't care. My eyes followed Edmund as he vanished up the road.

He could even make Puritan black look good.

Ann's conversation with Abigail faded into the background as I thought about Edmund. And all the places I might run into him.

I could practically hear music playing.

I was enthralled.

After that day, I always looked for Edmund every time I was in the Village. I made excuses to walk through the Village Square, just in case I might see him.

I even asked Joy about him.

"That guy?" She made a face like she'd bitten a lemon. "He's Ann Putnam's ex. I'd stay far, far away. Ann would *kill* you."

I swallowed. Joy's words struck me in the bones, but I couldn't stop thinking about Edmund. My heart pounded whenever I thought about him. I drifted off in class, I daydreamed on my walks.

A week flew by and I still hadn't see Edmund. I was convinced that he had moved away, or died, and we'd never meet.

And then I saw him again.

I was sitting with the Glass Girls, bundled against the cold but still claiming our usual lunch spot. Abigail and Mercy were debating what color apron they'd wear if we were allowed to wear anything but white—Mercy was pushing for purple, while Abigail defended blue—when Edmund strolled by.

My breath caught in my throat. Was he looking at me? He was kind of far away. I tilted my head to watch him walk toward the Village Square.

Ann let out a loud sigh. "It's like he's stalking me."

"Who?" Mercy asked, the topic of aprons suddenly forgotten.

"Edmund Hale. He keeps showing up during lunch break. Someone should remind him that we broke up."

Mercy looked from Ann to me. "I thought he was looking at Cavie."

My pulse pounded in my ears as Ann clenched her jaw. There was practically smoke coming from her ears. Then, in an instant, her face transformed so quickly I wondered if I'd imagined it. "That's a good idea, Mercy."

"What idea?"

"Maybe we can help Edmund get over *me* by introducing

him to Cavie."

My mouth went dry. I shifted on the hard ground, the soil's icy cold sending shivers through me.

Was Ann really offering to help?

Ann seemed untouched by the chill. "Look, Cavie, it's obvious to everyone that you aren't going to give us a moment of peace until you talk to Edmund. You're obsessed."

I wanted to protest, but I knew she was right. I would kill for a chance to talk to Edmund.

But before I could form words, Ann continued. "We'll just have to plan a party or something so you guys can finally meet."

"Really?" I squeaked. Just the thought of standing next to Edmund set my pulse racing. In the back of my mind, a small voice warned against accepting help from Ann Putnam, but I told it to shut up. I was going to talk to Edmund Hale!

Ann put her hands together. "Enough about Cavie. Let's talk about tomorrow night."

Somehow, I'd forgotten about our meeting with Tituba.

"I'm scared," Mercy blurted out. "What if we get eaten by ghosts?"

"How would a ghost eat you?" Ann asked, rolling her eyes. "They're *non-corporeal.*"

Mercy turned to me. "Does that mean they're not corpses? That makes no sense. Ghosts are dead. Corpses are dead."

Abigail jumped in before I could figure out how to answer Mercy. "It means they're made of spirit, not matter," she explained. "Like, a ghost can walk through a tree. So they can't really eat you."

"I don't know about that," Mercy said, her eyebrows folded together with worry. "I'm pretty sure a ghost could eat me if it wanted to."

Ann rolled her eyes again. "Can we please stay on topic?" She glared at Mercy. "I can't spend my day explaining ghosts to you, Mercy." Ann looked at Abigail and lowered her voice. "So you live with Tituba. Did she say anything about tomorrow night?"

Abigail also dropped into a whisper. "She told me to bring an *egg* and a *glass.*"

"That's totally creepy," Ann responded. "An egg and a glass?"

"I have no idea why," Abigail said.

"Did she say anything else?"

Abigail leaned in. "She said to be on time. And make sure no one sees what we're doing."

Ann gripped her apron. "This is going to be so amazing," she gushed.

I glanced at Abigail and Mercy. Abigail was practically glowing after Ann's attention. Mercy was slowly chewing on a tendril of hair that had fallen loose from her bonnet.

Ann ignored the uneasy silence from her followers and started telling us about a new servant in the Putnam house. I let her words wash over me as I clutched a hand to my middle. The anxiety in my stomach that had bloomed since I saw Edmund Hale had been joined by another fear.

Why *did* Tituba want an egg and a glass?

SIX

A bank of fog washed in from the sea early Friday morning. I could smell the salt on the air even though the shore was miles away. It hugged the Village in an eerie embrace.

As if I wasn't already nervous enough.

On my walk to school, I jumped at the disembodied lowing of cows who were only paces away but hidden in mist. I heard the distant creak of wagon wheels on the road long before the shadowy carts emerged from the wall of white.

I pulled my cloak tight around my body and scurried into the schoolhouse.

Everyone was talking about the fog. How long would it last? Did we still have to do chores? Mr. Green even said he would let us leave early if the fog didn't clear by afternoon. We'd all heard the rumors of a boy in Salem Town who'd been trampled by a horse because the rider couldn't see him through the haze.

No one sat outside for lunch that day.

After an afternoon of listening to Latin recitations, and then struggling through my own, I was ready to crawl back in bed and pray that Saturday would dawn with bright blue skies.

But no such luck.

Instead, Mr. Green looked out the window and sighed. "The fog just doesn't look like it's going to lift," he admitted. "Let's end an hour early today. Your parents will probably need your help around the farms this afternoon."

The students, elated one minute, groaned at the mention of chores. The ghostly fields of Salem Village were surely full of lost animals, and once again I was thankful that my dad hadn't bought any cows yet.

Joy barely tilted her head toward me as we sat at the desk. "Tonight's the night," she whispered. "You're still going to meet in the woods?"

"That's the plan."

"Assuming you can find each other." Joy laughed.

I gave her a half-hearted smile, ignoring the tightness in my chest. In truth, unless the fog's white tendrils loosened their embrace on the Village, I wasn't sure I'd be able to find the circle hidden deep in the woods.

Or how I would find my way home from school, for that matter.

Joy seemed to notice my nerves. She gave my hand a quick squeeze under the desk. "Don't worry about it, Cavie," she said quietly, "Everything will be fine."

I squeezed back and dropped her hand when Mercy walked by. It wasn't easy to hide our friendship when we sat next to each other all day, with the Glass Girls only two rows behind us. We sometimes whispered, or tapped on the desk to each other. Our silent communication had somehow brought us even closer. And most afternoons we met in the glen by the school to talk. And to plot.

Tonight, my mission was to gather more dirt on the Glass

Girls.

And avoid being eaten by ghosts.

I waved at Mercy and followed her out the door. When Joy slipped past me, she whispered, "We'll talk tomorrow."

Ann walked through the door right after Joy. "Eww, why were you talking to Joy Titus?"

"She's always trying to talk to me," I said quickly, searching my mind for a reason. "I guess because we sit together?"

Ann shook her head at me. "You're so innocent, Cavie. It's obvious what's going on."

I stared at her with a blank face. My mouth was dry as desert sand. How much had she overheard?

"She only wants to talk to *you* because you're friends with *me*," Ann said.

I let out a breath.

Ann didn't know how right she was.

"Just watch out," Ann warned me. "You know what *she's* like."

"As if I would ever be friends with her," I said with a laugh. "She's such a loser."

Abigail joined us. "Are you talking about Joy Titus?"

"How'd you know?"

"I heard Cavie say 'loser.'"

"You're so bad," Ann exclaimed, giving Abigail a little shove. She turned to me. "Cavie, you've only had to deal with Joy for a few weeks. Imagine how the rest of us feel. She's such a waste of skin. I hope no one ever marries her."

I was about to point out Ann's contradiction—if Joy preferred the company of women, she'd probably rather not marry a man—but I stopped myself. I didn't want to make Ann angry.

"I could totally see her as a crazy old spinster," Abigail gushed. "That would be hilarious."

"Let's not let Joy Titus ruin our plans for tonight." Ann smiled wickedly. "Where's Mercy?"

I pointed to the edge of the woods where Mercy was staring at nothing. Ann rolled her eyes. She grabbed us by the arms and pulled us toward Mercy, away from a group of younger girls who were watching us through the schoolhouse window.

I still hadn't gotten used to being treated like a celebrity by the other girls at school. Once they knew I'd been accepted by the Glass Girls, they practically followed me everywhere. I heard them whispering about me, and one had even started wearing a bonnet that looked a lot like mine.

"Mercy, come on," Ann ordered. "We should talk about our plans. Especially with all this fog."

"But I saw a squirrel," Mercy protested.

Ann huffed her frustration and ignored Mercy. "We'll meet in the usual place, three hours after sunset. Abigail can set up the candles in the woods. And since it's so foggy, we should each carry a candle, too. Cavie, I wasn't sure if your family had candles, so I brought you one." She pulled a half-melted candle out of her bag and thrust it toward me.

I took it and quickly shoved it in my bag. Did Ann expect me to say thank you? I mean, it was 1692—who *didn't* have candles?

Ann didn't wait for a response. She had already moved on. "Any questions?"

"So, I guess I'll come with Tituba?" Abigail asked.

"Of course," Ann said. "She lives in your backyard. It would be pretty stupid not to walk over together."

Abigail's face fell at Ann's words.

"Go home and act normal," Ann instructed us. "And meet in the woods tonight. Be there, or else."

Ann let her ominous words float through the air until they seemed to fade into the fog. Then she turned on her heels and strode away. Our three sets of eyes were glued to her. In seconds, she, too, had been enveloped by the fog.

Abigail let out a long breath of air. "See you tonight," she said, trailing after Ann.

I turned to Mercy. "Thanks for walking with me last time, but I'm pretty sure I can find the place myself tonight."

She smiled. "Okay." Her earlier fears seemed to have vanished, replaced by her usual bubbly personality. She gave me a wave and left.

I was alone on the edge of the woods. The fog hugged me like a coffin. I felt suddenly claustrophobic.

But at least now I had an excuse if I got lost—or in case I chickened out. I could always say that I couldn't find the right spot in the fog.

I felt like a coward for giving myself that out, but I might need it.

~ ~ ~

The sun set, though it was hard to tell through the haze. I could practically feel the fog hanging outside my room.

I listened for the sounds of my parents going to bed. All afternoon I had gone back and forth about going to the woods. My mom had thrust a basket of yarn at me and said, "If you're going to fidget, at least do something useful." But I still couldn't concentrate.

When darkness fell, I made up my mind. I wasn't afraid of

magic, and I wasn't scared of getting lost in the woods. Ann's anger frightened me more than an empty forest. She knew how to destroy people with a few words.

And a small part of me was curious.

So when I heard my parents' door shut, I counted to one hundred and snuck down the stairs.

Before I left the house, I pulled out the candle from Ann along with a small tinderbox I'd taken from the kitchen. I struck the box and tried to light the candle. The wick wouldn't take the spark. Finally, I held the candle up to our fireplace, its embers still glowing deep red. Still nothing. I peered at the wick in the dim light.

It was shiny—and coated in some strange sticky material.

I sank onto the rocking chair.

Was Ann hoping my candle would go out in the fog, trapping me in the woods? I wasn't going to let that happen. I pulled out another candle and lit it easily. I slipped Ann's candle and the tinderbox into my wide cloak pocket, just in case I worked up the courage to confront her.

Yeah, right.

I pulled open the front door and was greeted by a solid wall of dark fog. The temperature had dropped, and my breath came out in tiny swirls that joined the cloud settled over the Village. I was glad to have a thick shawl draped around my shoulders. I scurried down the road, stealing a glance over my shoulder at my house. Was the dim light of my candle visible from the second story rooms? I wasn't going to wait and find out.

The flickering light of the candle cast strange shadows on the fog.

I strained my ears.

My breath was the only sound. Apparently the birds had all

flown south to avoid a Salem winter. I couldn't blame them.

Bile rose in the back of my throat. I willed myself forward, afraid that if I stopped I would simply run home.

After what felt like an hour, I slowed. I had to be close to the path that ran into the woods. But everything looked so different in the fog. I silently paced to the edge of the road and searched for something that jogged my memory, a particular tree or bend in the path.

But everything was camouflaged, as if Salem Village had donned a disguise.

My pulse quickened, and my searching grew frantic.

Was Ann in the woods laughing at me? Was she watching me struggle?

But then I heard a noise. I froze in place and tilted my head toward the sound.

It was faint, but it sounded like Ann Putnam.

I pushed into the woods, ignoring the dense underbrush as it swatted against my legs. After a few minutes, I saw the circle of lights burning through the fog.

I had found them.

I breathed a sigh of relief and scolded myself for letting my fears take over.

Ann and Mercy were standing in the circle of candles.

"What took you so long?" Ann demanded. I searched her voice for any hint of duplicity, my hand reaching for the faulty candle in my pocket. But if she had intentionally sabotaged me, she covered it well. "We were starting to worry," she added in a lighter tone.

I wasn't about to admit that I'd gotten lost. "My parents stayed up later than normal, so I couldn't sneak out. But I came as fast as I could once they went to bed."

"Then why didn't you take the path?" Mercy asked. Ann and I glared at her at the exact same time.

I heard a rustling from the woods. Tituba emerged, a heavy bag on her arm, with Abigail trailing behind her.

"Finally," Ann said sharply.

Tituba's mouth flattened into a thin line. "This place will do." She dropped the bag in the small clearing.

I watched Ann. A look of uncertainty passed across her face in a flash and vanished. Was Ann nervous, too, about Tituba's promise to show us real magic?

If she was, she hid it well.

We waited for Tituba to speak. Instead, she bent over the bag and rustled through it. After a minute, she stood, but her hands were still empty. "Tonight we are going to call up the spirits to speak to us."

Mercy gasped. "But isn't that . . . witchcraft?"

Abigail spoke with a shaky voice. "Minister Parris gives sermons against that sort of thing."

Tituba sighed. "You girls have been playing with powers you do not understand. You have been using weak love charms and children's curses. Tonight will be different."

Ann opened her mouth. I expected her to protest, to defend her Burning Book. But something stopped her. My eyes darted back to Tituba. I saw why Ann hesitated. Tituba's eyes glowed golden in the candlelight and her face was like granite, grim and cold.

She looked like a queen.

Tituba's voice grew louder. "Tonight we are going to see the future with the help of the spirits. What do you want to learn about your futures?"

The four of us looked at each other. Questions flooded my

mind. If Tituba could really tell the future . . . How much longer did I have to stay in Salem Village? Would I ever move back to London?

Would Edmund Hale ever notice me?

I swallowed. I might doubt magic, but I'd kill for answers to my questions.

Ann spoke up, and of course we all deferred to her. "We want to know about our future husbands," she declared. "If they're rich and powerful and handsome. And where they live. And when we'll meet them." Her voice didn't shake at all. If I hadn't seen the flash of fear in her eyes, I would have believed her act.

"I can show you that," Tituba said quietly.

Mercy gasped. Abigail clapped her hands together.

My reaction was no different. I froze in place, my heart pounding in my chest.

"You brought the egg?" Tituba said to Abigail.

She reached into a pocket and pulled out a single egg, along with what looked like a wine goblet. "Is it the right kind?" she asked as she handed them to Tituba.

"Yes, this will work." Tituba held up the egg. "We are going to create a portal to the spirit world, to see what the future holds for you." She cracked the egg with one hand, quickly separating the yolk from the white. She poured the white into the glass and tossed the shell, still cradling the yolk, into the woods.

Then Tituba beckoned us closer.

Ann stepped forward eagerly. I followed her, my body buzzing with nerves.

"You will look into this glass. The answers you seek will be found there. You will see them before your eyes." She waved her hand over the glass and began chanting in a language I didn't recognize.

Ann leaned over the glass. "When will we see it?" she demanded.

Tituba glared at her. "Not until I say you can," she replied harshly. "Now don't interrupt me again."

My nerves evaporated and I barely stifled a laugh. No one spoke to Ann Putnam that way. Certainly not a West Indian slave.

But Ann ignored the insult. She was transfixed by the glass, her eyes wide as she stared into it. Tituba continued her chanting. I wondered how long it would take for something to happen.

Unless it was all fake.

Then Tituba fell silent.

Abigail gasped. "Did it . . . did it change?"

I leaned in and gazed at the egg white. It did look different—it had become milky and opaque. I shivered and told myself it wasn't magic. It was probably just a trick of the light.

"Now you may ask your questions," Tituba said. She held the glass over a fat candle, and the goblet sparkled with yellow light.

"Me first," Ann said quickly. She took a slight step closer to the glass and spoke directly at the egg white. "Who will I marry?"

Tituba sighed and shook her head. "You cannot ask that kind of question. Here, let me show you. We have to start with something simple." She directed her question at the glass. "Show us the profession of Ann Putnam's husband." Tituba waved her hand over the egg white. Ann nodded eagerly. "Watch, now. Watch closely." Tituba was gently swirling the glass with her right hand.

Ann suddenly gasped.

"Did you see that?" she sputtered. "I saw . . . I saw a pile of money!"

"Yes," Tituba confirmed. "The sign was clear."

My eyes darted from Ann to Tituba and back to the glass. I hadn't seen anything. But I was farther back.

Had they really seen the same vision in the glass?

"That means he's going to be rich," Ann crowed. "Maybe a banker. Or the governor!" She clasped her hands together as if she were a bride holding a bouquet. "I have more questions about my husband," she said to Tituba.

"That is not the way it works," Tituba explained. "Now we will go around the circle and ask the same question for each girl. After that we will pose a new question."

Ann's deflation only lasted for a moment. "Fine. Ask about Cavie. No, Abigail. Do Abigail next."

If Ann couldn't have her way, she could at least control who went next. And of course she used the opportunity to let us know where we stood in her hierarchy. Abigail didn't try to hide her delight. I snuck a glance at Mercy, who hadn't even made it into Ann's top two, but her eyes were trained on the glass. She didn't seem to care about the slight, if she noticed it.

Tituba reached out a finger to order Abigail closer. She nearly leapt to Tituba's side.

"I hope he'll be rich, too," Abigail whispered. "Rich like the Putnams." Her eyes darted to Ann, who ignored her. Ann had barely taken her eyes off the glass since Tituba started chanting.

Tituba waved her hand over the glass. "Show us the profession of Abigail Williams's husband."

Abigail leaned forward, her eyes wide. "What . . . what is that?" she asked, pointing. "It looks like . . ." She trailed off. It looked like a blob in the egg white to me, but I held my tongue. "Is it a book?" she asked Tituba.

"Yes," Tituba confirmed. "It is a book."

Ann leaned back and laughed. "Your husband is going to be a *nerd*," she chortled. "Maybe you'll marry a minister. I'm so glad I didn't see a book! "

"I don't want to be a minister's wife," Abigail sulked.

"Maybe it means he'll be an accountant," I said. "Or a professor."

"Really?" Abigail asked, but instead of looking at me, she looked to Ann, who rolled her eyes. Abigail was left chewing on her lower lip, anxiety written across her face.

Ann wasted no time. "Cavie next, Cavie next," she declared.

My feet dragged as I stepped closer to the glass. A shiver snaked through my body as I leaned over the glass. I recoiled at a strange heat that seemed to surround it. It was probably just the candle, but I thrust my hands into my pockets anyway to hide their shaking.

Tituba addressed the glass for the third time. "Show us the profession of Margaret Cavendish Lucas's husband." My head jerked up when Tituba spoke my name—how did she know it? But my eyes were drawn back to the goblet.

Tituba waved her hands over the glass. I gazed into the egg white and willed myself to see something. I licked my lips in anticipation and tried to tell myself that I didn't believe in magic.

The seconds ticked by, and still I saw nothing.

Ann grabbed my arm and I jumped. "A wagon wheel," she yelled. "I saw a wagon wheel!"

My pulse was still pounding. I tried to hide my nerves behind a smile. I hadn't seen anything in the egg white, but I didn't want to admit that in front of Ann.

"You agree that is what you saw?" Tituba asked me.

I nodded and squeaked out, "Yes."

"Cavie's going to marry a farmer," Ann said, challenging us with her eyes to disagree.

"It looked more like the wheel from a regal carriage to me," Mercy said. "Maybe Cavie will be the queen."

Ann scoffed. "Not likely. It sounds like Cavie is going to be stuck here in Salem Village, the wife of some farmer."

I let out a long breath and stepped back from the glass. If it really was a wagon wheel, did that mean I might marry Edmund Hale? I shook the idea out of my head and clenched my fists. I hadn't seen anything in the glass—so why had I accepted Ann's interpretation? Part of me knew that she was just trying to upset me, but part of me wanted to believe her.

"Mercy, hurry up," Ann said. "I want to ask more questions about my husband the governor."

Mercy stepped forward, throwing her silky blonde hair over her shoulder with one hand.

Tituba repeated the ritual. "Show us the profession of Mercy Lewis's husband."

I barely paid attention to the hand waving at this point. Instead I watched Ann's face. It was radiant in the flickering candlelight, the glow of the candle adding to the pale pink of her cheeks. All of her attention was trained on the glass.

Ann seemed so certain about what she saw in the egg white. Did she really believe in Tituba's magic? Or did she just want to believe?

Her perfect face held no answers to my question.

And then the light drained from Ann's face in an instant. A pallor came over her. "No," she gasped.

My eyes darted to the glass. Mercy shot back as if she'd been burned. She nearly trampled my foot. "Did you see it too?" she asked Ann.

"That can't be!" Ann said.

"What?" I asked.

"This is not good," Tituba said. "We must go from here." She pulled back the goblet so that it no longer glittered with the reflected light of the candle.

"What was it?" I asked, a rising tightness in my chest. My eyes jumped from face to face. I saw the same ashen look on each.

"Didn't you see it?" Abigail whispered. "It was . . . a coffin."

Mercy's voice shook. "Maybe it means I'll marry a coffin maker?"

Tituba shook her head. "This girl will be married to death," she declared. "She will find no husband, for she will be in her grave before her time."

Mercy let out a moan and started to cry. I put a hand on her shoulder, but it didn't seem to calm her. I could almost feel the fear emanating from her body. "It's not true," Mercy whined. "It can't be true!"

Ann stepped toward us, shaking her head. "But the spirits didn't lie about my banker," she said. "I'm sorry, Mercy."

Mercy's head snapped up. Fire flashed in her eyes. But instead of responding to Ann, she struck at the goblet in Tituba's hand. It flew to the ground. The goblet shattered in a tinkling of glass, and egg white splattered the leaves. "It's not true," Mercy growled. She turned and ran away from our group, enveloped by the fog.

For a moment, we were all frozen in place. Then Ann broke the spell.

"Great, now we can't ask any more questions." Ann folded her arms around her waist and tightened her lips.

"Shouldn't we go after Mercy?" I asked, looking from Ann

to Abigail.

Abigail's face was the picture of worry, but Ann brushed off my question. "She's rattled," Ann explained. "Mercy has these flights of fancy. She just needs time to calm down and come to terms with her fate."

My eyes widened. But what else could I do?

Everyone obeyed Ann's command to ignore Mercy. Abigail began to pick up pieces of the broken goblet, muttering that her uncle might notice it was missing. Tituba lifted her bag in one hand and the fat candle, still sputtering away and dripping wax, in the other. She glared at us. "Remember, tell no one about this. You have risen the spirits, and broken God's law. No one must know."

Ann sighed and rolled her eyes. "Of course we won't tell anyone," she said. "We aren't idiots."

Tituba's eyes locked onto Ann's. I thought I saw a hint of caution flash across Tituba's face, but I blinked and it was gone. I might have imagined it. "Let's go, Miss Williams," Tituba said, gesturing to Abigail. "We can do no more tonight." Abigail dropped the broken pieces of goblet she'd collected, leaving a mess behind her, and followed Tituba. She glanced over her shoulder at us—no, just at Ann—and winced.

Before Tituba's candle disappeared in the fog, Ann turned to me. "Put away the candles," she ordered. And then she vanished into the trees.

I was left standing alone in the middle of the fog-covered woods, in a circle of candles, with a broken glass and egg white scattered at my feet.

I shivered and started blowing out the candles.

SEVEN

A ray of sunlight snuck through my window the next morning.

The fog must have lifted in the night.

I stretched out in bed, piled under my blankets. I was glad for the sunshine, but it didn't erase my dark mood. Ann obviously believed Tituba's predictions, without any space for questioning. So where did my doubts fit in? Tituba's magic might have felt powerful in the dark woods, surrounded by flickering candlelight, but in the light of day the whole thing felt foolish.

And yet all three of the Glass Girls were convinced they saw the coffin in the glass.

Could I be wrong?

Had I been looking closely enough?

I pulled my knees to my chest. Whether or not I believed the magic spells, the Glass Girls certainly did. What would they do in school on Monday? Would they act like nothing had happened?

And how was Mercy?

With a groan, I pushed off the covers. I had to get up eventually. Not just because of my parents, but because Joy had made me promise three times that I'd meet her this morning by a little island in the creek behind the Village Square. She had to be dying to hear about the previous night.

But what could I tell her? I wasn't even sure what had happened.

Still, I couldn't leave Joy wondering. She might even worry if I was okay and come to the house looking for me. How would my parents react if Joy showed up in her black bonnet, asking if I came home last night?

I swung my legs out of bed and slipped into in a simple dress. It was technically dark blue, but hopefully it wouldn't raise any eyebrows among the Puritans. My family's lack of attendance at church had already caused some trouble, according to my dad. Minister Parris had approached him in the Village carrying a Bible. When my dad said he attended church in Salem Town—which wasn't true—Minister Parris had narrowed his eyes and encouraged us to come to his next sermon.

Did my dad know about the rivalry between Town and Village? I didn't want to explain it to him. He'd laughed off the encounter with Minister Parris as a funny anecdote about small-town life.

I wasn't so sure. His run-in with Parris only made it obvious that we weren't just newcomers, we were outsiders.

I grabbed an apple on my way out the door, barely waving to my parents as I breezed by. I mumbled something about meeting a friend in the Village, and my mom called after me, "Oh, that's nice. Have fun!"

The bright blue sky was jarring after a day encased by fog. I squinted in the light and shoved the apple into my bag. It was a crisp winter day, already early February. Fresh snow coated the grass, as if the fog had left behind footprints. New England was so different from the damp, grey winters in London.

The cold air burned my chest as I breathed in, and my exhales were white clouds.

I had to hurry. I needed to make a stop before I met Joy.

The road was hard and rutted under my feet, but I pressed on. This time, in daylight, I could see the small path off the main road that led into the woods. With a glance to either side, I stepped into the woods.

In minutes, I was back in the circle of candles. I hadn't followed Ann's orders last night. Instead of putting away the candles, I'd run home like a coward. In the dark, surrounded by fog, the woods had taken on an ominous cast. But now, in daylight, I wondered what had frightened me. Sunlight filtered through the bare branches of the trees and picked up hints of orange and red in the leaves coating the ground. I found the hollow stump with the candle bag I'd seen Mercy use earlier. I picked up each candle and wedged the full bag under the stump.

Then my eyes stopped on the sparkling glass.

I tried to squint and imagine it was a sheet of ice, but I knew the truth. I couldn't leave Minister Parris's shattered goblet in the woods. Someone else might find it. I gathered up the pieces quickly, my nose wrinkling as I tried to avoid touching the dried egg white. I looked around the clearing for a place to hide the glass. In the end, I used a fallen branch to scratch a hole in the hard ground. I sprinkled dirt over the shards and set a rock on top.

Before I turned away from the clearing, I set my foot on top of the rock and pushed down. The sound of glass crunching sent a shiver up my spine.

Something rustled in the dense underbrush. I jumped, my head whipping around to look for the source of the noise.

A squirrel. Just a squirrel.

Blood pounded in my ears. I had never been so skittish before, not even back at the girls' academy in London when we tried to prank each other. Something about the Village made my skin crawl.

I left the clearing behind and made my way back to the road. Once I reached the Village Square, I followed Joy's directions. In minutes, I came upon a narrow path leading to the stream. If I kept heading north on the road, the stream crossed under a bridge a hundred yards away. But this path led to an island upstream from the bridge, and Joy promised it was always deserted.

I tried to enjoy the stroll through the woods. Frosted leaves crunched under my feet. A cold breeze cut through the bare trees. But I couldn't stop shivering.

When I reached the island, Joy was nowhere to be seen. I settled down on a boulder, rubbing my arms as I watched the water trickling between the rock and the shore.

A few minutes later I heard someone approaching through the woods. My nerves screamed but I forced myself still.

It was just Joy.

She bound out of the woods, her arms already splayed apart. "Cavie, you have to tell me everything," she gushed. "I saw Mercy this morning and she looked like she'd seen a ghost." Joy hopped across the narrow stream onto the island and settled on a rock near mine.

How could I explain what happened? I pulled my cloak closer around my body.

Might as well start at the beginning. "Tituba used an egg white to predict the future."

"And?"

"And Mercy wasn't happy about what she saw."

"Stop being so cryptic, Cavie."

I leaned back on the rock and sighed. "It's hard to explain. Tituba said a bunch of chants over a goblet, and we asked questions. We were supposed to watch the egg white to read a message from the spirits. Ann wanted to know about our future husbands."

Joy rolled her eyes. "Why am I not surprised?"

"Ann bossed everyone around, as usual," I continued. "But you should have seen her face when Tituba scolded her."

"Ann Putnam, scolded by a slave? Oh, I wish I'd been there."

"Ann pretended like it never happened. She ignored Tituba and told the rest of us what to do."

"So, what did the spell reveal about everyone's husbands? Let me guess: Ann's is the best."

I had to smile. "The spirits say Ann will marry a rich banker. Or the governor. She hasn't decided. Ann declared that Abigail will marry a minister because she saw a book in the egg white. Abigail wasn't happy."

"Did she stand up to Ann?"

"Of course not." I shifted on the boulder. "But we didn't get very far before something really strange happened—" I began, but Joy cut me off.

"Cavie, do you believe in magic?"

I shrugged my shoulders and pulled my arms around my body. "I don't know."

"I believe in magic. Don't give me that look!"

I tried to hide the surprise from my face. Joy wasn't a Puritan, so I'd just assumed she didn't believe in magic. But why not? Most people swore it was real. And, to tell the truth, I wasn't completely sure myself.

Joy rolled her eyes. "I've lived in Salem Village long enough to know that magic is forbidden. And if Puritans don't like it, it must be cool. But I bet a lot of people who claim to know magic are lying."

"Like the Glass Girls and their Burning Book," I said. "I don't think they were really casting spells."

Joy gave me a serious look. "Is that how it felt when Tituba was doing magic?"

I swallowed and looked down at the stream. I couldn't put my feelings into words. "Maybe it was just the fog, or the candles. But something did feel different. It's like my skin was humming during the spells." I frowned. "I can't explain it."

"Then do you believe the predictions?"

I shook my head right away. "No. Ann told us what she wants our futures to be."

"What did she say about your husband?"

"Ann saw a wagon wheel and decided I'll marry a poor farmer and stay in Salem Village."

"But Ann knows you hate it here."

"It doesn't mean anything. Ann's probably just trying to upset me."

"Kind of like what she does with Abigail?"

"Exactly." I trailed a finger along the edge of the boulder. "I know she's doing it, but somehow I keep getting pulled in." I kept my eyes down. It wasn't easy to admit to Joy that I craved Ann's approval. But if anyone could understand, she would.

"Ann's always been like that," Joy said quietly. "She's fickle. Someone will hold her interest for a while, but then she'll turn on them. She makes you feel like you have to compete to be her friend."

Her words sent a shiver through my body. "You're right." Our eyes met for an instant, but I looked away.

Joy's voice hardened. "But what freaked Mercy out? What happened after that?"

It was easier to tell the story than to think about Ann's games. I jumped right in. "I don't know how to explain what happened. Tituba asked the spirits about Mercy's future husband, and suddenly everyone went pale. They all swore there was a coffin in the egg white."

"A coffin?" Joy said slowly.

I didn't want to remember the terror on Mercy's face or Ann's cold tone. "Mercy started crying because Tituba said it meant she was going to die. And Ann was really mean about it. She told Mercy the spirits don't lie, so she should accept her fate." The words poured out of my mouth.

"That's awful," Joy breathed. "What did Mercy do?"

"She smashed the glass and ran off. After that, everyone just left."

Joy's mouth hung open. "What a bitch."

"Ann?"

"Of course, Ann. Can you believe she'd do that to Mercy? Wait, don't answer. I shouldn't be surprised. No wonder Mercy was so pale this morning."

I pressed my lips together. For a minute, I listened to the stream bubbling next to me. Glittering fragments of ice clung to the wet rocks. In a few days, it might be frozen. It might not run again until spring. I watched the water sparkle in a ray of sunlight and thought about how quickly things could change.

"Cavie?"

I looked up to see Joy watching me with a worried expression. "Sorry. It was a weird night."

"It sounds like it," she said, but her look of concern didn't vanish. "I wonder what school will be like on Monday."

I shook my head. "I have no idea."

Joy reached out and took my hand in hers. The contact was so unexpected that I almost jerked back. But I stopped, drawn in by Joy's serious expression. "Someone has to stop Ann," she said.

I slowly pulled back my hand. "You're right." How could I explain to Joy that in spite of Ann's cruelty, and last night, I still wanted to be a Glass Girl? I liked having friends. I liked it when the younger girls whispered about me.

Ann was unpredictable, but the air around her felt charged with a kind of power.

And would Edmund Hale have given me a second glance if I hadn't been sitting with the Glass Girls that day?

Ann wasn't perfect, but neither was I.

Maybe we didn't have to destroy the Glass Girls. Maybe I could show Ann how to be nicer. I knew Joy would laugh at the idea, but Ann liked me. She always asked me to sit right next to her.

Maybe I could talk to her.

Maybe I could make Joy happy, but also stay friends with the Glass Girls.

That was a lot of maybes.

We sat silently in the woods, the air dead still. I snuck a glance at Joy. I couldn't read her expression. Her lips were pursed and she was gazing off into the woods.

I shifted my weight on the boulder. "Well, I should get back to the farm." I stood, my legs stiff from the cold rock.

"We'll talk on Monday?"

"Of course," I promised. I left the island and didn't look

back.

~ ~ ~

On Monday, my feet dragged as I walked to school. I hadn't seen Joy since Saturday morning. In fact, I hadn't seen anyone all weekend. I'd given myself a self-imposed exile on the farm, where I kept busy weeding the overgrown fields.

My stomach churned as the schoolhouse came into view. Was it possible to change Ann? Or would she somehow become even worse? If the effort blew up in my face, Joy would be furious.

Over the weekend I'd spent hours pulling weeds and thinking about the Glass Girls. Abigail was miserable because she thought Ann was mad at her. Mercy was depressed because she thought she was going to die. If only Ann was nicer.

Ann. I couldn't just *ask* her to be kinder. I had to give her a reason.

So what did she want?

And on top of all that, I had no idea how Friday night's adventure would color Monday morning.

But when I walked up to school, the first person I saw was Mercy. The rosiness in her cheeks had returned and she was smiling as she talked to Dorothy Marsh. As I watched, my eyes grew even wider when Mercy threw her head back and broke into laughter.

This was the same girl who thought she was going to die a few days earlier?

Ann Putnam grabbed my arm and pulled me aside. Where had she come from?

"You can't say anything about Friday night," she whispered.

"I know. I would never tell anyone."

"Good." She narrowed her eyes as if she didn't believe me.

"At least Mercy's better?"

Ann shook her head and let out a deep breath of air through her nose. "Not really. She's only smiling because I talked to her at church yesterday. I made up some story about how the magic wasn't real and it meant nothing. You know Mercy. She completely believed me." Ann leaned toward me and lowered her voice even further, until I could barely hear her. "It's sad, really. The poor girl will never marry."

My mouth fell open. That was Ann's attempt to help Mercy? She lied right to her friend's face—and in church, of all places. And now Ann was whispering behind Mercy's back about how she was going to die.

And I thought I could change Ann Putnam. Was I fooling myself?

Ann narrowed her eyes at me. I tried to hide my look of shock. But I still stumbled over my words. "You were just trying to help. And look how happy Mercy is."

That earned me a thin smile. Ann turned her gaze back to Mercy, who was still laughing with Dorothy. "I'm so glad you understand, Cavie. You just get me."

I held my face blank even though my stomach flipped. Was Ann right? Could I guide her in the right direction with compliments?

It was worth a try.

"You just want what's best for Mercy. There's nothing wrong with being a good friend."

"Speaking of that, I should tell Mercy to change her bonnet. That one makes her look like a whore."

My thoughts scrambled again as I stared at Mercy's bonnet.

It looked like the same one she wore ever day.

Ann's voice broke through my daze. "Anyway, you should totally come to this party a week from Friday," Ann said.

I gave a little shake of my head, but it didn't clear the fog in my mind. "A party? Puritans have parties?"

Ann let out a single laugh and playfully slapped my arm. "Of course we have parties! It's at Edmund Hale's house, too. His parents will be in Boston for the weekend so he invited everyone over. It's going to be crazy."

A party at Edmund Hale's house? My heart practically skipped a beat. All my worries about Mercy and Ann vanished in a flash. I'd finally talk to Edmund. What was his house like? Who would be there?

And what did Ann mean when she said the party would be crazy?

"So do you want to go?" Ann asked sweetly.

"Of course!" I breathed. My heart was pounding so loudly that I wondered if Ann could hear it. It sounded like a drum to me.

"I figured, since you have a huge crush on Edmund."

I opened my mouth to object, but nothing came out.

"I thought so," she said, grinning like a cat with a canary in its sights. "This will be the perfect chance for you to talk with Edmund."

I could almost feel my knees shaking under my white apron. "Really?" I squeaked.

"Geez, Cavie, don't make it so obvious. Boys hate that," Ann scolded. "Anyway, we'll meet here once it's dark so we can walk over together. Don't tell your parents." Before I could answer, she walked into the schoolhouse, leaving me alone on the dirt path.

A party at Edmund Hale's house. I floated into the school and sat down next to Joy, who raised the corner of her lips at me in a silent question. I shook my head once to let her know we couldn't talk.

I didn't want to talk to Joy. I just wanted to think about the party.

When Mr. Green started class, I snuck a glance at the back of the room. Mercy was glowing like she'd been cast as the Virgin Mary in a Puritan nativity scene. But Ann was sitting by herself.

The spot next to her, where Abigail always sat, was empty.

EIGHT

Somehow, the strange episode in the woods faded to the back of my mind. Instead, I spent my waking hours imagining the party where I would finally talk to Edmund Hale. Joy elbowed me at school on Wednesday because I didn't even hear Mr. Green ask me a question.

On Friday, Joy pulled me aside after school.

"What's gotten into you?"

"Nothing." I couldn't tell Joy about the party. It was only a week away. What if she wanted to go? It would ruin everything.

"You're acting different." Her hands were on her hips and her black bonnet hung down her back, exposing her dark hair.

I lowered my voice. "I'm just acting like a Glass Girl. You don't want to make Ann suspicious, right?"

Joy chewed on her lip, her face the picture of worry. She gave a nod. "What's our next move?"

"Shhh, Ann's coming." I stepped away from Joy and wrinkled my nose at her.

Did Joy talk about anything but Ann?

And anyway, my plan to reform Ann was working. A little. I

told her that Dorothy Marsh's dad knew the governor's son, and now Ann was being really nice to Dorothy.

It was a start.

Ann pulled off her bonnet with one hand as she walked over. Her hair cascaded down her back. "God, I hate this thing. It's so oppressive." She gave Joy a sideways glance. Joy sighed loudly as she stomped away. "You should ask Mr. Green if you can move to the back row with us."

"But that's Abigail's seat."

Ann gave a tiny shake of her head. A tendril of golden hair slipped over her shoulder. "Abigail isn't here."

I suddenly realized that Abigail hadn't been in school all week. "Is she okay?"

"She's got a cold or something," Ann said, looking disinterested.

"Oh. Should we take her some soup?"

Ann let out a laugh. "You're too much sometimes, Cavie." She swept her hair back. "I'll see you next week. Don't forget the party."

As if I could forget.

That Monday, I realized that Abigail's young cousin, Betty Parris, wasn't in school either. Betty sat in the very front row, as one of the youngest girls in our class, and I wasn't sure how long she'd been out. I wondered if her family was visiting a relative or something, but Ann would have known.

I convinced myself to stop by Abigail's house later that week.

But by Friday all I could think about was Edmund Hale's party. I ran home from school and headed straight to my room to pick out my outfit.

I had some beautiful dresses from our time in Virginia and

London, one in an irresistible blue satin. But what did Puritans wear to parties? I reached up to touch my hair, uncapped as it usually was at home. Would the girls wear bonnets? My stomach jittered with nerves.

I held up the blue dress and felt the silky fabric between my fingers.

Then I set it back on my bed.

I should have asked Mercy or Ann what they were going to wear.

And then I pictured Ann laughing at my dress and asking if I was pretending to be the daughter of an earl. My face flushed just imagining it.

Finally, I picked a plain black dress. I didn't want to stand out too much. I packed away my apron, pulled back my hair at the nape of my neck, and watched for the sun to set.

As I waited, I picked up my crisp, white bonnet and traced the hem with my fingers. At school, the girls always wore their bonnets. Only the Glass Girls—and Joy, I realized—dared to take them off for a few minutes, but even that was risky if an adult saw. I shifted my legs, but I couldn't get comfortable. Darkness had fallen outside, but I was trapped. My hand tightened around the bonnet.

I couldn't leave the stupid thing behind. What if all the other girls were wearing bonnets, except for me? I finally shoved the white cap into the pocket of my cloak, just in case I had to pull it out at the party.

And then it was time to repeat my Friday night ritual of sneaking out of the house. It was getting easier every time.

I hurried to the schoolhouse, my breath leaving a ghostly trail behind me. I didn't see anyone along the way. Puritans were pretty serious about going to bed when the sun went down.

When I reached the building, Mercy was standing in front, twirling the edges of her long, dark cape between her fingers.

She wasn't wearing a bonnet, either. I breathed a sigh of relief.

"Finally," she said. "Come on, let's go before someone sees us."

"What about Ann?" It was Ann's idea to meet at the school, after all.

"Oh, Ann's already at the party." Mercy looked over her shoulder. "Hurry up, we really don't want to run into someone."

She set out on a road that ran east, into Salem's farmlands. I hurried to keep up with her. Mercy's legs weren't long, but she was fast. A swirling chain of dead leaves danced in our wake. But we didn't see anyone.

Soon we'd left behind the buildings clustered at the center of the Village. Mercy's pace slowed and I caught my breath. The houses were spread out, surrounded by empty fields. I'd never come this way before. Maybe that's why I never ran into Edmund Hale. Did he even know my name? My pulse quickened again at the thought of seeing him.

I had no idea how far away Edmund lived but it felt like we'd been walking forever. I was just about to ask when Mercy pointed. "That's his house."

It was a small building, maybe only three rooms in all, set in the middle of a bare plot of land. A thin path led from the road to his door. We were still a quarter-mile away, but I could see light pouring from the windows, and I could even hear the distant sound of voices.

I didn't see any other houses off the road. It was the perfect place for a party.

As we walked up the path, the noise from the house grew

louder. I heard the hum of conversations, punctuated every few seconds by a loud laugh or a yell. The sound of music rose above the voices. A fiddle spun out a fast-paced tune and I could hear singing and stomping feet accompanying the music.

"Ann wasn't kidding about Puritan parties," I muttered to myself.

"What?" Mercy swiveled her head to look back at me.

"Nothing."

When we reached the door, Mercy pulled it open. A wave of sound and light hit us. When my eyes adjusted, I saw dozens of young Villagers talking and dancing.

None of them wore black.

The girls had donned brightly colored gowns in blues, greens, and even red. My throat tightened as I took in the scene. Where had they bought those dresses? Surely not in Puritan Massachusetts Bay Colony. And how did they hide the forbidden colors from their parents? Then I saw their hair, styled in imitation of the latest fashions in Europe, piled in ringlets atop their heads. Each of their cheeks held a rosy ring of blush. As we stood in the doorway, Mercy threw off her cloak and revealed a low-cut pink satin gown that I had never seen before.

My jaw hung slack. I had never expected to find Versailles in a backwoods colonial village.

Thank goodness I hadn't worn my bonnet.

Mercy elbowed me, raising an eyebrow at my plain black dress, which was peeking through my open cloak. "Geez, Cavie, have you never been to a party?" she teased. "You look like a regular *Puritan*!" She laughed and wandered off, leaving me to fend for myself.

I stood out like a crow among peacocks. I wanted to turn around and run home, but what would Ann say? And I'd miss my chance to see Edmund Hale.

I slipped out of my cloak and made sure my bonnet was hidden deep in the pocket. After adding my cloak to the pile by the door, I inched along the wall, trying to blend in with the plain thatched wood. Who were all these people? I recognized a few girls from school, but most of the revelers were strangers. And some looked much older than sixteen. They must have come from outside the Village. Had they walked all the way from Town? It was freezing cold and dark as a tomb, plus the woods were full of wolves and even more dangerous creatures.

I ducked my head to hide the flush in my cheeks. This was a party. It was supposed to be fun, but I was acting more like a prudish goodwife than a teenager.

Standing in the corner wasn't helping. I raised my chin and plastered a smile on my face. No one had noticed me yet, but I wasn't going to spend the party hiding. I left the dancing and loud conversations of the main room behind and walked into the kitchen.

A crowd of boys stood around a wooden barrel sloshing with liquid. I searched for Edmund, but didn't see him. As I watched, they dipped a ladle into a hole in the barrel's lid and scooped the drink into wooden cups, which they threw back with a chorus of hoots.

One of the boys saw me watching and held out a cup. "Want some apple jack?"

I held up a hand, waving off the cup. "What's apple jack?"

He grinned. "I guess you're not from around here?"

I gave a small shake of my head.

"It's an apple liquor. You freeze hard apple cider and let the water evaporate. It's amazing. And Edmund's parents have an entire barrel!"

He reached out to offer the cup again. I stepped back. I'd had a few sips of wine at Christmas dinner, and one time a trader in Virginia offered me a taste of rum that burned when it went down my throat. I had enough sense to know it wasn't a good idea to start drinking apple jack.

"No, thank you," I said. The boy turned back to his friends as if I didn't exist and downed another cup of the drink.

I left the boys and wandered back into the main room, looking for Ann or Mercy. The swirling dancers, now arranged in lines, were bowing to each other. After bowing, they stomped on the ground and spun around in pairs. It was a discordant cross between a waltz and a peasant dance. I stepped back to avoid being caught up in their exuberance and bumped into the hearth. A candle rocked dangerously close to the edge and I threw up a hand to steady it.

My stomach tilted. I'd already felt out of place in the Village. The party only made it worse. My cheeks burned as I relived my long, anxious debate over whether to wear a bonnet, when the other girls were baring their shoulders and ankles, downing apple jack, and dancing with unmarried men.

I didn't understand the rules of Puritan society. And I didn't know how Puritan teenagers broke those rules.

I hunched my shoulders, pushing down the shame that washed over me like an ocean tide. I wanted to pull on my cloak and leave.

But then I heard Ann's distinctive laugh.

My head whipped around. She was emerging from the bedroom door. And she was holding hands with someone who stepped out behind her.

It was Edmund Hale.

My breath caught in my chest and my body went ice cold.

Why was she with Edmund?

Why were they holding hands?

And then Ann looked across the room, right into my eyes, and smiled. She even gave me a little wave with the hand that wasn't currently clutching Edmund Hale's.

I couldn't look away, bewitched by her presence. She looked amazing in a light blue gown with her hair in gentle, honey-colored waves cascading down her back. My black dress burned like a bonfire, its drab, flat shape crying out that I could never compete with Ann Putnam.

And I didn't dare look at Edmund.

Time seemed to stop as I stared at them. And then I broke the spell.

My eyes darted to the front door. I nearly tripped over my feet as I ran to get my cloak.

As I fled, I ran into Mercy.

My ears were pounding so loudly that I could barely register her words.

"Are you leaving already, Cavie?" She looked over her shoulder at Ann, still holding hands with Edmund on the opposite side of the room. "Yeah, they got back together. Didn't she tell you?"

I shook my head. Hot tears of rage welled up in my eyes. I looked up at the rough wooden ceiling and blinked back the tears.

How *could* she?

Mercy chattered on, oblivious to the firestorm of emotions coursing through my body. "I guess Ann realized she wanted him back, or something."

"Or something," I repeated quietly. "Excuse me."

I grabbed my cloak, still at the top of the pile, and whipped it around my body. I wasn't going to hang around to watch Ann drape herself on Edmund Hale right in front of me.

She knew I liked Edmund. And she invited me to his party.

Why?

Just so she could throw it in my face? So she could smile and laugh about courting the guy that I liked?

I was halfway out the door when Ann threw an arm around me, pulling me back into the room. "Cavie! You're finally here!"

I recoiled from her touch as though she was a reptile. She stepped back, a hurt look flashing across her face. My first instinct was to apologize, but I pressed my lips shut.

"Are you leaving?" She wrinkled her eyebrows and tucked her chin to her chest. Then she glanced down at my demure dress and pursed her lips. Her silence spoke volumes. I put a hand on my hip, daring her to say something. Instead, she twirled a loose strand of hair between her fingers. "If this is about Edmund . . ." she started, then stopped herself. "I should have warned you. I know you used to have feelings for him, but you also knew that he was my ex. And sometimes those feelings just come back."

I *used to* have feelings for him? Her feelings just *came back*?

No.

Ann was watching me closely. I had no idea what my face looked like, but I didn't really care.

"Whatever." I pushed past her to go out the door.

"Cavie," she said, grabbing my arm. "I hope you don't blame me. After all, it's not like he even knows who you are."

Was that supposed to make me feel better? Or was it just another one of Ann's digs?

I didn't care. I stormed out the door and didn't look back.

On the long, cold walk home I wiped tears from my face. I

replayed that moment when I saw Ann and Edmund holding hands. I imagined running over and slapping Ann in the face or scratching at her flawless hair. The perfect comebacks were on my lips now, but I had been so shocked that in the moment my mind was blank. I should have expected something like this from Ann Putnam.

NINE

I couldn't hide my depression from my parents. On Saturday, I stayed in bed long past chore time, and when I finally pulled myself from the covers I moped around the house all morning, ignoring their worried glances. Pretending that everything was fine would have required too much energy.

After a breakfast of already-cold porridge, I sank into the rocking chair that my dad had bought in Salem Town. I picked up the knitting needles from the woven basket at the base of the chair and set them on my lap. But instead of continuing to work on a quilt, I stared into space and let my mind wander.

I jumped when my mom spoke.

"What's wrong, Cavie?" Mom bit her bottom lip. It was the fifth time she'd asked me the same question.

Dad whispered, "Probably boy troubles. She's sixteen after all."

I scowled and set down the half-finished quilt. I didn't want to admit that he was right, so I asked to be excused and stood. As I was headed for the front door, I heard my dad say, "See?"

I wanted to slam the door behind me, but I didn't. Instead, I stormed off in the opposite direction from Edmund Hale's house, away from the Village and into the silent woods of Massachusetts. A few cattle grazing along a stream were my only companions. The road dwindled into more of a path, wide enough for a horse but too narrow for a wagon. I walked until my feet ached and my anger had burned out.

I sucked in a deep breath of air and looked up at the bare tree branches spreading their arms over the path.

The sun had dipped from its zenith. It was past time for me to go home.

I turned back and retraced my steps. The walk seemed somehow longer on the way home. My stomach growled noisily. Then, when I was almost within sight of my house, I saw someone ambling down the road ahead of me. The figure waved and strode toward me.

Just my luck. It was Mercy, of all people. What was she doing here, so far from her own house?

"Hi Cavie," she said with a wide grin. "Where did you go last night? We all missed you!"

I looked over her shoulder toward my house and pictured the brown bread with butter that my mom served for lunch. I gave her a halfhearted smile. "Oh, you know."

"Was it because of Ann and Edmund?" Her round blue eyes and pale pink cheeks made her look like a porcelain doll. "You really shouldn't be angry with Ann. Everyone said they were eventually going to get back together."

Well, no one told me. Not even Ann, when she was pushing me to talk with Edmund. And why was Mercy here, anyway? Had Ann sent her to find out if I was desolate?

I vowed not to let a single inch of depression show on my face.

So I threw back my shoulders and looked Mercy in the eye. "I wasn't feeling well." It wasn't the best excuse, but I just wanted to change the subject. I couldn't keep talking about Ann and Edmund.

Ann and Edmund. Even their names made my stomach turn.

"Did you catch what Abigail has?"

Mercy's response caught me off guard. I had completely forgotten about Abigail's absence from school. I'd been too focused on myself. A grimace flitted across my face.

"Abigail is sick?"

"Didn't you hear?"

"Apparently I don't hear much around here."

Mercy either ignored or didn't register my frustration. "She and her cousin Betty have been sick for two weeks. Everyone's talking about it."

The knot in my stomach tightened. "Is it serious?"

Mercy wrinkled her eyebrows. "I don't know. Minister Parris called in a doctor. I'm sure he'll figure out what's wrong."

The last time I'd seen Abigail, she was vanishing into the fog after we'd called up spirits in the woods. Had it really been two weeks ago? I looked away from Mercy. "That's terrible."

"Ann says Abigail is probably still upset about *the magic*." Mercy whispered the last two words, even though we were standing alone on an empty road.

My eyes narrowed. "Ann said that?"

"Yeah, Ann says that Abigail takes magic pretty seriously."

I frowned. Tituba had predicted that Mercy would die, and yet Mercy seemed fine. But somehow Abigail was so upset that she couldn't leave her house?

Or maybe Ann was spreading rumors. Again.

It was probably just a cold. I told myself not to worry about Abigail.

But then I was left thinking about Ann and Edmund again.

Why was Mercy here, anyway? What did she want from me?

"I have to go," I told Mercy abruptly.

Her mouth felt open. "Oh. Okay."

She looked genuinely surprised. A new wave of guilt crested in my chest. "Look, Mercy, I'll see you Monday at school. Okay?"

She broke into a smile. "Great!"

I walked to my house, glancing back when I reached the porch. Mercy was still standing on the road, watching me. She gave me a quick wave before I went inside.

~ ~ ~

On Monday my skin began to prickle before I'd even reached the schoolhouse.

Groups of girls and boys stood outside the school whispering to each other. I looked from one face to the next and saw the same emotions replicated everywhere: terror and anxiety.

Had something awful happened? Another Indian raid? Had France declared war on the colonies? My mind raced with fantastical fears as I looked for Joy—she would know everything.

Joy was standing alone at the edge of the clearing. I hurried over. "What's going on?" I asked in a low voice.

"Didn't you hear?" she whispered back, her eyes darting around the schoolyard.

My pulse quickened. So something terrible *had* happened. "No. Tell me."

Joy sighed. "I forgot that you don't attend the Puritan

church. Of course you haven't heard." She leaned in closer and lowered her voice. "Minister Parris gave a strange sermon yesterday."

I wanted to ask Joy why she'd been at the sermon—she wasn't a Puritan, after all. But her skittishness unsettled me. I swallowed my question and looked her in the eyes. "Come on Joy, just tell me."

Joy bit her bottom lip and cast a quick glance over the other students. When she looked back at me, her face had gone white. "He said that Betty Parris and Abigail Williams are *bewitched*."

My breath caught in my chest. *Bewitched?* The word echoed through my mind. I tried to speak but stumbled over my words.

I'd heard of bewitchment, of course. The broadsheets sometimes carried tales of children assaulted by demonic forces. But there had to be another explanation. Two girls didn't want to go to school—that didn't mean witches were attacking them.

I swallowed hard. "What did he mean?"

Joy folded her arms tightly around her middle. "You know how Abigail and Betty haven't been in school?"

"Yes, of course." Suddenly the words tumbled out. "Mercy said that Abigail was upset because of what happened in the woods. She made it sound like Abigail wasn't that sick."

"I heard it's pretty bad. Last week Minister Parris called in a doctor to check the girls. The doctor couldn't find a natural cause for their illness."

I shook my head. "But why would he suspect a witch?"

Witches. They were just stories told to scare children. At least, that's how it had been in London. There weren't even witch trials in England anymore. Hanging witches was something that happened in the past, or only in the backwaters of the globe. Not in an educated city.

With a shiver, I remembered that I was in a backwater of the empire. London might have stopped believing in witches, but they still haunted the woods of the Massachusetts Bay Colony.

Joy's voice snapped me out of my thoughts. "I'm not sure what the doctor said," she admitted. "But Minister Parris didn't hold back in his sermon. He said there are people in Salem Village who've sold their souls to Satan. He said he could smell brimstone in the air. And he said the witches are attacking Abigail and Betty. I saw three goodwives faint. But that's not the worst part. He said the community has to find the witches."

My stomach clenched. I blinked as I tried to formulate a response. Didn't Parris have a responsibility not to terrify his parishioners? I looked around at the frightened schoolchildren. One girl was even crying. "And now everyone is afraid," I whispered.

Joy nodded. "They executed a witch in Boston a few years ago for tormenting children. Cotton Mather wrote a whole book about it."

That's right—Joy had told me about the book a few weeks earlier. The washerwoman accused of making girls curse during sermons. I remembered the conversation, but it felt like a lifetime ago. Then it struck me. "Wait. Didn't you say Minister Parris has a copy of the book?"

"Yes," Joy said, her eyes narrowing as she leaned even closer. "And now he thinks his girls are being attacked by a witch just like in Cotton Mather's book."

I raised a hand to my temple and stepped back. I could feel a headache starting to crash over me. "But don't you see—he's obsessed with a book about bewitched children, and now he thinks his own children are bewitched. It can't be true."

Joy sighed. "You don't understand, Cavie. Cotton Mather is

a hero around here. Everyone reads his books. A few Villagers have even visited Boston just to hear his sermons. If Cotton Mather says there are witches in the Massachusetts Bay Colony, everyone believes it."

"So now everyone thinks they're surrounded by witches." I looked at the girl who was still crying. Was she afraid she might be the witches' next victim?

"Minister Parris said the witches could strike anyone. He said they would target the most vulnerable people in the community, like the children," Joy said. "So after the sermon, all the parents freaked out about witches. They told their kids to watch out, never accept food from anyone, say their prayers, all that stuff."

As Joy spoke, I watched the youngest children, closest to the door of the school. A group of girls stood in a circle holding hands. Their mouths moved in silent unison and their eyes were screwed shut.

The whole thing made my stomach turn.

And I knew something Minister Parris didn't. How many Friday nights had Abigail Williams spent out in the woods casting spells on people? Or reading from their Burning Book? The Glass Girls might have even targeted some of the girls praying for protection from the witches.

The last time I'd seen her, Abigail was calling up spirits to predict the future.

But now Abigail was the *victim* of witchcraft?

A fire sparked in my chest. I grabbed Joy's arm and pulled her even closer to the edge of the woods. "You know what Abigail is like. She always wants to be the center of attention. She's practically frantic if she thinks someone else is stealing center stage."

Joy broke my gaze and looked at the ground. "She's

obsessed with status and popularity," Joy whispered. "But do you really think . . ." She trailed off.

I couldn't say the word that was on my mind: *faking*. Instead, I danced around it. "It seems like something she would do, right?"

"Maybe." Joy fiddled with her apron. "And the timing. Minister Parris has a lot of enemies in the Village. But now everyone is rallying behind him."

I looked back at the other students. Were they watching us? Joy and I had carefully maintained the fiction that we weren't friends. But here we were, whispering about conspiracies in full view of everyone. "We can't be the only ones questioning the story."

Joy shifted her feet. The air crackled with nervous energy. "I've heard some grumblings, but nothing concrete. Most people seem convinced the threat is real. They're already talking about how to find the witches."

I swallowed and hoped my panic wasn't written all over my face. Fear coursed through my body, and I felt the weight of my secret pressing down on me. I was the only one who might speak out about Abigail's obsession with magic—Ann and Mercy would never tell, and I couldn't imagine Tituba saying anything.

But who could I tell? And who would believe me? I was new to town and I wasn't a Puritan. Plus, I was a teenage girl. Minister Parris and his followers would never listen to me.

And somewhere in the back of my mind, I wondered if I was wrong. What if Abigail wasn't faking? What if it was true?

Were there evil forces in the Village?

Had we unleashed something dangerous that night in the woods?

Then I saw Joy's expression change in a flash. She went pale and ducked away from me so quickly that I almost stepped after her.

I spun around to see what had scared Joy off.

It was Ann Putnam. Of course.

The last time I'd seen Ann, she was cozying up with Edmund Hale. A blaze of anger whipped through my body, but it flickered and faded like an extinguished candle. My problems paled in comparison to the fear coursing through the Village.

And then I realized something. If Abigail was faking, I might not be able to do anything. But Ann could.

Her eyes were wide as her gaze swept over the clusters of frightened students. A frown flashed across her lips for a second and vanished. She spoke to me without taking her eyes off the weeping girl. "Can you believe everyone's talking about *Abigail?*" She said her name as if it were a curse.

"I guess everyone's worried."

Ann whipped her head around, glaring at me. Fire flashed in her eyes. "She just has a cold or something. And suddenly everyone's acting like she's famous."

Ann's reaction surprised me, but it shouldn't have. I pulled back and bit my lip. Of course Ann was jealous of Abigail. Ann was used to being the leader of the Glass Girls. She was used to all the attention.

And, I thought darkly, as soon as I liked Edmund Hale, Ann had to get him back.

But Ann hadn't said anything about Minister Parris and the witches. Did Ann really want to trade places with a girl that everyone thought was being attacked by Satan's minions? A shiver snaked up my spine. Maybe Ann craved attention so much that she didn't care about the terror infecting the schoolyard.

I planted my feet on the ground and pushed away my

worries. I needed to know if Abigail was lying. Panic was already sweeping through the town. But Abigail would never talk to me behind Ann's back. No, I had to convince Ann to help me, somehow. As long as Ann was obsessing about Abigail's popularity, she'd be useless.

I had to quench her jealousy.

I lowered my voice and tilted my head toward Ann. "You're Abigail's best friend."

"Abigail was a nobody before we were friends," she shot back.

"I bet everyone wants to talk to you."

She bit her lower lip and started nodding.

"Ann, you should tell the younger kids to calm down. They'll listen to you."

"Of course they'll listen to me," she said with a glare. "They practically *worship* me. God, Cavie, sometimes I forget that you're brand new to school."

I bit back a retort. I didn't want to press my luck.

Ann spoke again, in a lower voice as if to herself. "Why hasn't anyone asked me about Abigail? Are they *stupid?*"

And just like that, Ann's jealousy had been replaced by irritation. All because I'd guided her in that direction. Maybe I *could* use Ann to stop the panic.

Before Ann stalked over to break up the prayer circle, I grabbed her arm. "Maybe we could visit Abigail after school?"

She looked at me, the corner of her mouth tight. "Visit Abigail?"

"You know, to see how she's doing."

She rolled her eyes at me. "I get that. But why do *you* want to come? I thought you didn't like Abigail."

My breath caught in my throat. "No, I like Abigail," I

stumbled. "I'm worried about her."

"You barely even know Abigail," Ann reminded me.

Panic fluttered in my chest. I had to go with Ann. How else would I know if Abigail was lying? I pressed my nails into my apron. "But you'll need someone with you, in case, you know. In case it's true."

Ann looked at me like I had two heads. "In case what's true?"

"In case she really is being attacked by witches."

Ann laughed, a harsh, barking sound. "You don't really *believe* that, do you Cavie?"

I froze in place. Ann thought Abigail was lying, too? But what about the magic in the woods? Did she think that was real?

Or was it all a game to her?

My face must have shown my confusion. Ann laughed again. "Calm down, Cavie, you can come if it means that much to you. But don't say anything to Mercy. You know how she gets. She doesn't have a level head like us."

Without waiting for me to respond, Ann stalked off toward the prayer circle.

I let out a long sigh. Talking with Ann left me out of breath, as if I'd run a marathon. Somehow, I'd gone from confidante to outsider to ignorant child, and back to confidante in a matter of minutes.

It was like quicksand. I never knew where I stood with Ann.

I watched as a growing crowd of students gathered around Ann, who was holding court as if she were Queen. My stomach knotted.

At that moment, Mr. Green rang the bell to start school. We dutifully filed into the schoolhouse. More than a few girls had red-rimmed eyes. Mr. Green tried to ignore the tension in the room. He rapped the wall with his ruler and jumped into a dry lesson on grammar. Joy nudged my knee under the desk, but I waved her off. I was trapped in my thoughts, still puzzling over my relationship with Ann.

Then, a wail cut through the air. Everyone fell dead silent. One of the younger students, Charity, was crying. She was twelve, right on the cusp of reason, and in Puritan Salem Village she was supposed to know better. The seat next to her was empty, though—her best friend Betty Parris was home in bed. The poor girl had to be terrified.

Mr. Green stammered, "I said *which*, not *witch*. 'Behold the Lamb of God, *which* taketh away the sin of the world.' John 1:29."

But Charity kept sobbing. I stood up before I realized what I was doing. "I'll take her out for some fresh air," I said to Mr. Green. He nodded and looked relieved.

I shuffled off the bench and took Charity's arm, leading her outside.

Charity had fallen silent, but tears still streamed down her face. She pulled out a handkerchief and blotted her cheeks.

"Are you okay?" I said gently. "Do you want to sit down over here?" I led her to the hill where the Glass Girls usually ate lunch.

"But . . ." she sputtered, sniffling through her nose.

"What?"

"That's where Ann Putnam eats lunch," she finally said. "She might get mad if I sit there."

I stared at Charity. She was so afraid of witches that a homonym brought her to tears, but apparently she was even more afraid of Ann Putnam. "Well, I eat lunch with Ann Putnam, and I say you can sit here."

Charity watched me warily until I sat, and then she settled down next to me. "I'm so embarrassed," she apologized, wiping a last tear from her eye. Her cheeks flushed with shame. "I can't believe I started crying in class."

"Are you worried about Abigail and Betty?"

She nodded. "And I don't want to get bewitched," she said quietly.

The poor girl looked on the verge of tears again. I put a hand on her forearm. "You'll be fine, I promise. And I'm sure Betty and Abigail will feel better soon."

Charity jerked back and met my eye. "But what about the witches?"

My face fell. I couldn't contradict Minister Parris, but poor Charity needed reassurance. Otherwise she wouldn't make it through ten minutes of class without falling apart.

And so what if there *were* witches in the Village? If they practiced the same kind of magic that Tituba and the Glass Girls were doing in the woods, the Villagers were safe.

A current of ice snuck up my spine.

What if I was wrong?

That didn't matter right now. I squeezed Charity's arm. What would a Puritan say to comfort her? "The best thing you can do now is pray," I said. "For Abigail and Betty, and for yourself."

Charity looked up at me. "And that will protect me from witches?"

Did prayer protect against witchcraft? I didn't know the official Puritan line, but I certainly wasn't going to openly deny the power of prayer. "That's all you can do," I said.

"I'm very good, so I bet God will protect me," Charity said.

My stomach sank at her words. Did Charity think her friend Betty Parris wasn't good? If she had been attacked by witches, would the taint of witchcraft stick to her?

But it wasn't my responsibility to set Charity straight. I wouldn't even know where to begin. So I changed the subject. "I'm going to visit Abigail and Betty this afternoon." At least, I thought I was still invited. Ann might still change her mind. "What if we meet here tomorrow morning before school and I'll tell you how they're doing?"

Charity's face lit up. "Yes, I'd like that." Ann wouldn't be happy if she learned I was supplanting her role as the source of news about Abigail. But maybe she wouldn't find out. She'd be too busy telling her adoring followers about poor sick Abigail to notice me talking with Charity. I hoped.

Charity gave me a weak smile. "Thanks, Cavie," she said. We sat in silence for a few more minutes before we headed back into the schoolhouse.

Charity might feel better, but my body rolled on a wave of emotions.

I hoped I was doing the right thing.

TEN

I waited outside the schoolhouse long after the other students had left. Ann was still inside. When she finally walked out, she was smiling. In fact, she was the first person I'd seen smile all day. I wrinkled my nose. Was Ann actually *excited* to go see Abigail?

I hid my reaction behind a blank face. I had to stay in control of my emotions.

"Cavie, I was waiting for you. Hurry up, we don't want to make Abigail wait."

I bit the inside of my cheek. She'd been waiting for me? Not likely. And Abigail didn't even know we were planning to visit, so a few minutes wouldn't make a difference. But I wasn't going to contradict Ann. I fell in next to her and let her lead the way to the Parris house.

"Isn't it *so sad* about Abigail and Betty?" Ann said as we walked toward the Village Square. The trees thinned out and the buildings drew closer together.

"Yes," I murmured.

"It's like a *tragedy,* a real live *tragedy* that they're being tormented in this way." She shook her head and frowned. "I hope the people responsible will be found. And brought to justice," she added, her hands balled into fists.

So this was the new Ann Putnam—renegade supporter of poor afflicted girls.

Fortunately the walk to the Parris house didn't take long. I was running out of responses to Ann's passionate declarations.

But Ann stopped when the house came into view. I nearly ran into her. "Who are all those people outside Abigail's house?" Ann murmured.

I followed her gaze and saw a crowd of more than a dozen in front of a two-story thatched house.

Ann's eyebrows folded together in worry. "Come on, Cavie, let's go see." She marched up to the house and I trailed behind her.

The buzz of conversation enveloped us before we reached the porch. Everyone seemed to be talking at once.

"I can't believe what those poor girls are enduring," one man was saying to his neighbor.

"It's shameful. Downright shameful!"

A woman's voice said, "I heard the girls have been crying out constantly for relief."

"How sad that no one can help them."

I clenched my teeth. They were spectators, hoping to catch a glimpse of the sick girls. I watched Ann from the corner of my eye. For an instant, she seemed cautious, but in a flash she straightened her back and stood tall. "I can't wait to see my dear friend Abigail." Her voice cut through the conversations. Everyone fell silent and looked in Ann's direction. Then a woman right in front of us stepped to the side so that Ann could pass. The crowd parted, and Ann walked straight up to the porch.

I froze for a second and then scurried after her before the path vanished.

"I hope she's feeling better," Ann projected from the porch. "I've been praying for her every day."

Someone in the crowd actually choked back a sob at Ann's words.

Really?

I was intimately familiar with Ann's acting voice—she put it on whenever she spoke to adults. But it felt so transparent. And yet she'd turned a crowd of Villagers worried about Abigail and Betty into her own audience with a few words and a pouty lip.

Ann tugged her bonnet close to her face as if she'd just noticed the crowd watching us. Or, rather, watching her. She closed her eyes for a second and then turned and opened the door without knocking. I hurried to keep up with her.

As soon as Ann shut the door, the hum of voices grew outside. But inside, it was pitch black and silent. It took my eyes a moment to adjust. The curtains had been drawn, and there were no candles inside to light the room. Did Minister Parris dislike the attention from his neighbors? Or maybe he hoped the dim house would promote health.

"Abigail's room is this way," Ann said, pulling me toward the stairs.

With a start, I saw a shadowy figure sitting in the corner of the room. We had walked in without invitation or warning. My chest tightened. Then the form fell into place. A tall, thin man, bent over a desk, scribbling something. A letter? A sermon? It had to be Minister Parris. He looked over and we locked eyes for an instant. I had seen him around the Village, but never in such close proximity. His eyes had an intensity to them that rattled me.

Then he looked at Ann. "Ah, the young Miss Putnam," he said, his voice rough from disuse. "Here to visit Abigail and Betty, I hope?"

He seemed a man afflicted. His red-rimmed eyes spoke of sleepless nights, and the shadow of a beard on his face meant that he had dropped the Puritan commitment to cleanliness. In spite of Joy's warning about his sermon, it wasn't until I saw Minister Parris myself that I truly understood. Here was a man assaulted by demons. And it looked like he was barely holding them off.

A chill passed through my body. How ill were Betty and Abigail, really?

"Of course, I just had to check on dear Abigail and sweet Betty," Ann said in a treacly voice. "And this is my friend Margaret."

I jerked at the sound of my name.

His steely gaze returned to me. "I haven't seen you at church, Margaret." He laid the quill down gently next to his missive.

I tried to keep my voice from stammering. "My family just moved to the Village recently. We attend church in the Town."

"It is critical for a community to worship together," Parris admonished me. His eyes were the deep blue-grey of the sea after a storm. "I do hope we might see you at the *Village* church some time soon."

I nodded, my breath trapped in my chest.

After a moment, he indicated the stairs. "Please go ahead. I hope you can cheer them up." He picked up his quill and returned to his writing.

Relief washed over me as Minister Parris turned away. I

could easily picture him standing before a congregation, railing against witches. No wonder Charity had burst into tears in class.

But Parris seemed to have no effect on Ann. She traipsed up the narrow staircase, leaning back to whisper to me, "Us Putnams support Parris." I shot a glance back at the minister, but his head was bent over his desk. Ann continued. "He's a great minister."

We were at the top of the stairs. Ann stopped outside the door on the left. This time, she knocked gently and waited for permission to enter. When a weak voice invited us in, Ann pushed open the door.

The room was nearly as dark as the hallway, but a narrow strip of light peeked in between the window frame and the heavy curtain. The small room contained two beds—in the one closer to the window, Betty sat up looking positively cheerful. I swallowed at the sight of her. I had been prepared for many things, but a rosy, smiling girl was not one of them. My gaze jumped to Abigail, who was in the other bed. Instead of a smile, her mouth hung open in surprise. She looked a little pale, but otherwise she was completely unchanged.

After two weeks away from school, and all the rumors that they were on their deathbeds, I had expected something more grim.

"Ann," Abigail breathed. "You're here to visit me?" Her voice squeaked with delight.

Downstairs, Minister Parris was acting like his daughter and niece had just been given last rites. But up here, it was a regular slumber party.

Ann sat at the foot of Abigail's bed. I closed the door and stood awkwardly between the beds.

"Of course I came to see you. How are you doing?" Ann

asked. "Everyone has been *so* worried about you."

"We're feeling better, thank you," Abigail said. "We might even be able to come back to school in a few more days."

Ann's lips were pressed together in a flat, bloodless line. Her tender demeanor vanished and her eyes narrowed.

She was *upset* that Betty and Abigail were recovering?

Of course. If they recovered, Ann would lose her chance to lord her connection to Abigail and Betty over everyone in town. The crowd outside the Parris house would dissipate, and with it Ann's social currency would vanish.

The blood rushed back into Ann's lips as she broke into a smile. She looked like a cat who had cornered a mouse and knew he was guaranteed a meal. What could have changed her mood so quickly? I braced myself for her next words.

"You know how the Devil works," Ann said solemnly. "He might lighten his attack one day just to redouble his efforts the next. Didn't you hear about the poor Goodwin children?"

The children in Boston, again. Everyone was talking about it. I needed to find a copy of Cotton Mather's book and read it for myself.

"Oh yes," Betty said. "Father read it to us. Those poor children. I can't imagine how badly they must have suffered."

"And do you remember what happened when the witch was identified and executed?" Ann asked patiently, adopting the tone of a teacher.

Betty frowned as she thought for a moment. "They didn't recover right away. Is that what you mean?"

"According to Minister Mather, they didn't recover at all. When the witch died, their torment increased sevenfold. Can you even imagine? At the moment they expected to get well and recover, the poor children were struck down by Satan."

Abigail sat silently during Ann's speech, her face blank. But Betty's lower lip trembled. She looked on the verge of tears.

"That won't happen to us, right, Abigail?" Betty asked her cousin. "Because Tituba said she would cure us."

"What?" Ann said sharply. "What did Tituba say?"

Betty gave a little gasp as if she had revealed a secret she wasn't supposed to tell. She looked to Abigail, who gave her a little nod. Betty gripped the quilt on her bed with both hands as she spoke. "Tituba said that she could use magic to cure us."

I shifted my weight. The conversation was getting dangerously close to revealing our activities in the woods. If anyone learned that we'd performed spells, we'd be in terrible trouble.

I tried not to picture Minister Parris's blazing eyes.

"Does your father know about this?" Ann asked Betty quietly.

Betty shook her head. "We didn't tell him. Tituba told us not to. But she promised she could help."

Abigail's eyes shifted from Ann to me and back. The blood had drained from her face. "I do think Tituba might be able to help us," she said weakly. Abigail had been so excited to see Ann only minutes earlier, but now she looked even smaller in her bed.

Ann sighed and tilted her head at Abigail. "And what exactly is Tituba going to do?"

Betty's smile returned. She was oblivious to the crackling tension between Abigail and Ann. "Tituba knows how to break curses. She learned it in the West Indies. She's going to bake a cake with our urine in it, and then she'll feed it to some dogs. She said it will reverse the magic and we'll both be cured."

Ann recoiled at Betty's words. "Gross." She looked back to Abigail. "I just want to make sure you're both okay. If you want,

Cavie and I will watch to make sure Tituba does everything like you said. If she leaves out a step, she might make things even worse." I opened my mouth to object, but Ann silenced me with her eyes. "You two should stay in bed and rest," she added, adopting her nurturing voice again.

"That's nice of you, Ann, but it's really not necessary," Abigail protested. She pulled at the hem of her sleeve and frowned.

"Abigail, what kind of friend would I be if I didn't look out for you?" Ann said. "Now you both need to relax. Stay calm and rest. I'll pray for you. And I'll go talk to Tituba right now."

Ann didn't wait for a response. She marched out of the room, pulling me in her wake. She was like a force of nature, like a magnet that drew me behind her, my mind scrambled.

Once the door was firmly closed, Ann raised her eyebrows and said, "We're going to make sure *that* doesn't happen."

My voice caught in my throat. She had lied right to Abigail's face, and I was following her mutely. At the bottom of the stairs, Ann avoided the room where Minister Parris still worked and exited through the back door. "Tituba lives out here in a shed or something," Ann told me.

My heart hadn't stopped pounding. "What are you going to say to her?"

"Just wait and see." She walked up to a small shed that couldn't provide much protection from the New England winter and knocked on the door. A moment later it swung open and Tituba stood before us. "Hello Tituba," Ann said in an authoritative voice, her hands on her hips. "Betty and Abigail told us about your plan with the urine cake."

Tituba crossed her arms in front of her body and stayed in the doorway. "Yes. The cake will help the girls feel better. I have seen it work in a number of other cases." Her eyes dared Ann to contradict her.

Ann continued, ignoring Tituba's challenge. "Abigail and Betty changed their minds. They don't want you to feed the cake to the dogs after all." She cocked her head to one side. I felt a charge pass between them. "They're going to pray that God will deliver them from the Devil. As you know, the only source of relief from the Devil is the Lord." Ann punctuated her words with a staccato rhythm.

Tituba frowned. Her hand flickered to her neck for a moment before it dropped back to her side. "They don't want me to make the cake?" She looked at me. "Are you sure?"

I froze with my mouth hanging open. How could I contradict Ann? I wasn't going to side with urine cakes over Jesus.

Ann took a step closer to Tituba, raising a finger in warning. "And don't mention your plan to anyone. I'm sure Minister Parris would hate to learn that his own slave was promoting an ungodly remedy."

My skin tingled. I looked down at my hands. My knuckles were white from gripping the hem of my apron. There was no mistaking the threat in Ann's words.

The fire had gone out of Tituba's eyes. She gritted her teeth together as the silence stretched on. "Fine," Tituba said brusquely. "If that's all, I need to get back to my work." She closed the door before Ann could reply.

Ann turned to me, a grin spreading across her face. "And that's how you do it," she said to me. "You should be taking notes, Cavie. I'm teaching you some important lessons."

My jaw hung loose as I stared back, stunned into silence. Ann was *proud* of how she had frightened Abigail and Betty, and then manipulated Tituba.

And she expected me to applaud her.

Was I just another member of the audience to Ann? Another player she could direct?

I couldn't force myself to respond. My stomach was churning violently.

If I opened my mouth, I might not be able to hold back my retching.

ELEVEN

This couldn't last forever.

I tried to tell myself that things would get back to normal soon. Betty and Abigail would return to school, the terror over witches would fade from people's minds, and I could pay less attention to Ann Putnam and more attention to my studies.

But the queasy feeling in my stomach refused to fade away.

How could it, when I had just seen more evidence of Ann's skillful manipulation? She had the crowd outside the Parris house holding their breath to hear her next words. Betty and Abigail listened rapturously while Ann wove tales of demonic diseases. And Tituba bent to Ann's will—how could she not, when she was a slave?

My stomach couldn't relax, because I couldn't stop thinking about Ann.

How far would she go?

Were there any boundaries she wouldn't break?

I slept poorly and woke up with a foggy haze hanging over my mind. I dragged myself from the warm bed and prepared for school. I could already picture the scene in front of the schoolhouse. Everyone would crowd around Ann as she told tales of poor Abigail sick in her bed and innocent little Betty tormented by the Devil.

I shook off the prediction and left the house with a heavy cloak weighing down my shoulders.

The walk seemed longer than usual. A coat of fresh snow draped the world in white. The woods crowded the road as if they had somehow grown overnight, and they were dead silent, without even a birdsong. If only I could flee from the icy crush of winter like the birds.

My feet crunched through the snow, where not even a horse's hooves or wagon wheels had disturbed the road.

When I saw the schoolyard, it was like my vision come to life. Crowds of girls stood together, no more than a quiet murmur breaking the silence. Some of the older boys glared at the woods as if hoping for some ghoul to emerge that they could battle.

But the scene was missing a critical piece.

Where was Ann?

Why would she be late on this day, when she was guaranteed to be the center of attention?

I dragged my feet. The answer couldn't be good.

I threaded my way through the crowd, avoiding eye contact. In a way, I was like Ann's understudy. If she wasn't around, people would come talk to me. Everyone knew I ate lunch with Ann and the Glass Girls, and the rumors about Ann's visit to the Parris house might have included my small part. I kept my head down to avoid getting drawn into conversations about Abigail and Betty.

But before I made it to the door, I stopped and jerked my head around. I suddenly heard what the girls were talking about.

Abigail and Betty weren't the names on the lips of my fellow students.

Instead, I kept hearing Ann's name, repeated again and again.

The breath caught in my chest. I grabbed Charity's arm. "What's going on?" I whispered, not wanting to draw more attention. "Did something happen to Ann?"

Charity's face was white. Her hands shook in mine. "The Devil attacked Ann Putnam," she moaned quietly. One of the girls next to her began to sob.

It landed like a punch to my gut. "What do you mean?"

Charity leaned closer, her eyes wide. "The witches came after Ann, just like they attacked Abigail Williams and Betty Parris. Ann's one of the afflicted."

Charity dropped my hands and turned to comfort her crying friend.

I stood, speechless, near the doorway of the school. Ann was *afflicted*? I didn't believe that for one second. A tremor rattled my hands and I gripped my apron firmly to still it. I'd seen Ann just yesterday. She'd been fine. More than fine. She'd been bragging about threatening Tituba.

And now she'd mysteriously fallen ill overnight?

I drew in a sharp breath of air as everything fell into place. Ann wasn't being attacked by witches. No. She'd upgraded her role from town gossip to town victim. She'd seen the crowds outside of the Parris house and made a calculated choice. If she was under attack by demonic forces, women would weep for her, and *her* name would be in everyone's mouth.

I balled my fists until my knuckles gleamed white. My teeth ground together, sending shock waves through my jaw. Ann was terrifying all these children just to draw more attention to herself.

How selfish was she? Did she care at all about the people she hurt?

Apparently not.

I swore that as soon as school was over, I'd march to Ann's house and tell her it had to stop. I knew what we'd done in the woods, and I knew how she'd tried to scare Betty and intimidate Tituba. This game had gone on long enough. It wasn't funny anymore.

I'd make her listen to me.

When Mr. Green rang the bell for school, the room was half empty. The back row was deserted—Mercy wasn't in school, either. Joy whispered to me that most parents had kept their children at home, just in case the witches were trolling for new victims. And no one could concentrate on the lesson. Mr. Green had to halt his lecture a number of times because of crying girls, and a few even ran out of the schoolhouse and didn't return.

Mr. Green let us leave early, but this time no one cheered or celebrated. The remaining students filed out of the building in complete silence. No one lingered to talk.

I caught Joy's eye as we walked out. She fell in next to me as I stomped toward the Village Square. I didn't want to confide in Joy, not on the road surrounded by other students, but I couldn't leave her completely in the dark. "I'm going to talk with our *friend*," I whispered.

She nodded, her eyes glued to the road ahead of us. "Good."

Joy only spoke that one word, but it communicated volumes. And I felt better, walking next to Joy through the melting snow. I didn't feel so alone.

Dozens of Villagers were standing in the square. I saw more than one goodwife hug her child returning from school as if we'd survived a death march. Other mothers shook their heads at the mothers who'd allowed their children to venture to school, whispering that it was much safer to keep vulnerable young ones at home in order to protect them from satanic assault.

As if the Devil couldn't get through their thin wooden doors.

I schooled myself not to show my disgust with the terrified Villagers. They didn't know any better. For all they knew, witches were descending on Salem Village to destroy everyone. It wasn't so different from the Indian raids that had plagued the colony, except this time the enemy was invisible.

And Ann's illness was proof, to them, that the witches were growing stronger.

I knew Ann's house on sight, even though I had never been invited over. It was a large two-story building just past the Village Square. A wide swath of fields trailed from the back of the house. The Putnam farmlands. It was one of the biggest houses in the Village—her family was rich, by Village standards.

I stood at the bottom of the porch steps and took a deep breath. I couldn't put off the confrontation forever. I forced myself forward and knocked on the door.

A woman who looked like Ann's older sister answered. "Hellllloooo," she called out in a surprisingly cheerful voice. "I'm Ann's mom. Are you one of Ann's friends?"

I nodded and introduced myself. She led me into the front room, which was the exact opposite of Minister Parris's dark and solemn house. Where the Parris house held only bare chairs and blank walls, the Putnam house was decorated in pillows, throws, and curtains of all colors. It was like walking inside a confectioner's shop.

Ann's mother grinned at me. "Just so you know, I'm very close with Ann. Some people even think we look like sisters."

My eyebrows shot up. Goodwife Putnam was wearing a fitted bodice that would have drawn disapproving eyes outside of her house. Her apron was tied so tight around her waist that I could see her contorted flesh spilling out below the band. She did look young, I guess, but her bubbly smile had a hint of strain. Her daughter was upstairs ill in bed, but Goodwife Putnam seemed to care more about impressing me than nursing Ann back to health.

Or maybe she knew Ann wasn't really sick.

Goodwife Putnam watched me, waiting for a response. I fumbled for something to say. "Um, that's great. I like your bonnet."

A smile spread across her face. She waved a hand at me. "You're too kind. And you have great taste—this bonnet is from London."

"Oh, wow."

"I'm sure you want to run up to see Ann. But just remember—I'm not like the other goodwives. A little sinning keeps things interesting, right?" She gave me an exaggerated wink.

I forced the corners of my mouth back, but it might have read more like a grimace than a grin. I was here to accuse Ann of faking a satanic attack, and her mother wanted me to know that she's cool? I was breathless, as if I'd just run a mile. How was I supposed to respond?

I looked up the stairs, shifting my weight.

"Go on upstairs, it's the first door on the right," Goodwife Putnam finally said.

Relieved, I raced up the stairs. It turns out I didn't need directions—when I reached the top, Ann's door was obvious. Her name was carved into the wood with intricate painted flowers woven into the letters.

I knocked gently.

"Mom, leave me alone," Ann yelled from inside.

"It's Cavie."

There was a pause on the other side of the door. I strained my ears and caught the sound of whispers. A minute later, Ann said, "Fine. Come in."

When I pushed open the door, my jaw dropped. It was the most elaborately decorated room I'd seen anywhere in my life. And it was here, in Puritan Salem Village.

Ann's enormous bed sat in the middle of the room, braced by four posts with a billowing pink and white canopy on top. A padded divan sat next to the bed, alongside a beautiful armoire covered in an elaborate pattern of carved vines and leaves. There was a mirror hanging on the wall, as well as a hand mirror sitting on a dark table in the corner next to a very expensive boar-hair brush. The walls were covered with art—reproductions of Renaissance and Baroque classics. The room was at least twice the size of my own, and the ceiling was much higher.

I was so distracted by the decorations that I barely noticed who was sitting on the bed with Ann—it was Mercy.

"Like my room?" Ann asked in her sickly sweet voice. She sat cross-legged on the comforter, wearing a dark pink dress that definitely would have gotten her in trouble outside of the Putnam house. Her cheeks were as rosy as ever and her golden hair hung loose around her face, the smallest hint of a curl at the ends.

She looked the picture of health.

"It's . . . nice." I stood awkwardly by the door.

"I know, my parents spoil me," Ann said, staring at me from the bed. "They told me to be careful about who I let in here, because I could get in trouble for having some of this stuff."

I looked around again. That must be true. Puritans weren't big fans of mirrors, for starters. And I'm sure Minister Parris would have a thing or two to say about the giant pink pillows on Ann's bed. "I won't tell anyone," I promised.

"How was school today?" Mercy asked.

"It was fine." The fire that had carried me to Ann's door had been doused by the surprises within the Putnam house. First Ann's mother, and now this room. I blinked slowly and tried to remember why I'd come.

Ann tilted her head. "Weren't people talking about me?"

I swallowed. "Yes," I admitted. "I heard you aren't feeling well?"

Ann snorted. "That's what they told you?"

"Not exactly."

"Why are you playing games, Cavie? Just tell me what they said."

I let out a deep breath and licked my lips. "They said the witches attacked you."

As soon as I gave the answer Ann wanted, her demeanor toward me changed. She smiled and pointed to the divan. "Don't just stand over there, Cavie, come sit with us. I'll tell you what happened."

I wanted to call Ann a liar, or grab Mercy and pull her away. But instead, I quietly sank onto the seat. It was the most comfortable place I'd sat in the last two years. Inside, I burned with shame for not calling Ann out immediately. But I told myself that I should at least hear her story before I accused her of faking.

Ann looked from me to Mercy. She seemed to sit up straighter now that her audience had doubled. She took a dramatic breath and began her tale. "Yesterday, after we visited Abigail and Betty—"

"And Tituba," I interrupted.

Mercy's head jerked toward Ann. Apparently Ann had left Tituba out of earlier versions of the story.

"And Tituba," Ann added reluctantly. "Anyway, after I came home, I started to feel these invisible pinches. Almost like someone was in the room with me, right here, but I was alone."

Mercy shivered at that and looked around the room as though someone might jump out of the armoire or emerge from under the bed. I stopped myself from rolling my eyes.

Ann continued. "And then, suddenly, I felt burning hot, as though the fires of hell were in this very room."

Mercy gasped, but Ann kept her eyes on me. It felt like she was measuring my response to her story. I gave in to the pulling weakness inside me, that told me to play my role so Ann wouldn't be disappointed. "That sounds terrifying," I said weakly.

"Oh, it was," Ann said. "But I didn't even tell you the worst part." She paused, and raised an eyebrow at me.

She wasn't going to continue unless I prompted her. I had to act my part if I wanted to hear her story. "What happened next?"

"Well, I was pretty frightened after the pinching and the burning. I told my mother that I wasn't feeling well. She sent me straight to my room in case it was a fever. But I knew it was no ordinary fever. So of course I pulled out the Burning Book." She picked it up from the bed, where it had been sitting amongst the pillows. "And things in the book had *changed.*"

"Changed how?" My stomach was rolling. I put a hand on the arm of the divan to steady myself.

"Just look," she said, holding it open to the section about

our classmates.

I leaned closer. My pulse pounded in my ears.

"There's a page for Abigail," Mercy burst out. "And none of us wrote it!"

No. I shook my head. That wasn't possible. Ann must have written it herself—but the handwriting didn't look like hers.

"And look what it *says*," Mercy exclaimed. "It's the names of the witches who are cursing her."

A shiver passed through my body. I could believe that Ann would write a fake page about Abigail—but would she really accuse strangers of being witches?

Of course, they weren't strangers to Ann. These were people she had known her whole life. What possible reason could she have for lying?

I felt suddenly hot. Could I be wrong? What if there were invisible forces at work? My eyes darted from the book to Ann's face.

Ann looked almost serene, sitting on the bed. She suddenly reminded me of a fresco I'd seen of the Virgin Mary in Paris, draped in blue, calm and perfectly composed.

She certainly didn't look like the victim of satanic magic.

My eyes darted back at the book. I leaned on the edge of the divan and tried to make out the names, written in red below Abigail's. I didn't recognize the first two: Sarah Good and Sarah Osborne. But the next one stood out.

"Tituba? You think Tituba's a witch?"

"I didn't say that—the book did," Ann said flatly. Her eyes flashed with intensity. "We saw her do magic in the woods with our own eyes."

Mercy shook her head. "I knew something was wrong with that woman," she said solemnly.

My mouth was as dry as the Sahara. "But you wanted Tituba to do magic for you," I pleaded to Ann. "She was only doing what you asked."

Ann shook her head. "We know she has powers." She turned to Mercy, laying a hand on her arm. "And no one needs to know about that night." Ann's eyes jumped back to mine. "We *all* swore that we would never tell."

My voice finally caught up with my racing mind. "Ann, you can't be serious. You know what they do to people accused of witchcraft, right?"

"Of course. We all know about the poor Goodwin children and that terrible laundry woman who tried to torment them into an early grave. They were right to hang her."

"And you would send Tituba to a similar fate?"

Ann's eyes dared me to accuse her of something, but I couldn't form the words in my mouth. Every time I tried, my tongue tripped and I simply froze. I saw satisfaction bloom in her eyes, as if she had known I wouldn't challenge her.

"*I* didn't do anything," Ann said, her face blank. "I didn't write these names in the book. I didn't make Abigail and Betty sick. I certainly didn't pinch myself." She pulled up the sleeve of her dressing gown and showed me a row of bruises on her arm. "There are dark powers at work in the Village."

"And we have a responsibility to do something about it," Mercy added. "So that's why we chose to act."

My breath caught in my lungs. A frantic energy swept over my body. "What did you do?" I asked Mercy, and then turned to Ann. "What did you do?"

Ann leaned back on the bed as if we were at a spring picnic. Her voice was light, unencumbered by the weight that was crushing me. "I'm going to tell my father the names of the witches who have been tormenting us," Ann said calmly. "It's our Christian duty to protect the community and protect ourselves."

I stared at her without blinking. "You're going to start a witch hunt," I whispered.

Ann stared back. "Maybe Salem Village needs one."

TWELVE

Did Ann know what she was saying? Her cool, green eyes and relaxed pose said that *she* had nothing to fear from a witch hunt—and, I admitted to myself, she was probably right.

Everyone knew that witches were cranky, old women, the kinds of people you didn't want living next door. Witches put a curse on your cow when you refused to give them milk if they came begging at your door. Witches made your crops wither in the fields because they hated good Christians. Witches gathered in the woods at secret meetings, where they danced around a bonfire and trampled crosses.

Then again, Ann *had* been sneaking around the woods doing magic for months.

But no one would look at Ann Putnam, perfectly put together Puritan Ann Putnam, and think she was a witch. Her cream skin and blonde hair were stamps of the Lord's approval. No one would believe that Ann Putnam had sold her soul to the Devil.

A shiver snaked through my body as I watched Ann warily. I clutched my arms tightly around my waist. Ann might look beautiful on the outside, but I knew she was rotten at her core, like a bushel of apples infested with worms.

My mind raced as fast as my heart pounded. Ann would send Tituba to the fires—no, in the English colonies they hanged witches, they didn't burn them. Ann would drape a noose around Tituba's neck, and for what? Tituba might have offered to bake a pagan urine cake, which surely Minister Parris would see as a dangerous willingness to bend the rules of a Christian community, but she hadn't done anything more than Ann and the other Glass Girls. Hadn't they also put curses on people? Hadn't they wanted to see into the future?

At least Tituba's motives were pure. She had offered to show us magic because of *our* desire, not her own. And she had tried to cure Betty and Abigail before Ann stepped in and twisted things.

But Ann didn't hesitate before throwing Tituba to the wolves.

Ann's words replayed in my mind. *I'm going to tell my father the names of the witches.* Would she really do it? And what else might Ann tell her father? Would she tell him about the urine cake?

A new thought struck me, sending my stomach rolling. How many more names might appear in the Burning Book?

I had to say something, I had to stop Ann, but my mouth was too dry to form words. My thoughts were thick with worry, as if the fog that sometimes overtook Salem Village had settled in my mind.

I had to stop her. But how?

Sitting there in Ann's room, I was paralyzed by fear. And I acted like a coward.

I scrambled to my feet and mumbled something about getting home before dark. This time, Ann's placid grin reminded me of a painting I'd once seen replicated, some Italian woman drawn by Da Vinci. Ann knew her words unsettled me to my core, but she just sat there smiling.

I left the room and stumbled down the stairs.

A voice called from the kitchen. I jumped before I realized it was Ann's mother. "Don't forget to come back for a visit! You don't even have to wear a bonnet in *this* house."

I didn't respond. I flew out the door and away from Salem Village, moving as though I was in a dream. The voices around me were muted to my ears, but I still jumped at every sound. I wished with all my heart that it was only a bad dream, that Salem Village itself was a mirage. I imagined waking and finding myself back in Virginia, or even better, in London.

Of course, it wasn't a dream. And when I finally made it home, my mom's first words were, "Did you hear what's been happening to the girls in Salem Village?"

I collapsed onto a chair in the living room, breathing heavy. "Yes," I whispered.

Her face compressed into a mess of fine lines. She leaned forward as if she wanted to spring from her seat to comfort me. I waved her off and drew a slow, steady breath. But the worry stayed on her face.

"You aren't afraid of witches, are you?"

I was shaking my head before she finished her sentence. "No."

"Good." Her eyebrows inched back to their usual position. "People here in the colonies are a bit behind the times. Back in London this sort of thing hasn't happened in a while. It just strikes me as so . . . provincial."

Relief coursed through my body. Finally, someone who agreed with me. I had to watch my words so carefully in the Village, where questioning witches could brand me as a heretic, or worse. But at home, I could voice my fears—not about Ann, I couldn't go that far, but at least about the Villagers.

The words tumbled out. "The children in town are terrified that they'll be snatched away by witches and thrown into a cauldron. And the parents are even worse. Half of the mothers kept their children home from school today, as if they could protect them."

Mom's eyes widened as she listened. After a pause, she spoke. "It's hard for me to imagine that people are so worked up over rumors."

Of course she was surprised—she barely left our ten acres of land on the edge of Salem Village. She hadn't seen the girls weeping outside of school, the mob outside the Parris house, or the worried goodwives shutting their doors tight, as if wood could stop a witch.

"You should go to the Village Square," I told my mother. "It's flooded with men talking about how to protect the community from witches. They're convinced that the Devil himself is sitting out in the woods plotting against Salem Village."

She pulled the quilt tighter around her legs. When she spoke again, her voice was quieter. "I might suggest that to your father." She watched me. "He was quite adamant about moving to Salem Village."

"What about you?"

"I had my reservations."

I sat up straighter. My parents had always seemed like a united front. "Why?"

She sighed. Then she looked out the window into the haze of dusk. "I've had more exposure to the Puritans than your father. You know I grew up outside of London. There was a small community of Puritans that lived near my town."

I found myself leaning forward. "What were they like?" I hadn't heard many stories about my mother's life before she met my father, got married, and had me. There was something so weird about picturing my mom at my age.

"They were nice enough, most of the time. But there was one . . . incident. They accused our Anglican minister of being a tool of Satan. As you can imagine, that didn't go over well. He was a respected minister who had served in our town for decades."

"Then why did the Puritans attack him?"

"This all happened when I was quite young," she cautioned. "And within a few months the Puritan community had moved, I think to Amsterdam or even the colonies. I can't recall. As for their complaint with the minister, it had to do with one of his sermons. It was so long ago. They disagreed with his interpretation of Scripture. As you might have noticed, Puritans can be pretty intense about Scripture. But there were rumors that the Puritans were planning to attack our church. Fights started breaking out between the Anglicans and the Puritans. It was a bad situation."

She fell silent, lost in the world of her youth. I let the silence grow before I spoke again. "And so you didn't want to move to Salem Village?"

She gave a small nod of her head.

"But Dad insisted?"

At that, she frowned. "It wasn't like that." I could see her weighing her next words carefully. "You're still so young, Cavie. You don't know what it's like to be a wife. Your dad and I talked about my concerns. He's always receptive to my input, as it should be. And I was wary of Puritans, but we weren't going to avoid the Massachusetts Bay Colony because of a single event that happened when I was just a girl."

"But things are different, now." I spoke cautiously. "Maybe we should think about leaving."

My mother shook her head. "Your father just finished planting for the spring, and he'll never agree to leave before harvest. We committed to staying for at least a year or two." Her tone changed and she leaned back in her seat. The girlish voice of her past faded, and once again she was firmly in parent mode. "I understand that the transition to a new community is always difficult, but we have to give it a try. It wouldn't be right to run at the first sign of trouble. And it seems like you've made some friends here?"

Until that moment, I'd managed to forget about my "friends." I wasn't going to tell Mom that three of my new friends were playing starring roles in the growing witch panic.

Or that I'd only befriended them to ruin their reputations.

I didn't think my mom would be very proud of that. The Glass Girls were playing a game, but then, so was I. Ann was willing to risk Tituba's reputation, and maybe even her life, to gain power, but how different was I, really? Before I even knew Ann, I had plotted with Joy to destroy her life here in Salem Village.

Was I no better than Ann?

My mom's words shook me from my thoughts. "Don't you think the panic will die down soon?"

I thought back to Ann's words and the chill in her eyes when she proclaimed her innocence. She saw herself as a victim of circumstances beyond her control. Ann hadn't even flinched when I warned her that trials and hangings might be next.

Had Ann already gone to her father with the names of

witches?

What would he do next?

If Ann told anyone, it would set a dangerous process in motion. The Puritans would never dismiss an accusation that Villagers were dallying with Satan. I had no reason to think that any of those women were guilty. But how could I stop Ann?

The question kept echoing in my mind, without an answer.

Did I think the panic would fade? Not as long as Ann Putnam saw it as a way to get attention.

I cleared my throat before I answered. "No, I'm not sure it will die down." My conviction sounded weak, though in my heart I felt certain.

My mom reached down to her basket of knitting. I felt her slipping further away, unconvinced of the danger. "You're probably just nervous," she said, her attention on the knitting needles. "Now why don't you go see if your dad needs help in the fields."

I stood, my legs wooden. I replayed my mom's words in my head. She had reservations about moving to Salem Village, just like I did. And yet here we were. It didn't seem fair.

Or maybe it felt wrong because right now, I wanted to be anywhere else. My mom had brushed off my worries as if I were just a child. But I hadn't confided in her about Ann. I had held back, because I was afraid of disappointing her.

And maybe I was afraid to admit how easily I'd agreed to destroy the Glass Girls.

My mom thought things would die down because she didn't know the depths girls were willing to go to be popular. That *I* would go. She couldn't comprehend someone like Ann Putnam. Maybe there hadn't been girls like that back in England when she was young. Or, who knows, maybe an English version of Ann

Putnam riled up the Puritans near my mom's town with outlandish claims about Satan.

I didn't know how far the violence had gone, but I could imagine.

And maybe things died down back in England because the Puritans decided to leave town.

My mom glanced up at me, questioning me with her eyes. Were my thoughts written on my face? I turned away, grabbing my cloak as I walked outside to find my dad.

Was I wrong to blame all Puritans for the behavior of Ann Putnam? I wasn't a Puritan, but I was still guilty of my own sins. I looked across the empty fields, dark with freshly tilled soil.

But no. There *was* something different about the Puritans. I felt it.

Maybe they expected too much. Their fathers claimed to be a "city on a hill," and declared that God's favor shone on the Massachusetts Bay Colony. But what about the children? At only eleven or twelve, they were expected to act with decorum at all times, to uphold the dignity of their faith and family. Any misstep would bring heaps of scorn and possibly exile.

That was a lot of pressure for a bunch of teenagers.

Was it surprising that kids rebelled by dancing to fiddle music and drinking apple jack at parties? Or running off to the woods to try magic? If the Puritans weren't so anxious to prove they were Godly, would it matter if a girl claimed she was being attacked by a witch?

I pulled my cloak closer to my body. The brilliant blue sky looked just as it did above London on the rare clear winter day. And maybe Salem Village wasn't so different from Europe— thousands of witches had been executed on the continent not that long ago.

But Europe had left witch trials in their past. They were a distant memory for me—I'd never witnessed one in my lifetime. I'd only heard about them from old stories. It was a thing of history books, not current events.

And yet in this corner of the English Crown, witches still haunted the forests.

Were the Puritans to blame for that?

I walked into the field, the soil giving slightly under my leather boots. The edge of the wood looked dark and foreboding, cutting a ragged line between the brown earth and the blue sky. The woods felt endless here on the edge of town. A man could walk a thousand miles to the west without meeting another living soul.

I froze. Every exhale left a hazy white cloud around my face that dissipated between breaths. We truly were on the edge of the civilized world, a small outpost of light in a dim corner of the globe. Every day I overheard stories of Indian raids and girls being carried off to live in the woods, or families on the frontiers being slaughtered. So many of the students at school lived with uncles or cousins because their parents had been killed by Indians, or bears, or the unstoppable crush of a New England winter.

It was easy to imagine dark forces in the woods, because they were real. Salem Village *was* under attack, but our enemy wasn't a fallen angel. Our lives, carved out on the edge of a massive continent, were under assault by nature, by man, by reason itself.

We weren't meant to be here.

The back of my neck tickled as if I were being watched. I spun around but saw nothing. Nothing except for the woods, always there, and our house, which looked even smaller compared to the vast stretch of sky above it. I fought the urge to run inside and slam the door. I knew, deep in my chest, that a door couldn't stop the forces that plagued Salem Village.

The problem was much bigger than Ann Putnam.

~ ~ ~

The next day I awoke with a pounding headache.

I'd been awake most of the night thinking about the witch panic. About *my* role in it. What if I'd visited Abigail sooner? Or what if I hadn't told Ann to use her position as Abigail's friend for attention?

But that was all in the past. Once Ann Putnam told her father the names of the witches attacking her, it would be over. I couldn't stand up and call Ann a liar, or reveal the Glass Girls and their Burning Book. I couldn't walk into the Village Square and start ranting about circles of candlelight in the woods.

That would be a good way to paint myself as a witch.

I couldn't prove anything, and I was a newcomer, an outsider that didn't even attend the Village church. I might not fit the stereotypical image of a witch, but if Ann wanted to, she could surely set the Village against me.

In a sweaty panic, I saw a torch-wielding mob descending on our house. In the inky black night of Salem Village, anything was possible.

When the sun rose, my skin still carried the clammy tremors from the night. I wanted to stay home, but my mom pushed me out the door with a small satchel of food. I looked warily at the edge of the woods and stuck to the very middle of the road. Every noise set my nerves on edge. Even the wind through the trees sang a melancholy tune.

I still couldn't shake the sense that something in the woods was watching me. I understood, now, how easily panic could spread.

If Ann had already told her father, would I arrive in the Village to find the sheriff arresting witches? Or worse, a mob of men descending on those poor women's homes, ready to take matters into their own hands?

But when I reached the school, it looked just like it had the day before, except there were even fewer students. Mr. Green's face was contorted with concern. He raised a handkerchief to wipe his brow three times before classes even started.

At least there wasn't a mob carrying torches.

I searched the classroom for the one person I wanted to see today—not the Glass Girls. They'd stopped attending school. But there, leaning in the corner of the room, I saw Joy, still wearing her all-black uniform.

Before I could walk over, Mr. Green rang the bell to start class. I dutifully sank into my seat. The entire back row, along with most of the front row, stood empty. When Joy slipped into the seat next to mine, I risked a whisper. "We need to talk."

She gave a nod, her eyes trained on the front of the classroom.

With so few students, the morning recitations flew by. As lunchtime approached, Mr. Green sighed and leaned back on his desk. "That's all for today."

A boy in the second row raised his hand. "You mean we can go home?"

"Yes."

The benches squeaked as students stood to file out of the building. There was none of the typical exuberance for a half-day off from school. Even the younger students had picked up on the mood in the Village. There would be no celebrating in the schoolyard.

As the other students quietly walked home, Joy pulled me aside. We hurried down the road toward the deserted clearing. Neither of us spoke on the walk, but as soon as we arrived, Joy turned to me.

"Is it true you went to see Ann Putnam yesterday?" Before I could open my mouth, she peppered me with more questions. "Did you hear about the other girls? What did Ann say? Was Mercy there?"

I blinked. "Wait—what other girls?"

"Three more girls claim that they're being attacked by witches. Including Mercy."

I shut my eyes and took a deep breath. I should have known. Of course Mercy would join Ann's charade. And once Ann made it popular to be afflicted by witches, of course other girls would join in. I looked up at the clouds flowing eastward across the clearing. For a minute I felt dizzy. "Which girls?"

"Elizabeth and Alice Booth. They're in our class. The sisters who sit together near the window."

I remembered the names. "They're the ones who almost look like twins, right?"

"They're less than a year apart. And they worship Ann Putnam."

I'd been focused on the panic infecting the adults in Salem Village, but how had I missed how Ann's act would play to her fans? My stomach knotted. I couldn't get swept away by the darkness. Joy was my friend and my only ally in stopping Ann Putnam. I had to stay focused.

I sucked in another deep breath and released it slowly.

Joy was watching me. A muscle in her cheek twitched.

"Cavie, I . . ." She lowered her voice. "I thought you might be wrong about Abigail, before. I thought maybe Minister Parris was right that the Village was infested with witches. But when Ann claimed to be sick, it just seemed like too much to believe. I've known Ann Putnam my whole life. I'd believe she's a witch before I'd believe she's being attacked by them."

I raised a corner of my mouth in a half-hearted smile. I hadn't known Ann as long as Joy had, but her words echoed my own feelings.

At least I wasn't the only one questioning Ann's story.

Joy pulled a book from her bag and held it out to me. "This is Cotton Mather's book about the Goodwin children. You should read it."

I nodded and took the thin volume. I wanted to flip it open and pour over it right there in the glen, but we had more urgent matters to discuss. Reluctantly, I slipped it into my bag for later. "I have to tell you what happened at Ann's yesterday."

"You did visit her! I heard a rumor, but I wasn't sure if it was true."

"People are spreading rumors about who's visiting Ann's house?"

Joy rolled her eyes. "The entire Village is obsessed with Ann Putnam. It's disgusting."

"It gets worse," I said in a whisper. I swallowed before I continued. "Ann thinks she's the victim in this entire story. She told me without an ounce of hesitation that the witches are out to get her." I pictured Ann, sitting on her bed with the Burning Book on her lap, content as a lion after a meal. I remembered the row of bruises on her arm. Bruises she must have inflicted on herself. I shivered. "And she really does believe it. She's convinced herself that it's true."

Joy didn't answer at first. We were frozen in the glen like statues, our icy breath mingling. Then her voice broke the silence. "Did she name the witches?"

I nodded. "She has a whole list. She pretended the names just appeared in the Burning Book. And she's going to give the list to her father."

Joy's breath caught in her throat. "I'll bet you a thousand pounds she'll go to her grave before she reveals the Burning Book. How could she?"

"It would make her look guilty." That book could turn Ann from victim into villain in seconds if anyone else saw it. No wonder she guarded it so closely. It was a marvel that she hadn't tried to destroy it yet. "But the names alone will do enough damage."

The silence stretched longer and longer. Even the woods were deadly silent. Not a single creature stirred in the depths of winter. I raised my eye to catch Joy's. "I'm glad you believe me that Ann's making this up." I didn't know how else to thank Joy. The words didn't seem enough. But her presence here proved that I wasn't alone.

Joy voiced my thoughts. "What should we do now?"

The same question had tormented me for days. Yesterday, I'd felt hopeless. If the problem was bigger than Ann Putnam, there was no way to stop it. But today, standing with Joy, a glimmer of hope burned in my chest. Alone, I might not be able to stop the panic. But together, we had a chance.

Still, every plan I came up with had a problem. We couldn't prove Ann a liar with the Burning Book, not when she watched it so closely. We couldn't go to Minister Parris—he'd never believe two strangers over his own daughter and niece. And I'd tried to talk to Ann, but she wouldn't listen to reason. I saw the same process of hope and disappointment playing out on Joy's face. She bit her lip and tugged at the hem of her bonnet.

I pulled in a sharp gasp of air. "Ann wants attention, right?" An idea was starting to form in the back of my mind.

"That's why she made up the whole story."

"What if people stopped paying attention?"

With a shake of her head, Joy dismissed my question. "That would never work. The Villagers are too caught up in the witch panic already."

"No, that's not what I mean. What if Ann thought someone else was getting *more* attention? You should have seen her when we saw the crowd outside of Abigail's house. She practically turned green with envy."

Joy didn't look convinced. "What would you do?"

"I could tell her that everyone's outside of the Parris house? Or try to convince her that no one's talking about her anymore?"

"It might backfire. What if she does something even more drastic to get attention?"

I sighed. Joy was right. Manipulating Ann hadn't worked so far, so why did I think it would work now? Ann was impossible to trick. She'd already thought out everyone else's moves three steps in advance. She would have made an amazing chess player, if she had the patience for the game.

Frustration seeped into my voice. "This is like fighting a hydra. Whenever we come up with a plan to get rid of one head, more pop up."

"But we have to keep trying."

"Should I go back to Ann's house, then?" Joy started to nod, but I reached out and grabbed her arm before she could speak. "What about Abigail?" My pulse raced. "Two days ago, Abigail said she was feeling better. She thought she might come back to school this week. And then Ann falls ill." The thoughts were swirling in my head. I struggled to order them. Joy watched me, one eyebrow raised. "What if Abigail thinks Ann is trying to steal her place?"

Joy didn't look convinced. "Abigail must be used to that."

"No, see—Abigail might suspect that Ann's lying."

Hope coursed through my body. It was the closest I'd come to a plan that might work. If Abigail thought Ann was faking, she might be able to convince Minister Parris to back down from his claims about witches. And what if Abigail hadn't heard that Ann was planning to accuse Tituba? Would Abigail defend Tituba over Ann? I wasn't sure how close Abigail was to the woman, but they'd known each other for years.

I had to act now, before Ann shared the list of names with anyone else. Once that happened, it would be too late.

I tried to explain my thoughts to Joy, but she was still skeptical. I convinced her that it was at least worth a try. I vowed to visit Abigail the next day to drive a wedge between her and Ann.

Joy and I talked in the glen for hours, until the winter sun had dipped below the tree line and our hands were tingling and red from the cold. When dusk forced us to part, we promised to meet before school the next morning to continue our conversation.

But by the next morning, it was already too late.

THIRTEEN

The witch attacks were spreading.

My mom woke me with the news: school had been canceled because of the outbreak of afflicted students, which had risen from six—Ann, Abigail, Mercy, and Betty, plus the Booth sisters—to nine overnight.

My stomach dropped.

Three more girls were wailing that witches tormented them. How many would there be tomorrow, or the next day? There were six hundred souls in Salem Village. The fire could get much hotter before it burned itself out.

Only a day earlier, I'd dragged my feet all morning to avoid school, but now I threw on my cloak and begged my parents to let me visit the Village Square. The news only increased the urgency of my mission. I had to talk to Abigail right away.

Once my parents had extracted a promise that I would return before noon to help in the fields, they let me leave. I flew out of the house and down the road.

A bank of clouds had settled in overnight. The brilliant blue sky had been replaced by a low, gray ceiling. It felt like the world was pressing down on me.

Panic climbed up my neck once I reached the Village Square. The entire square was packed with people in an uproar, whispering about witches and gossiping about who might fall ill next. I still didn't know if Ann had given the names in the Burning Book to anyone. I strained my ears for word of Tituba, or Sarah Good and Sarah Osborne, my entire body rigid with worry. But thankfully, the only name on people's lips was Ann Putnam.

Maybe she hadn't told anyone yet.

Maybe there was still time.

I was caught up in a stream of people moving toward the Parris house, rumbling that their minister needed to take a stand against the dark forces. I searched the crowd for Joy, hoping that a familiar face would calm my pounding heart. Part of me wanted to run home and stay in my house until the hysteria died down, but my guilt proved stronger than my fear.

I had a plan. I couldn't abandon the Villagers now.

Joy was nowhere to be seen. Either she'd already heard school was cancelled and stayed home, or she had come and gone before I arrived. Or she might be trapped in the pack of people on the other side of the Village Square, standing outside the Putnam house.

I peeled away from the crowd before we reached Abigail's door and crept between her house and its neighbor into her backyard. I stopped in the dark gap between the structures, drawing in a few unsteady breaths now that I was alone.

Dizziness spun around me. I put up a palm and rested it on the sturdy wood of Abigail's house. I tried to ground myself in something solid. Joy wasn't there to help, but I could still do something.

I had to convince Abigail that Ann was lying.

Voices from the front of the house jolted me out of my thoughts. A man loudly proclaimed that something had to be done. A woman's cry joined him, lamenting for the poor, innocent children.

I pictured how I must look to the crowd: a girl, standing alone in the shadow of the house, with my hand pressed against the building. I pulled my palm back as though singed. All the picture needed was a black cat to convict me.

I could never drop my guard. I had to be above suspicion at all times.

I raced to the back of the house. Tituba's small hut stood there, the windows dark as if no one was home.

Had Ann already accused Tituba of witchcraft?

Had Tituba fled, or been arrested?

"Cavie."

I jumped at the sound of my name and spun around. Betty Parris was standing on the back porch, watching me. I held a hand to my heart and tried to still its pounding. "Betty, you scared me."

She was dressed in her typical black dress with a white apron, instead of the nightclothes she'd been wearing a few days ago. The color had returned to her cheeks and she stood firmly on the porch without wavering. I breathed a sigh of relief. At least one of the afflicted was healing.

Betty was still watching me with her wide brown eyes. "What are you doing back here?"

"I didn't mean to startle you. I was coming to visit Abigail, and the front of the house . . ." I trailed off.

"I can hear their voices from my room," Betty confided. "Father says I can get out of bed now, but he wants me to stay in the house just in case my torments return. But I get so lonely and bored in my room that I try to listen to the voices. And sometimes I sneak out here, for fresh air."

"And Abigail? Is she better, too?"

Betty glanced over her shoulder, back at the door. She lowered her voice. "Father says she has to stay inside, too, but she's recovered. She's in the kitchen making a pie, or maybe rolls. Something with baking." She gestured that I should follow her inside.

When Betty swung the door open, I saw Abigail standing near the stove, her arms covered in flour. She leaned over the table, beating a pile of dough. When she heard us, she turned and smiled, brushing a piece of hair out of her face. Her fingers left a white trail of flour where her hand had touched.

She didn't seem surprised to see me. For a minute, I wondered how much Abigail had heard about the panic in the Village, and what she knew about Ann. Had Minister Parris shielded her out of concern?

Abigail turned back to the dough without speaking.

I stepped toward her. The floorboards squeaked under my feet. "Hi, Abigail. Betty says she's feeling better. How are you?"

"I'm better," she said in a distracted voice. Something was different about her. The fire in her eyes had been dampened. Was it because of the illness, or something else?

"What are you making?"

"It's just some bread," she said. "I've always liked baking. The precision, I guess. And I like seeing the dough rise." She struck the ball again with a closed fist.

I hadn't pegged her for the baking type.

Betty watched us from the corner of the kitchen. I shifted my weight, trying to avoid the squeaky floorboard. "I'm sure you've heard a lot about what's happening in the Village."

Abigail didn't answer. Instead, Betty spoke. "Father doesn't want us to pay attention to that terrible Village gossip. Isn't that right, Abigail?"

Abigail nodded as if she were barely listening. "Yes, Betty, he wants to make sure we continue to recover."

Betty looked at me and spoke quietly. "He stays in the study all day and most of the night. He's writing something. But I don't see how, with the shades drawn. It's too dark to see the end of your quill."

Abigail spun around, brushing off her hands on her apron. "Betty." Her tone held a warning.

Betty's eyes shot open. The edges of her eyebrows folded down in hurt. Had Minister Parris told them not to talk? Had Betty violated some family pact? She turned back to me and began to babble. "Of course, we still hear things. We aren't complete shut-ins."

Before Abigail could silence her again, I asked, "What kinds of things?"

"Earlier this morning Ann Putnam visited—" Betty began, but Abigail cut her off, taking a step toward us.

"Betty, leave us," Abigail commanded. Her hands were on her hips and her eyes flashed with intensity. Betty wasn't the only one who cowered under Abigail's glare. Her mood changed fast as quicksilver. It caught me off guard.

Maybe Abigail didn't want me to know Ann had visited.

Maybe that meant Ann hadn't told her father yet.

Betty sulked and took her time leaving the room, dragging her feet as she headed for the stairs. Abigail and I watched her back, until she vanished and the creaking sounds of her feet faded away.

We were alone.

I had to take control of the conversation. "I visited Ann yesterday," I said in a quiet voice. "She told me about the Burning Book."

Abigail's forehead wrinkled. "Why would she tell you?" Her voice was barely loud enough for me to hear. "She said that I was the only one who knew besides Mercy."

I shrugged. It was time to play my part. Time to drive a wedge between Abigail and Ann. "I don't know why she'd lie to you. That's strange." I paused for a moment. "Ann even showed me where the names appeared in the book. Did she show it to you?"

Abigail gave a small shake of her head, her eyes wounded. "She said it was too risky to bring the Burning Book over." She swallowed hard. "She really showed you?"

"She must trust me," I ventured. I locked eyes with Abigail. "After all, I was in the woods with you when Tituba called up the magic to predict our futures."

"That's right," Abigail whispered.

"Ann wanted my opinion about what she should do next."

At that, Abigail squeaked and threw a hand over her mouth. "She did? She wanted *you* to tell her what to do?" She sank into a chair near the stove, nearly stumbling as she sat. The raw dough lay on the table, completely forgotten.

I tilted my chin back. "I guess you've been out of school for a while. Ann and I grew a lot closer while you've been gone."

Panic flashed across Abigail's face. She gripped her apron so hard that flour rained to the floor.

Abigail's worst fear was being supplanted in Ann's hierarchy, and here I was, exploiting her anxiety. I took a deep breath and told myself it was for a good cause. Yes, I was manipulating

Abigail, just like Ann had toyed with Tituba, but I was trying to help.

Abigail looked down at the floor. "I didn't realize. I didn't even know that Ann was afflicted until she visited me today."

It was too perfect. "You didn't?" I tried to pour shock into my voice. "But why wouldn't she tell you earlier? Or send you a message, at least? We were all talking about it before school yesterday. Everyone in the Village must have known before you."

I watched Abigail's face fall again. She squirmed in the chair and turned her eyes down. Was she holding back tears? I refused to feel an ounce of guilt. Someone had to stop Ann, and if that meant upsetting Abigail, it was worth it.

Abigail mumbled, "I guess she thought I was too sick. Or something."

In that moment, I could twist the knife—when Ann and I visited Abigail only a few days earlier, Abigail had told us she was recovering. Ann knew, the very day she claimed witches pinched her, that Abigail wasn't ill.

But I hesitated. I didn't want to be cruel. Abigail was fragile, and one wrong word could easily turn her against me. So I kept my mouth shut.

Finally, Abigail looked up at me, her brow furrowed. "I don't know why she wouldn't tell me." She stood slowly and returned to the dough, her back to me. "What names did you see in the Burning Book?"

She wanted to know if Ann had lied to her about that, too. I silently calculated my answer. Would Ann have held back any of the names? Tituba, maybe? I could make Ann look bad if I gave different names—but if Ann had given all three names to Abigail, she'd discover my deception soon.

"Sarah Good, Sarah Osborne . . . and Tituba."

Abigail half turned toward me, her hands once again coated in flour. The shakiness had vanished from her voice. "That's what she told me, too."

Her confidence in Ann might have returned, but I'd make sure it didn't last. "But you don't think . . . Could Tituba really be a witch?"

Abigail's frown returned. Before I could decode her expression, she turned back to the dough. She pounded it again, her strikes lighter than before.

Earlier that week, Abigail had been willing to put her life in Tituba's hands, wagering that the urine cake would guarantee her health. And I'd seen the way Abigail acted with Tituba in the woods. I wouldn't go so far as to call them friends—Tituba's bondage made that impossible—but they were friendly.

Abigail spoke, barely loud enough for me to hear. "It's . . . difficult for me to picture Tituba as a witch. In spite of the magic she showed us in the woods. She's lived with Minister Parris since before I moved in a decade ago. If she wanted to hurt me, she wouldn't have to go through all the trouble of bewitching me." She tilted her head toward me and gave a weak smile. "She could just put poison in my food or strangle me in my sleep."

Her joke didn't lighten the mood in the kitchen.

Internally, I catalogued my progress. Abigail was worried about her position with Ann. She was questioning whether Ann's list of names was true. But I still had to give her a reason to believe Ann was faking her illness.

I'd led her to the edge. Now it was time to push her over.

I leaned against the wall and absentmindedly traced the wood grain with my fingers. "Everyone in town is so worried about Ann. At school, I barely heard anything but Ann, Ann, Ann. Mr. Green even let us out early yesterday because so many people were in tears."

Abigail's shoulders stiffened, but she kept her back to me.

"And it's not just at school. There's a prayer circle outside Ann's house all day and night. As soon as word of Ann's illness spread, the Booth sisters fell ill, and three more girls were struck this morning. I guess they're so worried about Ann that they've worked themselves up into a frenzy. Even Minister Parris was in the Village Square this morning praying for Ann."

That finally forced Abigail to spin around. Her cheeks burned red and her hands were balled into fists at her side. "But I saw her a few hours ago and she looked fine. She snuck up to my room without even knocking." She paused. "Ann didn't look ill at all."

"Spiritual torment can take many forms, I guess." I shrugged my shoulders as if Ann's healthy appearance was completely normal. "Ann must be in a great deal of pain even if she isn't showing it."

Anger flashed across Abigail's face. She almost stepped toward me, but stopped herself. I could see the questions piling up in her mind. Would she draw the obvious conclusion? Abigail knew Ann better than I did. She must have seen Ann make similar calculations in the past—when Ann saw an opportunity to build her status, she always took it.

Then the fire drained from Abigail's body. She almost collapsed before my eyes. When she finally spoke, her voice came out in a hoarse whisper. "I guess I knew Ann was popular, but I didn't realize she was *that* popular."

Abigail's sudden change left me unbalanced. I was glad for the solid wood of the wall behind me, or I might have faltered.

If only I could peer into her mind and see what she was thinking.

But it was past time for me to leave. I didn't want to press my luck. "I better go. Ann asked me to visit her every day while she's feeling ill." I watched Abigail closely for a flare of jealousy, but her face was blank. Her hands hovered over the wooden bowl of dough as if she'd been frozen in place. Finally she gave a weak nod.

I slipped out the door.

I sucked in a deep breath of crisp winter air as I stood on the back porch. My words had shaken Abigail, but I was left wondering if I'd achieved my goal.

This was going to be harder than I thought.

FOURTEEN

The Village Square rumbled like a Roman Arena.

When I finally worked up the courage to peek back into the square, I almost darted back into the shadows of the Parris house. The crowd had grown in size, and anger pulsed through the air.

My heart pounded as I watched them. These were the men of Salem Village, called up to protect their youth.

Their voices blended together and struck a discordant note. I could barely make out any words. Until my eye caught on a tall, older man with a sharp nose and a hint of gray in his dark hair. I didn't recognize him. He stood at the edge of the mob, only ten feet from where I remained hidden by shadows, and his face was contorted with rage.

"Someone needs to call the Governor," the man shouted.

His companion, a shorter, younger man, still wearing his black hat, shook his head vigorously. "We can't just sit around doing nothing."

The taller man jostled the Villagers at his elbows. "The longer we wait, the more those poor afflicted girls suffer."

This brought a chorus of support. Encouraged, the man leapt up on a bench, his sharp profile clear from my position. "The girls must know who's tormenting them," he shouted. Heads from across the square turned in his direction. "Once we have the names, we can do something to defend our children."

The names. *The names.*

Maybe Ann hadn't told anyone, yet. Maybe it wasn't too late.

His companion on the ground spoke to the crowd. "Hathorne's right."

The man called Hathorne raised an arm. "Will we cower before this threat? Or are we men?" His growing audience roared their assent.

No. This was exactly what I wanted to avoid—a mob demanding justice. Once the names wiggled out of Ann's control, anything could happen.

"If you're a good, Christian man, follow me now to Putnam's house. We know what to do with witches."

"Hang them!" voices from the crowd began to chant. "Hang them!"

My blood turned to ice in my veins.

Hathorne waved to silence the crowd. "They knew how to handle witches in Boston back in '89. *'Thou shalt not suffer a witch to live.'* The words are right there in the Holy Book. So follow me to Putnam's!" He jumped down from the bench and pushed through the crowd.

I was frozen in place, my thoughts clamoring through my mind. I could hear a pounding in my ears—was it my blood, or the sound of stamping feet rushing to Ann's house?

Would Ann hold back? Or would she start naming "witches" for the mob to lynch?

I couldn't follow the crowd. It was too dangerous.

So I forced myself to go in the opposite direction, back behind the Parris house, and I ran, breathlessly, toward Ann's house. Something pushed me to get there before the mob.

But my race had been for nothing. I slid up the side of the Putnam house and arrived before Hathorne's mob, but another crowd had already gathered in front of the porch. Ann's father stood tall on the top step, holding court for an audience of mostly men.

And Ann stood next to him, the corner of her mouth turned up in a faint grin.

As I caught my breath, Hathorne's mob joined the men already watching Putnam. A rumbling passed through the crowd like distant thunder drawing near.

Ann's father raised a piece of paper above his head. I squinted, but I was much too far to make out the writing. "Fellow Villagers. I know you share my concern to protect our precious children against witches." He laid his other hand on Ann's shoulder. She gave a pout. "I have here on this paper the names of three witches."

My breath caught in my throat. I nearly choked.

It was too late.

I was too late.

The crowd gasped and muttered at Putnam's revelation. Hathorne pushed himself to the front of the mob, nodding along with Putnam's words.

"I am going to turn this list over to the Sheriff of Essex County, and then I'll send a copy to the Governor himself," Ann's father vowed.

The men let up a whooping cheer at those words. Nausea swept over me. I reached out a hand to steady myself on the side of Ann's house.

Two words raced through my mind over and over again. *Oh no. Oh no. Oh no.* I'd never be able to stop this mob. Thomas Putnam was one of the most powerful people in Salem Village. Who would ignore his calls for justice?

Putnam lowered the list of names and waved it at the crowd, waiting until they fell silent. "Now, some in Salem Village may doubt the reports of witchcraft," he began. Boos from the men interrupted him. "I agree, I agree," Putnam said. "But we must find compassion within ourselves to reach out to the skeptics. We have to convince them that the threat is real."

Hathorne frowned from his front-row position. "How do you suggest we do that, Putnam?" he called.

"Just listen," Putnam continued. "We have to tell them the story of my dear Ann. Poor Ann's noble and Puritan suffering is an example that all of us should follow. And who would dare deny the tales of her agony?" He gestured to Ann, who stuck out her lower lip in a pantomime of anguish.

My own lip curled at her play acting. I wanted to leap on the porch and slap that look off her face. But my eyes darted back to the crowd. They were enthralled by Putnam's speech. What would they do if I challenged Ann so publicly?

It might be even worse than hanging.

Ann's father leaned closer to her. "Tell them, Ann," he said.

Ann took a step forward. The crowd hushed to hear her voice.

"For several days I have been tormented," she began in a weak voice. Her eyes swept over the crowd and focused on the distant horizon. "I have been pinched at all hours of the day, until I can get no rest at all. I have heard the sounds of wailing, which no one else could hear. I have felt terrible pains shooting through my body, with no source of relief." Her voice carried through the air, the mob completely still. The only sound was a woman sniffling. I searched the crowd and saw several women dabbing their eyes with handkerchiefs.

Who would dare deny Ann's torment?

I would, for one.

But I didn't have any allies in this particular bunch.

Ann's tale continued. "I have seen the specters of our fellow Villagers. They appear before me and torment me viciously. No one else can see them. I tried to be brave—" she dropped her head and a single tear rolled down her cheek—"I confronted one of the specters and told her to leave me alone. But she only laughed and said my troubles would never end."

I leaned forward on the balls of my feet. *Specters*? What was she talking about? Could Ann have taken the idea of ghostly apparitions from Cotton Mather? I vowed to read his book as soon as I could get home.

Then it struck me. The specters served a purpose. Ann could accuse women of witchcraft without showing the Burning Book to anyone. She wouldn't have to reveal her own secrets.

One of the men in the mob cried out, "Who was the woman?" A chorus of calls repeated the question.

Hathorne stepped forward when the voices faded. "Tell us her name!"

Ann bowed her head, lifting a willowy arm to her temple. "I fear revealing her name lest she redouble her attacks against me." Ann's father put a protective arm on her shoulder.

Hathorne's fists were balled at his sides. "We'll make sure that doesn't happen." He turned to the crowd. "We'll have her arrested today. She won't be able to torment anyone else." The men behind him were quick to agree.

Thomas Putnam whispered something to Ann and then

spoke to the crowd. "My daughter will do the right thing. These women must be exposed for their crimes."

Ann nodded weakly as she lowered her arm. She stood taller and threw her blonde locks over her shoulder. "I know you'll protect me," she said, speaking to the crowd as much as to her father. "I recognized the specter right away. It was Minister Parris' slave, Tituba."

The men erupted into calls for Tituba's arrest. The fury rolling through the mob sent a shiver through my body. I pulled my cloak tighter, but the chill had settled in my bones.

The words the men hurled at Tituba—they would have earned a mouthful of soap at another time. They called her a cannibal, Satan's handmaiden.

I stepped back from the house, ready to run if the mob's violence erupted.

And if I feared for myself, what would happen to Tituba?

Ann's father waved the crowd to silence and turned to Ann. "Tell them what you saw her doing."

Ann bit her lip, as if the next words were difficult to speak. Somehow, her gaze found me, hiding in the shadows. I tried in vain to read her expression. But her steely gaze gave away nothing.

When she spoke, her voice rang loud in the square.

"I saw her doing magic."

The mutters and curses rolled through the square. But I barely heard them. Would Ann really admit she'd practiced magic in the woods? It would make her look as guilty as Tituba.

She'd never dare.

But could she spin it some way that would shield her?

And would that protection extend to her friends who'd been in the woods with her?

I stepped back so quickly that I bumped into the rail of the house next door to the Putnam's. If Ann would throw a noose around Tituba's neck so easily, could I be next?

Ann's next words caught me off guard. "I saw her outside Minister Parris's house. She was making a magical cake to cure Abigail and Betty."

That never happened. I screamed in my head, but of course I couldn't say anything out loud. Yes, Tituba had planned to make the cake, but Ann stopped her. I *knew* Ann was lying—but who would believe me?

"Tituba was using all kinds of foul substances," Ann continued. "She told me she was going to feed the cake to some dogs. And she stole urine from the chamber pots to bake in the cake." A woman gasped. "I knew it was wrong," Ann pleaded, and if I hadn't known the truth I would have believed every word. "Minister Parris taught us a saying: *he who knows how to heal knows how to harm.*"

So that was her angle.

Another tear streaked down her face. "I think Tituba was making the cake to show Minister Parris that she could cure the girls, when really *she* was the one tormenting them." Ann wobbled on her legs and looked close to fainting. Her father stepped in to steady her.

"Are you ill?" a panicked voice called from the crowd.

Ann's body went completely stiff. Her arm darted out as if pushing away an invisible attacker. The crowd gasped. Ann cried, "She's attacking me! She's angry I told you the truth!"

Hathorne took another step toward the porch, uncertainty written across his face. Ann's father clutched her close. Another voice in the crowd yelled, "We have to find Tituba!"

"Tell us the other names," Hathorne said. "We'll have them

arrested right now!"

"Look, the Sheriff!"

The crowd split to let the man approach the Putnam house. He was surprisingly young, not yet thirty, with ashy brown hair and a prominent widow's peak. I'd never seen George Corwin before, but apparently the crowd had drawn his attention.

Corwin stepped onto the porch and approached Ann. "Tell us the names." He spoke in a voice barely loud enough to carry. "I can have those women in jail within the hour."

Thomas Putnam kept one arm around Ann while he handed the paper to Corwin. The Sheriff took it and quickly scanned the names. Once he finished reading, he turned to the crowd. "I'll need help."

"Just tell us who to arrest," Hathorne vowed. His voice sent a chill through my veins.

Corwin strode off the porch, trailed by a group of men. "We'll arrest Tituba first. Then Sarah Good and Sarah Osborne."

The mob broke apart, but dangerous energy still pulsed through the Village. A group of women rushed to Ann to see if she needed anything after her attack. She let them lead her inside, but before she vanished, she caught my eye again. Her icy glare sent another shiver through my body.

It carried a warning not to cross her.

I drew back between the houses, my chest tight. I could hear Corwin and his followers banging on the Parris door to arrest Tituba.

Everything was spiraling out of my control.

I ran home without looking back.

FIFTEEN

I was gasping for breath by the time I reached my house.

Neither of my parents were home, thankfully, so I could race up the stairs and shut myself in my room to read Cotton Mather's book. I pulled it from under the corner of my mattress where I'd hidden it two days earlier and threw myself down on the bed to read.

The title stood out in stark black on the front page. *Memorable Providences Relating to Witchcrafts and Possessions.* I ran my finger over the words at the bottom: "Boston, 1689." My hand trembled as I stared at the page.

A woman had lost her life that year because of the story in this book.

But I had to read it. Ann might have taken her tale about spectral attacks from Mather.

I skimmed the beginning of Mather's tale about the family of John Goodwin, a mason in Boston, and his six children. I flipped through the pages quickly, searching for Mather's description of the children's actions when they were being attacked. I had to force my hand not to shake as I scanned through the book.

Finally, I found it. One daughter had *strange fits*. Three of her siblings were soon seized by *similar tortures*.

I frowned.

Mather's words were so general. What did he mean by strange fits? He wrote that their contortions were "so very grievous that it would have broke a heart of stone to have seen their agonies." That sounded similar to Ann's performance, but not so similar that I could prove she was copying the Goodwin children.

Then, a few pages later, my heart dropped. Mather could have been describing Ann Putnam in this passage.

"They would make most piteous outcries that they were cut with knives and struck with blows that they could not bear."

Ann *must* have read this—it *had* to be the source for her performance. My pulse quickened and I pushed forward.

I searched and searched for a description of specters but found nothing. Ann might have invented them herself, or read it in another book. Still, this was proof. If I took this to the sheriff, I could convince him that Ann was only mimicking the Goodwins.

And then a line near the end of the book caught my eye. My throat tightened as I read Mather's words.

"I am resolved after this never to use but one grain of patience with any man that shall go to impose upon me a denial of devils or witches. I shall count that man ignorant who shall suspect, but I shall count him downright impudent if he assert the non-existence of things which we have had such palpable convictions of."

The book fell from my hands. I looked up at the bare planks of the ceiling. The most respected minister in the Massachusetts Bay Colony was staking his reputation on the existence of witches. Who was I to contradict him? If I ran to Sheriff Corwin, he'd probably just laugh in my face.

Why had I been so certain that the book would undermine Ann?

Nothing I'd done had stopped Ann. And then she'd smiled at me as she stood on her porch crying that witches were attacking her.

Ann was like lightning, faster than everyone else and too brilliant to look at. And there was no way to capture her for your own purposes.

Ann Putnam would always be Ann Putnam, no matter what I did.

But I couldn't hide in my room forever.

I picked up Mather's volume and stuffed it into my bag. I had to show it to Sheriff Corwin. Or Hathorne. Or *someone*. The coincidence was too much. And I'd never be able to forgive myself if I did nothing. I slipped my cloak around my shoulders and headed back to the Village.

My steps were heavy on the long walk. Only a few hours earlier I'd flown home as if chased by Satan himself, but now I felt no rush to return. What would I find in the Village this time? Another mob waiting to hear who Ann would accuse next? More girls, afflicted with the mysterious illness? My stomach was in knots picturing the possibilities. I tried to shove them aside and focus on my task. I slid one hand into my bag and grasped the book to remind myself that it was still there, still something solid I could hold.

At the last minute, I skirted the Village Square and took a different road. I didn't want to run into Abigail or Ann. Instead, I followed a narrow path that led to the jail. If Corwin had made good on his promise, I'd find him there.

When I rounded the last curve in the road and saw the low, squat prison building ahead of me, it was already surrounded by Villagers.

I took a deep breath and forced myself forward.

The crowd moved as if a living organism, beating with three names: Sarah Good, Sarah Osborne, and Tituba. Hathorne was there, holding court before an audience of men who hung on his every word. From what I overheard, Hathorne was vowing justice against the accused witches—except he left out the "accused" part. He seemed certain that the women were guilty and would soon hang.

All three women had been arrested.

Could they hear the calls for their necks from inside their cells?

And Sheriff Corwin was gone. He'd ridden off to Salem Town, or maybe even Boston, for reinforcements. News of our outbreak would soon be in the mouths of Puritans across the colony.

I deflated when I heard Corwin wouldn't be back until tomorrow at the earliest. And I couldn't show Mather's book to Hathorne—not with rage flickering in his eyes. He'd never loosen his grip on the mob who seemed to hang on his every word.

But I couldn't go back home now. Not when things were changing so quickly.

With a quick glance to make sure no one was watching, I ducked behind the jail. The building bordered a deeply wooded thicket of trees that was nearly impenetrable. I'd discovered that crowds tended to ignore everything except the front of the building. Here, the voices from the mob faded. I could even hear a squirrel chattering in a distant tree. It was nearly the end of

February, but patches of snow remained in the shadows behind the jail.

I inched along the edge of the building in the narrow strip between the wall and the woods' tangle of branches. The glowing light ahead had to be a window, perhaps from one of the jail cells.

I couldn't walk in the front door, but I might still be able to learn something from peeking in a window.

When I reached the small hole in the wall, I had to stand on tip toe to see inside. Metal grates almost blocked my view. I inched higher and higher, until—

I threw myself down, stifling a gasp. I'd seen Tituba, her wild hair hanging down below her bonnet.

I stilled my beating heart. I had to look again. Something pushed me to talk with Tituba—to reassure her that not everyone had judged her guilty without a trial.

But would I find her furious? Resigned? Afraid?

I barely knew the woman. How would she react to being arrested and thrown into a cell?

My stomach clenched with guilt. I'd been there when she spoke with Ann. I knew Ann was lying about the urine cake.

I had to help Tituba. I couldn't let fear scare me off.

And then I heard a voice from inside the cell—a man's voice.

Someone else was in the room.

I sealed my lips tightly. I didn't dare look inside again. Instead, I strained to hear his words.

"You surely must see the reason in what I say," the man's voice said.

Tituba's response was louder. She must have moved closer to the window. "I don't know why I should listen to anything you say." Her voice was defiant, in spite of her position as a prisoner.

I strained to pick out the man's next words. "You may feel that way now, but things can change quickly. Just consider what I've said."

Tituba scoffed loudly. "It's because of your niece and her *friends* that I have been falsely accused."

I nearly slipped and fell. The man had to be Minister Parris. And what's more, Tituba did blame the Glass Girls for her arrest—and she blamed me, too.

Minister Parris's voice grew sterner as he spoke. "You will never return to my house again," he vowed. "But I would rather your life be spared."

"My *life*," Tituba shot back. Her tone sent a shock down my spine. She was not speaking to him as a slave to a master. Her words dripped with venom. "If my life is in danger, it is because of your family." Anger coursed through her words, enough to make my mouth fall open. "Now leave me alone."

The cell was silent. For a minute I wondered if Minister Parris had heeded Tituba's command. I was about to raise myself up to look through the window when he spoke.

"Your insolence knows no bounds." Then, in a louder voice. "I will take my leave of you. But remember—confessing is your only option."

Confessing? Had I heard right? My mind tripped over what I'd heard. Just a moment earlier, Minister Parris said he wanted Tituba's life to be spared. Then why would he pressure her to confess?

I swallowed, my mouth suddenly dry. What would Parris gain from Tituba being branded a witch? She lived in his own home. She was accused of attacking his daughter and niece. His own oversight as a father and a minister would be called into question.

Had someone pressured Parris?

What had Joy said about Parris and the Putnam family? In the complicated alliances in Salem Village, were they friends or foes? I thought she said the Putnams supported Parris, but I wouldn't wager much on my memory. Was it possible that Thomas Putnam had asked Parris to talk with Tituba?

Did Putnam think Tituba's confession would verify Ann's claims?

I shook my head. None of it made sense.

I heard Tituba curse under her breath. That didn't seem like a smart choice for someone accused of witchcraft.

And then, silence.

My mind raced, but I held my body completely still. I huddled beneath the window, listening to the sound of my own breath. My eyes were locked onto a fallen branch, with a single wilted, brown leaf still hanging from it. Another branch cracked somewhere in the woods and I jumped. It was past time for me to leave. I couldn't risk being found sneaking behind the jail. If they caught me, I might end up on the other side of the wall, with no way to escape.

I scurried away from the prison, refusing to look back at the crowd still gathered outside the jail.

This time, I didn't avoid the Village Square. I had to find Joy and I didn't know where else to look. I searched every face I passed, glancing under a dozen downturned bonnets, but Joy wasn't there.

A new panicked thought floated through my mind. Ann Putnam hated Joy Titus. Would she accuse *Joy* of being a witch? I wouldn't put it past her. Would Joy find herself thrown into prison before this absurd witch hunt died out?

And what about me? Had I shown my cards too soon? Would Abigail run to Ann's house and tattle on me for talking about Ann behind her back? Would Sheriff Corwin bang on my door next, with a warrant to arrest me?

In the back of my mind, a voice tried to reassure me. Ann wouldn't go that far. She had her limits. If her entire performance was meant to bolster her popularity, she'd only target unpopular Villagers.

But I'd been wrong about Ann before.

She'd already stabbed me in the back by getting back together with Edmund Hale. And I never thought she'd openly accuse anyone of witchcraft. I'd been wrong about that—so could I also be wrong about Ann's limits?

Maybe Joy was in danger. Maybe she'd fled from town to protect herself.

Ann's wrath could easily burn more people before it faded.

It could burn *me*.

My hands shook with fear. I was frozen on the edge of the Village Square, unable to move.

I wanted to help Tituba and the other women, strangers to me but surely innocent, but I had to protect myself, too. I screwed my lips shut and silently vowed not to risk my own neck. My skin prickled and shame burned in my cheeks for my cowardly behavior, but I pushed down the bile rising in my throat and pressed on.

I would do everything in my power to stop Ann's witch hunt—but I had my limits, too.

I shoved my hands into the pockets of my apron and waited until their quaking had stilled. The breeze ruffling my dress carried a hint of spring, a promise of rebirth after the chill of winter. The earth would thaw, the snow would melt, and in a few weeks leaves might burst from dead branches. What would the Village look like by April? Would every woman be in jail, or under suspicion of witchcraft? I wanted to believe that the panic would fade, but I remembered my words to my mother. Now, I was even less certain that this would blow over without violence.

A movement caught my eye. I spun to look at a second-story window where the curtains had moved. A girl was peering out, watching me stand in the square. I didn't recognize her, but the feeling of being watched lit a fire under me. I reached into my bag for the reassuring solidness of Mather's book and hurried home.

It was almost dusk by the time I reached my house. I'd spent the entire day running back and forth to the Village, my pulse racing with each new discovery. It was only when I saw a light shining through the window that I realized I hadn't eaten since breakfast. I felt faint, like I might collapse at any moment.

When I pulled open the door, I saw Joy Titus sitting at the table with my mother. They were chatting and drinking tea, as if the world wasn't crumbling around us.

Joy raised an eyebrow at my appearance. I blinked and wondered what I must look like. Surely racing to the Village hadn't left me looking orderly, and sneaking behind buildings had left streaks of dirt on my white apron. The panic that had gripped me all day must have taken its toll, too.

"Finally," my mom said. "Your friend Joy has been waiting for quite some time." Her tone was light, but I felt a flush of embarrassment rise in my cheeks. I'd been worried that Joy was in prison or fleeing the Village, and she'd been sitting here with my mother the entire time.

"It's fine, Goody Lucas," Joy said. "I enjoyed the tea and

your stories about London very much." She was the model of politeness and decorum. But as soon as my mom turned to take the tea cups into the kitchen, Joy shot me a look that meant we needed to talk.

"Is it okay if we go up to my room?" I asked my mother. As the sun dipped in the sky, the bitter cold flooded back. I didn't want to go back outside, even if it would be more private.

"Of course," Mom called as she left the room. "Have a nice visit."

Something in her voice struck me—the clipped sound of her words. She wanted to talk to me, too. She must have heard the news from the Village, then, about the arrests.

But right now I had to focus on Joy. I led her upstairs to my bare room, which lacked all the trappings of Ann Putnam's. Instead of trinkets and decorated walls, a canopy bed and a chaise, my room had a simple bed, a single wooden chest, and a little stool for the bowl of water I used to wash my face every morning and evening. No mirrors, no decorations. The chest at the foot of the bed held my clothes and a few blankets. Two plain bonnets hung from pegs on the door.

Simple. More Puritan than Ann's room.

Joy must have seen that room, back when she and Ann were friends. In comparison, my room looked like a hovel. But I had more important things to worry about.

"We need to talk," Joy said quietly as soon as I closed the door.

"Yes, we do." I sat on the bed.

Joy gave the chest a glance and decided to perch next to me on the bed. "I assume you heard about Ann Putnam's little performance this morning?"

Had it really only been a few hours earlier that I'd watched

Ann fall into a fit and call out the names of witches to that angry mob? It felt like a lifetime had passed since then. "I was there," I told Joy. "I saw the whole thing."

Joy's eyes widened. "Did she really collapse on the porch? Is it true that a dark cloud covered the sun when she was being attacked by ghosts?"

Apparently the rumor mill in Salem Village was working at full force. "She didn't collapse, and there was no dark cloud. And it wasn't ghosts—she said specters. She pretended that Tituba's specter was pinching her, but only Ann could see it."

Joy's mind was lightning quick. "That way, she can hide the Burning Book."

I nodded. I pulled out Cotton Mather's book and set it on the bed between us. "Joy, have you read about specters before?"

Joy clenched her jaw. "Does Mather talk about them?"

"I couldn't find anything in here. I was skimming, so I might have missed it. But maybe Ann got the idea from another book?"

Joy was already shaking her head before I finished speaking. "I don't know. It's possible, I guess." She paused. "Everyone knows what specters are—the ghostly apparitions of a person still living. But I can't for the life of me remember where I learned that. Maybe Minister Parris mentioned specters in a sermon."

My shoulders slumped. So we couldn't prove Ann had stolen the idea from a book.

Joy must have read the disappointment on my face. "I could look through some other books, if that will help," she vowed. Then her face grew still. I could tell she was weighing her next words carefully. "I saw the Booth sisters this morning. I can't exactly go talk to Ann or Abigail, but they'll still talk to me."

In my obsession with Ann, I had forgotten about the other

afflicted girls. "What did they say?"

Joy raised a hand to her mouth and chewed on her nail. I wanted to shake the information out of her, but I tried to be patient. "They were almost frantic for news about Ann. They kept asking me about her ailments, and how she suffered during attacks. What did the attacks look like? Did her eyes roll up in the back of her head? And you know they're desperate if they came to me—everyone knows that Ann hates my guts."

"So they can imitate Ann perfectly." I rolled my eyes. "And everyone will believe them."

Joy locked eyes with me. "But that's not all. Think about it. If they were talking to Ann, or if Ann was giving them instructions, they wouldn't have to ask me."

I shifted my weight on the bed. Joy's intensity rattled me. "Isn't that a good thing? It means Ann doesn't have a plan. She's not coordinating with the other afflicted girls."

"No, Cavie, don't you see? If there's no plan, and the other afflicted girls want to imitate Ann, what will they do next?"

It struck me so hard that I almost recoiled. "They'll start accusing people of attacking them, too," I whispered. How hadn't I seen it earlier?

"And who can guess what they'll say? Ann, at least, has followed a predictable pattern. I don't know exactly why she named Sarah Good or Sarah Osborne, but I can guess why she accused Tituba."

I remembered that night in the woods when Tituba had spoken to Ann rudely, treating her like an equal instead of her better. Ann wouldn't tolerate that kind of slight. As if that weren't bad enough, Tituba knew Ann had been in the woods doing magic. Tituba was a danger to Ann—so of course her name would slip out when Ann fell into a fit.

Joy continued. "You don't know these people like I do. There have been rumors about Tituba's superstitious practices for years. But she's also made healing ointments for a dozen women. Sarah Good is a beggar, always asking others for assistance. The Villagers see her as a burden to the town. There were already whispers about her cursing people who refused to help her. And everyone knows that Sarah Osborne doesn't attend church. She's rude to people, which is a deadly sin around here. Don't you see? These women are believable witches."

I pulled my arms close around my body. Was the chill in the room coming through the walls? Joy was right. Quarrelsome older women, beggars, and healers could easily don the witch's hat. They were already thorns in the side of good society, so it wasn't a stretch for town magistrates to picture them teaming up with Satan to undermine their communities.

Joy glanced at the closed door as if she suspected someone was listening outside. Her voice quivered with fear. That struck me even deeper than her words—I'd never seen Joy so shaken. "The Booth sisters might follow Ann's lead and target women with bad reputations. But what if they don't? What if they accuse my mother? Or yours?"

My mother, a witch?

The thought was so ridiculous that I almost shook my head. But the Booth sisters didn't know her. She was new to town. Who would defend her?

"What can we do?" I finally said in a quiet voice. Three women already sat in prison, and others might soon join them. I couldn't shake the guilt clawing through my chest. I might not have named them, but I had played a role. I had told Ann how much attention Abigail was getting when she first fell ill. I hadn't stopped Ann when she lied to Abigail, and then to Tituba. I hadn't stood up to Ann when she showed me the names in the Burning Book.

Instead of acting, I'd snuck around playing childish games, teasing Abigail with tales of Ann's betrayals and hiding behind the jail eavesdropping on prisoners.

My stomach suddenly dropped. I'd forgotten about the conversation between Tituba and Minister Parris. What would happen if she confessed? That would set off an even bigger storm.

I grabbed Joy's arm, my breath vanishing in my chest. "Tituba's in prison."

A bewildered look crossed Joy's face.

"I was at the jail this afternoon," I explained, the words tumbling out. "I went around the back and found her cell. I heard her talking to Minister Parris."

"Parris?" Her eyebrows shot up.

"He told her to confess."

Joy's mouth fell open. Her eyes darted around the room. "Are you sure?"

"Positive. Tituba was furious. She even cursed at him. It makes no sense. Why would he want her to confess?"

Joy brought a balled fist to her face. She puzzled over my question for a minute. Then she looked up at me. "Parris is close with the Putnams. Thomas Putnam singlehandedly got Parris the job as minister."

"Would Parris tell Tituba to confess because of the Putnams?"

"It's possible. The Putnams pay the minister's salary. They give Parris firewood for the winter. And his congregation is full of Putnams. If he lost their favor . . ."

"He might lose his job?"

"More than that. His house is owned by the Village. If the Putnams turned against Parris, he'd lose his parsonage and his property."

"Would that be enough for him to tell Tituba to confess?"

Joy answered my question with another one. "Do you think she'll do it?" There was no need to say who Joy meant.

I tried to replay the conversation in my mind, listening for the silences between the words. "Tituba was furious at Parris for telling her to confess. She said it was his fault that she'd been arrested in the first place."

Joy's eyebrow rose, the shock of Tituba's rebuke written on her face. "We'll just have to hope that Tituba holds her tongue tomorrow."

"Tomorrow?"

"Didn't you hear? The examination of the accused witches starts in the morning."

My eyes darted to the window. It was already dark. Dawn was only a sunrise away.

Salem Village didn't waste any time when it came to witches.

My hands started shaking again. I clutched my skirt to still them. Until that moment, I'd convinced myself that Ann's folly could be stopped. But witch trials had a way of fueling more witch trials. It wouldn't be easy to derail the villagers. Especially if Tituba confessed.

Would Tituba resist Minister Parris's suggestion and proclaim her innocence?

Or would she bend under pressure and give voice to the dark suspicions spiraling through the Village?

SIXTEEN

The next morning I was up before the sun, before even the demented rooster who still plagued me every morning.

I couldn't sleep. I kept thinking about Tituba. What would she say in front of the assembled Villagers? And would Ann be at the examination? Would she testify against the accused witches?

Finally, the sun rose. I slipped out the door before my parents were up. If my mom knew about the arrests, she'd warn me to avoid the trial.

But I couldn't miss it.

On the cold walk to the Village, I forced my mind to go blank. Each step cost me something in anxiety and worry. I could almost feel exhaustion dragging down my limbs. It was the first day of March, but winter's grip had not loosened on the Massachusetts Bay Colony. Snow still lurked in the dark corners of the forest and there were no birds chirping in these woods.

My feet eventually carried me to the meeting house, where the examinations would take place. The tall building, surrounded by a ring of bare-branched trees, looked foreboding in my eyes. The clapboard sides would barely keep out a New England winter chill, but today the meeting house would be warmed by the bodies of the Villagers who had packed the space. I wriggled into the building—the first time I'd been inside—and squirmed past farmers and their wives until I was near the front of the room.

Ann, Mercy, and Abigail sat together in the front row, as if they owned it. How did they still carry an air of authority, even in this atmosphere? Sitting in the meeting house, Ann Putnam shone like a queen on her throne.

That was not a good sign.

I peered at Abigail—was there a hint of worry on her face? Something must have happened after we spoke yesterday, otherwise she wouldn't be sitting next to Ann Putnam.

Or maybe not.

Maybe Abigail had decided to side with Ann, as usual.

I wedged myself at the end of a bench a few rows back from the Glass Girls. I didn't want them to see me, but I couldn't take my eyes off of them.

The murmurs from the Villagers grew louder as time passed with no change. Finally, a tall man in black appeared at the front of the room. I jumped when I recognized him. It was Hathorne, the man who had led a mob around the village—was that only yesterday?

He stood behind the raised pulpit at the front of the meeting house. Of course—this wasn't church, but Puritans couldn't resist a pulpit.

"Silence," he ordered in a stately voice.

Was *he* in charge of the trial?

No. Hathorne had called for blood just yesterday, but today he was an impartial judge?

A shiver snaked up my spine.

Hathorne continued. "Today we will examine three accused witches: Sarah Good, Sarah Osborne, and Tituba, slave of

Minister Parris. The afflicted girls are here to testify about the actions of these three women. I would remind everyone that this is a legal proceeding and as such you must stay quiet and not interfere." He glared out at the crowd as though we had already violated his rule.

So it didn't matter that half the people in the meeting house had heard Hathorne quote the Bible to justify killing witches. I gripped the bench with my hands until my knuckles turned white.

"Sarah Good will be examined first."

A noise at the back of the meeting house drew all eyes. Sheriff Corwin was leading in the accused witch, dressed in rags that provided little protection against the cold. Her terrified eyes darted around the meeting house.

She clutched her belly with both hands—she was with child.

My heart broke as I watched Sarah led up the center of the room to a small table in front of Hathorne. Who could believe this disheveled, confused woman was Satan's henchman?

Hathorne was untouched by the poor woman cowering before him. He frowned at her, barking, "Why did you bewitch these girls?" He pointed toward the Glass Girls.

Sarah's mouth fell open and she fumbled for words. "I did not. I never did."

Hathorne, undeterred, moved on. "When did you meet the Devil?"

Sarah's jaw tightened. I saw a hint of the fire that must have frightened her neighbors. "Never."

"What evil spirits did you call to hurt these children?"

"I do not hurt them."

"Then what creature do you send to hurt them?"

"I do not hurt them."

Sarah's declarations did not slow Hathorne. He spoke in an even, calm tone, as if her answers meant nothing.

He's already decided she's guilty. I shivered again.

Hathorne finally turned to the afflicted girls sitting in the front row. Although he spoke to all of them, to my ears it sounded like he was addressing Ann alone. "Look upon this woman. Is she the one who attacked you?"

I leaned forward in anticipation. Ann could end this now.

A cry split the silence in the room. "She's attacking me!" It was Ann Putnam, writhing on the bench. "The specter of Goodwife Good is attacking me!"

My heart fell as the room erupted into screams and cries. More than one woman fainted, and men leapt to their feet as though they could single-handedly fight off an invisible specter to protect Ann Putnam.

Instead of watching Ann—I didn't believe her antics for one second—I looked to Sarah Good. Her face had gone pale and the fire in her eyes had vanished. Her eyes darted between Ann and Hathorne.

Everyone assumed she was guilty. The Villagers didn't want to hear Sarah's defense. They weren't after the truth. They only wanted blood.

So what could Sarah Good possibly say?

Sarah must have reached the same conclusion. She slumped in her seat and stared at the floor.

Hathorne's chilly voice cut through the tumult in the room. "Why did you attack Ann Putnam?"

"I did not," Sarah replied, her voice weak and hollow. "I did nothing to her."

Hathorne shook his head. I stole a glance at Ann, who sat calmly with her hands folded in her lap as if the attack had never happened. A faint smile rested on her lips.

"Why do you lie?" Hathorne demanded.

"I did nothing," Sarah repeated faintly.

"Then who hurt her?"

"I don't know. Ask Sarah Osborne or Tituba."

Hathorne jerked forward as if he'd caught a scent of blood. "Which of them did it?"

"I don't know. You arrested them."

"We arrested you, too."

"But I did nothing."

"Then who torments these girls?"

Sarah's eyes flashed back to Ann. Fear pulsed through her body. She had to know that Hathorne would not relent until she gave him what he wanted. A witch.

Bile churned in my throat—did I want Sarah to lie and accuse another, or be declared a witch herself?

Her hand drifted again to her belly.

"It was Osborne."

A whisper coursed through the crowd. Sarah's shoulders slumped, but Hathorne sat straighter. He leaned over and spoke to the man next to him who recorded the examination. "She told many wicked lies. Mark down that she resisted authority." He waved to Corwin to remove Good. "Take her back to her cell."

Sarah squeaked in protest when she realized that her accusation had not ensured her release. But she did not resist as Corwin led her away.

Minutes later, the sheriff returned with Sarah Osborne. She shook as he dragged her to the front of the meeting house. Had she spoken with Sarah Good? Did she know her fellow prisoner had accused her of witchcraft?

A lump formed in my throat.

The exact scene began to repeat itself with a different woman playing the role of accused witch. Hathorne asked the same questions in the same even tone, barely giving Osborne time to answer. Osborne denied everything. Hathorne pushed her to admit that she hurt the girls. Ann Putnam once again interrupted the examination, crying that Osborne's specter was attacking her.

Men balled their fists and women wept for poor Ann Putnam.

My skin crawled. I wanted to flee, but I couldn't move. The scene before me was captivating, entrancing. Once, during the crossing from London, I'd seen an abandoned ship, cast against the rocks and decaying into the sea. The shipwreck made my hands tremble. My mind populated the deck with passengers, tossed from the boat and drowning in the shallow waters.

I thought of that ship often, the way it had planted itself in my mind no matter how I resisted its siren song. The examination was something similar—it was a disaster, a calamity from which I could not rip myself away.

When Osborne refused to confess or accuse, she was replaced by Tituba.

Blood pounded in my ears. What would she say? Would she fall to Minister Parris's pressure and falsely confess that she was a witch?

Tituba's dark hair hung down her back and her head was bare. She stood straight, her tanned skin marking her as something different from the Puritans staring at her. Tituba glanced at the front row, where Abigail sat. Abigail flinched and slid lower on the bench.

Tituba didn't look nervous.

Had she already decided how she'd answer Hathorne's

questions?

"Tituba, you are the West Indian slave of Minister Parris," Hathorne started.

"Yes."

"And when did you first meet the Devil?"

Tituba didn't pause a second. "I have not." Her words were short and declarative. A wave of relief coursed through my body. If Tituba refused to confess, maybe the whole mess would fade away. Without more evidence, the trials couldn't continue. The only proof was Ann's accusations—and surely the Villagers wouldn't convict someone on Ann Putnam's acting skills alone.

"Why did you attack these girls?"

The questions were familiar by now, as were the responses.

"I did not. I never did."

Hathorne paused for a moment and glanced over his notes. "Did you not attack Ann Putnam?" he asked. His eyes raised and he looked at Ann.

I balled my fists. This wasn't right. Hathorne was practically asking Ann to have another "spell."

But Ann didn't move. She didn't yell or thrash.

And then I saw it—Abigail's hand clenched on Ann's arm. Was Abigail trying to stop Ann from testifying against Tituba?

If she was, someone should have told Tituba.

She looked at Ann and then Abigail. For the first time, I could see worry etched on Tituba's face. She had to be remembering the magic in the woods. Any one of the Glass Girls could testify against her.

And Ann Putnam could send Tituba to her grave.

I wanted to scream that the Glass Girls wouldn't tell what happened in the woods. Ann would never admit it—the whole thing made her look bad. And Abigail's hand was staying Ann's performance. Tituba had nothing to worry about from Ann Putnam as long as Abigail held firm.

But before I could do anything, before I could talk myself into interrupting the trial as Ann had without thought, Tituba spoke again.

Her voice dropped an octave. I could hear the trembling in her words. "I saw a dark man from Boston." Her face titled down while her eyes looked up, as if in a moment of prayer. But this was something much different.

What was she doing? Did she fear Ann's accusation? A confession was much, much worse than anything Ann could dream up. Ann's lies about ghostly apparitions and invisible attacks would never be allowed at the trial—they weren't proof. Ann was just a tool that Hathorne could use to force a confession.

And Tituba was giving Hathorne exactly what he wanted.

"What did the dark man look like?" Hathorne asked quickly.

"He wore black, and . . ." Tituba trailed off. "It was the Devil." I heard the Villagers around me gasp. Here, finally, was proof that Satan walked in Salem Village.

The corners of Hathorne's mouth tilted upward.

He had found his witch.

"What did he tell you to do?"

Tituba kept her eyes forward. "He told me to hurt people."

"And who did he tell you to hurt?" Hathorne pressed.

"I hurt no one. I told him I would not hurt the girls."

My head ached as I listened to Tituba's words.

"Who did you hurt?" Hathorne demanded.

"Some people." A woman nearby moaned at the answer, ignoring the fact that Tituba was contradicting herself.

"Who else was there when the Devil asked you to hurt

people?"

Tituba paused. "Sarah Good. And Sarah Osborne."

Why? My pulse pounded in my ears. Why would Tituba accuse anyone else? Had Minister Parris told her to name them? Or was she trying to please Hathorne? Surely Tituba wasn't naming others to save herself—she had just confessed to meeting with Satan and hurting people. There was no saving Tituba.

"What did you see them do?" Hathorne pressed.

"They hurt the girls."

"How did they hurt them?" Hathorne waited for an answer. When Tituba did not speak, he offered a clue. "Did they use *animals* to hurt the girls?"

"Yes." Tituba spoke quickly. She was an eager student. "I saw Sarah Good with a bird."

I'd heard the rumors that witches had animal familiars who carried out their bidding—everyone in England had heard those tall tales. And, apparently, so had this West Indies slave woman.

"And where did you witches meet?" Eagerness crackled in Hathorne's voice.

"In the woods. In a clearing." Tituba looked down. "At night, with candles."

I froze, my mouth drawn tight. Was Tituba about to accuse the Glass Girls of practicing magic? Accuse *me?* I bit my lower lip and forced my eyes away from Ann.

Had it really only been a few weeks ago that we crowded around Tituba, eager to learn of our future husbands?

But Tituba said nothing more.

Hathorne continued his questioning. His words came faster now that he received the answers he sought. "And how did you get there?"

Tituba scratched her face, her eyes roaming the room as if looking for another clue. "We rode on sticks," she finally said.

"And did you fly *over* the trees or *through* the trees?"

Tituba's mouth opened but nothing came out. She wasn't the only one who looked confused. What was Hathorne getting at? I had no idea what he was after, and I would wager that Tituba didn't either. How could someone fly *through* a tree?

Tituba frowned and pushed her foot against an uneven floorboard. Was Hathorne pushing her on some obscure debate between demonologists about witches' flight? The question had a hint of Cotton Mather in it. But how would Tituba possibly know the answer?

Oh, right . . . she had just confessed to being a witch.

To Hathorne, Tituba was a direct link to the spiritual world, someone who could finally answer the questions that plagued intellectuals. Was Satan made of spirit, or matter? Could demons control men's bodies? Did witches only dream their black sabbaths, or were they physically present? Mather had explained some of these debates in his book, and now Hathorne was going after the answers.

But I believed Tituba's confession about as much as I believed Emperor Charlemagne could rise from the dead and walk across the ocean.

Tituba gaped like a fish out of water, her mouth opening and closing. Couldn't Hathorne see that she didn't understand his question? After a moment she said, "We just arrive there."

Hathorne gave a little shake of his head and changed the subject.

I looked at the assembled Villagers, searching their faces for any hint of skepticism. Someone had to object to Hathorne's questions. They were ridiculous. Tituba floundered like a schoolchild, searching for the right answer when she had no clue what the teacher wanted to hear. Wasn't that proof that Tituba knew nothing about witches or the Devil?

If Hathorne really believed Tituba was a witch, why couldn't she answer even the simplest questions?

But all I saw on those faces was shock and fear. They didn't question Tituba's words—they had been taught not to examine dark matters too closely. Everything she said confirmed their bleak suspicion that their city was doomed, assaulted by evil forces that wanted the Puritans to fail. They were on the side of God, and thus Satan was their enemy.

What a farce.

I nearly missed the end of Tituba's examination because it came so quickly. She was on her feet, shuffling out of the room next to Sheriff Corwin before I could blink.

She had confessed to being a witch, and she had named Sarah Good and Sarah Osborne as accomplices. Did it matter that Tituba was the only one Ann hadn't accused of attacking her? Tituba was still headed back to a cell, just like the other women.

I placed a hand on my belly, which swirled and churned.

Had Tituba planned her performance, or did she choose to confess in the moment? It didn't matter. With her confession, the witch hunt had spiraled beyond Ann Putnam, and soon, like a raging wildfire, it would consume the entire Village.

If Satan had seduced one Puritan, there had to be more.

Hathorne turned to the men sitting behind the afflicted girls. "We know these poor girls are being attacked by witches," he said in a low, even voice. "We have clear evidence that these evil women must be brought to trial. As the Grand Jury, it is up to you to decide if we should begin a trial."

The examination had been aimed at this audience, then, of

Village men. They sat right behind Ann, a front-row seat for her act. And now Hathorne was telling them to order a trial.

I watched each man. They were steadfast, Puritan fathers who believed it was their duty to protect the Village. Unsurprisingly, they did not deliberate. Their foreman stood and nodded his assent, assuring that three women would be on trial for their lives.

Hathorne collected his papers as though the answer had never been in doubt. "I'll write to the Governor immediately," he told the men. "We need to convene a special tribunal to sit and hear the cases, as I'm afraid we do not have enough capable judges here in Salem. I will announce the Governor's reply as soon as I receive it. Because of the circumstances, I am certain he will want to address this matter with all haste."

With that, Hathorne dismissed the grand jurors and the rest of the crowd. The meeting house began to empty.

All I could hear were Hathorne's words from yesterday, ringing in my ears.

"Thou shalt not suffer a witch to live."

SEVENTEEN

The murmuring voices of Salem Villagers had drifted outside the meeting house, which was nearly empty. But the Glass Girls remained in the front row, next to the other afflicted girls, so I tucked myself in the corner of the room to spy on them.

Hathorne approached the girls, his mouth a thin, flat line across his face. "Children," he began. Ann flinched at the title. She was sixteen, after all, and in another year she might well join the ranks of goodwives in the Village. But she obediently sat and listened. "This must be a frightening time for you. I cannot promise that your torment will end now that we have identified several of your attackers." His eyebrows folded into an approximation of sympathy. I had no doubt that Hathorne truly did feel it was his duty to protect the Glass Girls, but that wasn't enough to make me feel an ounce of compassion for him. He was just as responsible for the coming trials as anyone else in Salem Village.

I couldn't read Ann's reaction. She turned her back to me, so I could only watch the golden locks hanging from the back of her prim white bonnet. Next to her, Abigail's head tilted down as if she was staring at her feet.

Hathorne continued in his softer voice, clutching his flat black hat to his chest. "Now, I need all of you to be strong. You will be the most important witnesses at the trial, so you must be prepared to speak up on your torments. Inform me immediately if anyone attacks you. *Anyone.*"

Ann would be a witness? No—that couldn't be right. What court would accept her ranting as evidence?

Hathorne looked each girl in the eye. Abigail seemed to pull back from his gaze, but I might have imagined it. "The witches are in prison, but the walls of the jail cannot contain their powers. They may still strike out at you. Or their allies might attack. They might have many accomplices who are still hiding their identities. So please protect yourselves and stay strong."

Ann spoke for the group. "Don't worry, Magistrate Hathorne. It is our Puritan duty to stand up against these forces of Satan. We won't let you down."

Hathorne gave a nod and settled his hat atop his head. "God protect you," he prayed. He turned and exited through a hidden door behind the pulpit.

Nothing but empty seats separated me from the Glass Girls. What would Ann say if she saw me? I spun and scurried down the exterior wall of the meeting house, slipping out before the Glass Girls had noticed me.

I had to find a way to talk with Abigail. Alone.

Her hand on Ann's arm had stopped Ann's thrashing spell. It might not be too late to use Abigail to stop Ann.

Minister Parris was standing outside the meeting house waiting for his niece. His eyebrows were low, and I could almost feel the rage emanating from him. I concealed myself behind a witch hazel bush—it just *had* to be witch hazel—near the entrance of the building and waited until Ann had stomped off toward her house. Then Abigail emerged, dragging her feet. I trailed Minister Parris as he walked her home. They didn't stop to speak with anyone on the short walk.

Why was the man furious? Hadn't he *wanted* Tituba to confess? He didn't say a word to Abigail, who hurried to keep up with him.

Once they were inside, I slipped into their backyard. Tituba's small hut stood abandoned and empty. How long would she be in prison?

How long would she be *alive*?

I shifted my weight from one foot to the other. My hands fidgeted with the hem of my apron as I waited. I kept my eyes trained on the upper windows of the house, on the room where Abigail and Betty slept.

The creaking of the back door caught me by surprise. There was no time to hide myself. But to my relief it was Abigail, alone. She carried an empty bucket, to draw water from the family well.

She saw me and froze. She eyed me with the same suspicion she'd given me yesterday.

I couldn't afford to hesitate. "Hello, Abigail."

"What are you doing out here?" she asked quietly. She closed the door tightly behind her and took another step forward.

"I saw what you did. Why did you stop Ann?"

"Who told you that? Did Ann say I stopped her?" Abigail's forehead wrinkled with worry.

"No—I saw you hold her back."

She bit her lower lip. I could almost see the question running through her mind. If I had seen her, who else might have noticed? "I'm starting to wonder," she said, then stopped. "Maybe you were right about Ann. She just seems . . . she enjoys this a little too much." Abigail's voice dropped to a whisper. "I was sick, I truly was. My uncle stayed up all night praying at my bedside, convinced I might die. I had hallucinations. I'm not sure if they were real or fever dreams. But Ann . . . She doesn't seem ill."

I swallowed hard. Abigail's doubts had already pushed her to hold Ann back—could I nudge her further?

Abigail continued. "Ann has always wanted to be the center of attention. I just . . . I didn't want to testify against Tituba. I don't believe her confession was true. She can't be a witch."

I took a step toward Abigail. I could see her white knuckles clutching the handle of the empty bucket. "I don't believe it either. I know we all practiced forbidden magic in the woods, but I don't think that makes Tituba a bad person. It doesn't make her a witch."

"I've known her for years," Abigail whispered. "If she was a witch, wouldn't I have noticed? I've never seen her sneaking off to cast spells. She wouldn't hurt anyone. She made medicines for me or Betty. She knows so much about herbs and remedies. But that doesn't make her evil." Abigail's voice cracked. She was on the verge of crying.

My eyes followed hers to Tituba's empty hut.

"Why did Tituba confess?" I whispered.

Abigail shook her head, blinking back tears. She was suddenly back in control, the confident girl I'd met when I first arrived in Salem Village. "I don't know. I even asked my uncle, but he refused to talk. I hate this. Everyone in the village is treating me like I'm so fragile, like I could relapse at any moment. I feel fine."

And she looked healthy. Her cheeks glowed in the crisp March air, and her dark hair shone in the sunlight. But everyone else in Salem saw a weak child who had to be protected from satanic attacks. No wonder Abigail was frustrated.

Abigail dropped the bucket to her side. Her tone changed again. "Or maybe she is a witch. Why would she lie? Why would she confess to something that wasn't true?"

"Maybe she was afraid," I shot back.

"Maybe." Abigail didn't sound convinced. But she, of all people, should understand the crushing pressure to conform. Abigail modulated every movement, every word according to what might please Ann. Was it so hard to imagine that Tituba was trying to please Hathorne, or Parris?

I tried to find compassion for Abigail. She had to feel isolated. Her doubts about Ann were bubbling up, the woman she had lived with for years had been thrown in jail, and no one was answering her questions. And here I was, the new girl who threatened her place with the popular crowd, pushing her this way and that.

Abigail deserved better.

But so did Sarah Good and Sarah Osborne. And Tituba. Ann wasn't just toying with people's feelings. She was toying with their lives.

The magnitude of the problem hit me. Hathorne had probably sent off his letter to the governor. I might have been able to stop Ann, given enough time. But how was I supposed to stop the judicial process she'd set into motion?

Abigail pulled the bucket back to her chest. "I better get the water before my uncle starts to worry."

My chance with Abigail was slipping away. Had I reached her? Was there still time to derail the trials? Abigail was halfway to the well by the time I managed my next question. "How's Betty? She wasn't at the trial today."

A dark cloud came over Abigail's face. "She's had a relapse," she said quietly. She turned toward the well and continued. "She's in bed resting."

"I'm sorry." I realized a moment later that I meant it. Betty was guiltless, even if her illness had fueled the search for witches.

"Thank you." Abigail hurried back into the house without looking back.

I stood for another moment, my eyes still drawn to Tituba's hut. Would the woman ever live there again? Even if her name was cleared, I couldn't imagine Minister Parris welcoming her back. And the Villagers wouldn't soon forget her confession about meeting the Devil.

I drew in a deep, even breath, trying to still my racing heart. It didn't work.

I slipped back into the shadows and avoided the Villagers crowding the square, every conversation about the same topic. I learned through whispers that a young Putnam boy had ridden off only minutes earlier to Boston, carrying Hathorne's letter. Salem's witches would soon be known throughout the Massachusetts Bay Colony.

I made for the glade, hoping to find Joy. I hadn't seen her at the examination that morning, and we had to talk. But the glade was empty. The sun shone on the smooth rock at the center of the grass, unaware of the chaos bubbling up in the Village. I sat, listening to the sounds of the woods. The tinkling of melting ice carried through the air, as did the rustling of leaves as chipmunks looked for food.

I closed my eyes and wished that I, too, could join the chorus of forest sounds and leave behind the unharmonious human world.

I don't know how long I sat on the rock, but at some point I heard steps approaching through the woods. My eyes flew open. Joy was standing before me.

"I didn't go to the examination," Joy said. "I snuck into Ann Putnam's house."

My stomach dropped. "Why would you do that?"

She sank onto a stump across from my rock before she answered. "I wanted to find the Burning Book. If we find the book, we can prove that Ann's a liar. And everyone was at the meeting house, so I knew she wouldn't be home."

I let out a shaky breath. Why hadn't Joy talked to me first? "And what if someone had seen you? They'd throw you in jail."

A flash of worry shot across her face, but she shook it off. "It doesn't matter. I couldn't find it." Her eyes dropped to the ground. "I looked on her bed. And under her mattress, and in her armoire. She must have moved it. Or destroyed it."

I shook my head. "She wouldn't take it out of her room. And she'd never give it to Mercy or Abigail."

"Then it's gone." Joy's voice cracked. She'd risked so much to find the Burning Book for nothing. Even though sneaking into the Putnam house was reckless, I had to admit it wasn't a terrible idea. But it was too late.

"That's not the only way to stop the witch hunt. Abigail kept Ann from testifying against Tituba."

Joy's eyes widened. "*Abigail* did that?"

I nodded. "I talked to her after the examination. She doesn't believe Ann is really afflicted."

"But she still sat next to Ann at the examination, right?" Joy snarled. Her intensity rattled me. Then again, Abigail had taken Joy's place as Ann's best friend. Joy acted like she hated the Glass Girls, but maybe she was jealous, too.

I considered my next words carefully. "So you heard what

happened."

"Everyone's talking about the trials. And Ann's *performance*."

"I can't even describe it, Joy. No one questioned Ann's fits."

"She's *Ann Putnam*. Even if someone doubted her, she's from one of the most powerful families in the Village. Why would anyone risk angering her father? Or standing up against the Putnams?"

"Even the men on the Grand Jury didn't say one word against Ann." I bit the inside of my cheek. I couldn't stop picturing Sarah Good, one hand on her swollen belly.

"Wait." Joy jumped to her feet. "I know someone who might take a stand against the Putnams."

"Who?"

But Joy didn't answer. She turned and ran from the glade, leaving me bewildered. Where was she going? Had she thought up another dangerous plan that she wasn't going to share with me?

I called after her, "Please stay out of trouble."

I don't think she heard me.

EIGHTEEN

I didn't go back to the Village.

The next morning my father told me to stay home. He'd heard about the witch trials from a neighbor, and he didn't want me to get caught up in the hysteria.

If he only knew.

My dad never gave me orders like that. I wanted to resist on principle, but I was tired. I didn't want to spend another day running around the Village trying to put out a hundred fires while a thousand more sparked. So I agreed.

As I sat mending socks with my mother, I tried to picture Sarah Good, locked in prison. Had they told her about Tituba's accusation? Did she know about the letter to the governor? We were less than twenty miles from Boston, so the governor's reply could arrive any minute.

My mom chattered on about the spring planting season and a cow my dad wanted to buy. I let her words wash over me without responding. Inside, my mind swirled with questions. What was Joy doing? Would she be waiting for me in the glade?

I jumped at every sound. We were so isolated out on our

farm, at the edge of civilization. No one came to visit. Everyone was probably avoiding their neighbors, with accusations of witchcraft brewing.

I went to bed that night feeling defeated. I'd accomplished nothing all day—except the socks—and I felt like a coward for hiding in my house. Sarah Good didn't have the same luxury. I might be the only person in the Village who could save her life, but instead I spent the day sewing.

Joy knocked on my door early the next morning, before the sun had crested above the trees. The sound made me leap out of my chair. I rushed to the door before my parents could stand. I slipped onto the porch to talk with Joy.

At least she wasn't in jail.

"You heard the news?" she asked.

"What news? I've been here."

"The governor authorized a special tribunal to hear the cases."

"Already?" I shivered and pulled my shawl around my shoulders. "Will the trials start soon?"

Joy nodded. I could see the worry written across her face. "There's more."

More? And suddenly it came to me. "Oh no. Did Ann accuse someone else?"

Joy's expression answered my question before she spoke. "Five more. They're already in jail."

Five. Five more people caught up in Ann Putnam's web of lies. Abigail hadn't stopped her, then. A chill shot through my body.

"But I have an idea," Joy said. "We might still have one chance to disrupt everything before the trials start."

I tried to focus on Joy's words, but my mind was swirling.

Who had Ann accused this time? Did I know any of them? How soon would Hathorne's grand jury send them off for trial?

Joy grabbed my arm. The contact shook me out of my thoughts. "The court has to rule on spectral evidence."

I released a long stream of air from my lungs and tried to hang on to the hope in Joy's voice. "The spectral evidence. If the judge won't allow it, Ann wouldn't be able to testify. She couldn't fall into fits."

"She might even be barred from the trials."

The idea blossomed in my mind. I'd almost given up on the idea after Hathorne's speech. But maybe there was still a chance. Nothing had stopped Ann yet—but could legal procedure? "If Ann isn't allowed to testify, the jury might not find anyone guilty."

"And if the judge says spectral evidence isn't allowed at the trial, it might be banned at Hathorne's examinations."

My stomach flipped as a new thought struck me. "But Tituba still confessed. Even without spectral evidence, she called herself a witch."

Joy didn't have a response to that. Her mouth was sealed shut in a sharp line. The silence stretched on, until I could almost feel the quiet of the woods pressing down on us.

The sound of a skittering rock made me jump. My eyes flew up. It was just Joy—she had kicked a pebble in her frustration. "We can't do *nothing*," she muttered.

I watched the edge of the woods, waiting for signs of life, but there was nothing but the deadly still of the last gasp of winter.

Joy was right. If we gave up now, I'd always wonder if I could have stopped the trials. I searched my mind for the right words. "If the judge threw out spectral evidence, maybe Tituba would take back her confession. I mean, didn't she confess because she thought Ann would accuse her?"

Joy's eyes darted up to meet mine. I saw a flicker of hope pass across her face. "Then maybe it isn't too late." She flew off the porch and then looked back at me with her eyebrows raised. "Come on!"

Her energy was infectious. I followed her to the road. "Where are we going?"

Joy didn't slow her pace. I almost had to run to keep up with her. "Didn't I tell you? I know someone who might be able to help."

I reached out to catch her arm, but she slipped away, hurrying down the road. "Joy, you have to slow down." She finally slowed to a fast walk. "Where are we going?"

Her eyes were trained on the path ahead of us. "We're going to see Joseph Porter."

"Who?"

"The Porter family—you know, the rivals of the Putnams. I should have thought of it sooner. They live on the edge of Salem Town, and they generally avoid the Village. But Joseph Porter won't ignore this. He hates the Putnams. And Minister Parris. Did I ever tell you about Parris's first sermon? It was insane. He knew the Porters didn't want him as minister, so he called them out as bad Puritans. The Porters were livid. They attend church in Salem Town now."

The rivalries of Salem Village were still foreign to me—I was just starting to get a grasp on the teenage cliques, and Joy was adding another layer to the mess of conflicts that plagued the Village. But if she thought Joseph Porter could help, I trusted her. So I nodded and matched her step for step.

We avoided the Village and took a small path that led toward the Town. I could feel Joy buzzing with energy next to me, but doubts still flashed through my mind. If Joseph Porter was so powerful, why hadn't he stepped in sooner? And would a rivalry with the Putnams and Parris be enough to motivate the man to stop the trials? *Could* anyone stop the trials at this point?

If Porter was smart, he'd see the risks in taking a public stance against witchcraft when public opinion was clearly against him.

"We're almost there," Joy muttered. I wasn't the only one who was breathless from the relentless pace Joy had set. "The Porter house is just through these trees. Their family's involved with trading, so they've made a lot of money recently. More than the Putnams, even though they've been buying up land. Right now, ships from England are worth more than Massachusetts Bay land." The house came into sight as the trees thinned. It was much larger than the buildings near the Village Square. I saw glass panes in the windows and a wide porch wrapping around the house, which faced a small pond.

In my eyes, it looked like a fortress. "And we're just going to knock on the door?" I was suddenly very aware of who we were—two schoolgirls from minor families in a backwater village. Would they even open the door for us?

Joy waved off my question. "He knows my family. And he's a curious man. He'll want to talk to us. Just remember—he would be a powerful ally. He might actually be able to influence the new judge."

A knot of worry tugged at my insides, in spite of Joy's confidence. It was one thing for us to vent our doubts about the trial to each other, but it was something very different to confide in a stranger.

But Joy walked up the steps as if she belonged and knocked

on the door. When it swung open, we saw a plainly-dressed woman wearing a demure white bonnet. "Yes?"

"We're here to see Joseph Porter," Joy said.

The woman—she must have been a servant, even though I hadn't seen many in Salem Village—nodded and stepped back. "I'll see if he's available."

"Tell him it's Joy Titus."

Where had Joy found that commanding voice? I was speechless as I watched her order someone else's servant around. Maybe I didn't know Joy as well as I thought.

The servant asked us to wait in the sitting room. Once we were alone, Joy leaned over and whispered, "I hope this works."

Before I could muster a response, the servant had returned. "This way," she said, leading us toward the stairs. I trailed a half-step behind Joy, the skin on the back of my neck tingling.

I followed Joy into a study, a richly-decorated room with its own small stove. The large window looked out toward the town. I could even see a sliver of the harbor. Two shelves of books faced each other on either side of a large mahogany desk, which was covered in papers. The man sitting behind the desk was thin and clean shaven, and though he wore dark clothes, he was not dressed like a Puritan. His thick padded jacket over a vest buttoned to his neck made him look more like a merchant than a farmer. I could tell at a glance that my mother would have described him as handsome. I had to agree when a smile stretched across his face.

"Joy Titus," he said. "You're the last person I expected to see today. And who is your companion?"

His blue eyes turned on me at the exact moment when the servant shut the thick door. I flinched at the sound, but didn't break contact with his eyes.

"Margaret Cavendish Lucas," I said, bobbing my head in a small curtsey.

"You wouldn't be John Lucas's daughter, would you?"

I tried to hide the surprise on my face. "Yes." I wanted to ask how he knew my father, but there were more pressing matters to discuss.

He signaled that we should sit in the seats across from his desk, and after we were both settled, Mr. Porter sank back onto his chair. "What can I do for you girls? I have to admit, I'm curious why you're visiting me."

"You've heard about the witches," Joy said flatly.

"Of course." Mr. Porter's voice dropped an octave and the smile vanished from his face. "And I've heard that Thomas Putnam and Minister Parris are behind the whole thing."

My heart pounded in my chest. Maybe Joy had been right—maybe we had found the one person in Salem Village who could stop the trials before anyone died. But Mr. Porter wasn't completely right. I opened my mouth to correct him and then closed it. Would he be angry if I contradicted him? My performance had drawn his attention. I could almost feel his blue eyes trying to read my secrets.

"Miss Lucas?" he asked in a quiet voice.

"It didn't start with them," I began. "Minister Parris's daughter Betty and his niece Abigail were sick. The doctor who visited them couldn't find a natural cause. That's what started the panic in the Village. Everyone assumed their illness was caused by magic." I stopped, unsure how to explain Ann's part in the whole mess.

Mr. Porter shook his head. "There are not many men of science in the Village, I fear. They spend too much time reading stories from that Cotton Mather instead of the writings of illustrious men like Isaac Newton. Newton has shown that many supernatural things have natural causes."

I suddenly felt like I was back in the schoolhouse. I had heard of Isaac Newton, though I had not read his works myself, as they were densely philosophical and mathematical. But a tutor back in London had raved about the man's abilities. I sorted through my mind, trying to grasp onto something to impress Mr. Porter. This was more important than getting a top grade on a paper—his confidence could make the difference in stopping the trials. "You mean like his predictions on comets?"

Mr. Porter gave me an appreciative look. "Exactly, Miss Lucas. The last generation believed comets to be a harbinger of doom, a sign of God's wrath. They thought a comet signaled the coming of plague." He paused for a moment, clearly enjoying his position as an authority. "And yet look at what Mr. Newton has shown. He has demonstrated that comets appear on regular and predictable orbits. They are not signs of anything, other than God's majesty in ordering the universe according to mathematical laws."

I had trouble following Mr. Porter's monologue, but one thing was clear—he was a follower of science, and that made him skeptical of claims about witchcraft and magic. And he didn't like the Putnams or the Parris family.

Still, I had to tell him the truth. "Mr. Porter, you should know. The girl leading the accusations, Ann Putnam, she's a friend. Sort of. But we know she's lying. She's making everything up because she wants attention."

Joy shot daggers at me with her eyes. She wouldn't have said anything about Ann. But if Mr. Porter was going to put his name on the line, he should know the whole story.

Mr. Porter's reaction surprised me. He waved off my

confession as if it were nothing. "She is only the means to an end," he said. "Putnam and Parris want an excuse to grab power, and she's provided it. I don't care about the schoolyard squabbles of Putnam's daughter."

He didn't understand. How could he help if he ignored Ann's role? I risked a glance at Joy, who leaned forward in her seat.

"Mr. Porter, we came here to ask for your help." She was desperately trying to keep the conversation on track. When I opened my mouth again, one glance from Joy stopped me. I sat back and let her drive the conversation.

"My help?" He raised one eyebrow.

"The governor is sending a judge to hear the trials. If reasonable Villagers don't speak up now, there might not be another chance."

I could see the skepticism on Mr. Porter's face. I ignored Joy's warnings and jumped back in. "You've heard of spectral evidence?"

The man's face soured as though he'd bitten into a lime. "The courts won't consider that reliable," he spat.

"They did during the examinations," I shot back. "Hathorne practically begged the afflicted girls to put on a show for the Villagers. Ann Putnam writhed and thrashed until everyone believed she was being attacked by a specter."

The corners of Mr. Porter's mouth turned down in a frown. "And everyone believed her performance?"

I nodded. "A few women even fainted. With a dozen questions, Hathorne had everyone convinced that the accused women were sworn witches. Not a single person questioned the evidence."

Mr. Porter stood. He pulled a book from the shelf and

flipped it open. I tried to read his face, but it was blank. He kept his eyes trained on the book as he spoke. "Such spiritual attacks are impossible according to the laws of nature. After all, Descartes himself tells us that all spirit is made up of matter."

I knew less about Descartes than Newton, so I kept my mouth closed. Joy made a similar calculation.

Mr. Porter looked up from the book. Again, I felt like a student, mind blank at just the moment the teacher asks a question. "You see," Mr. Porter explained. "If the women were in the meeting house when this happened, how could they possibly separate their spiritual essence from their physical being with no sign of change? If the specter is indeed material, activating it would involve some lessening of their body."

In truth, no one was watching the accused women when Ann was shrieking out. Had anything changed in their appearance? Sarah Good had grown pale, but perhaps that was a natural reaction to Ann's accusation.

Porter set down the book and turned his back on us, gazing out the window. "And you were hoping I'd publicly come out against the trials?" he asked quietly.

Joy and I exchanged a glance before she spoke. "We don't want innocent people punished for crimes they didn't commit."

I added quickly, "And spectral evidence goes against reason and science. It should not be allowed in the courtroom."

At that, Porter turned. He seemed to care more about science than about the innocent women locked up in jail. But if that helped us, so be it.

"I agree," he said. "The courts cannot be corrupted in that manner. That is the goal of any just society. However, I fear we may not live in a just society." He paused for a moment, musing over that thought.

"So you won't help us?" Joy asked. I could hear the anger in her voice.

"I will do everything I can to help without risking my position," Mr. Porter said.

But what did that mean?

I needed something concrete from our conversation. "Would you petition the judge to exclude spectral evidence from the trials?"

"I will do that," Mr. Porter agreed. I relaxed my balled fists and tried to smile. "But I must warn you that it is a dangerous climate to openly oppose the Putnams or Minister Parris. I will try to limit the damage they cause, but I cannot risk harm to my own family. I hope you understand that my decision comes not from cowardice but from self-preservation."

I tried to hide my disappointment. I knew why he felt the need to protect himself. Hadn't I felt the same way? Hadn't I wanted to protect Joy from falling on Ann's bad side and potentially being accused herself? I couldn't fault Joseph Porter for applying the same calculation to his family and his own reputation.

And yet I had hoped for more.

"Thank you," Joy said. "We appreciate your offer of support."

Mr. Porter smiled again, but under the surface I could sense he was glad our visit was ending. "Please, come see me again any time."

Joy and I stood at the obvious dismissal. At some hidden signal the servant swung the door open. We followed her from the study.

I wrapped myself tightly in my cloak as the chilly air swirled around us. We didn't stop to discuss our meeting. Instead we hurried away from the Porter house. I knew his study faced away from the woods that led back to Salem Village, but I couldn't help but feel like someone was watching us.

We didn't speak until we were surrounded by woods.

"I guess we have to wait and see what happens when the new judge arrives," I said quietly.

"I guess you're right." The fire had left Joy's voice.

Shouldn't we be celebrating? We were better off than we'd been before the conversation with Joseph Porter—at least now we had someone offering to help.

Then again, some small part of me had hoped that Mr. Porter would step up, write the governor a letter calling the trials a farce, and fix everything. As if he could single-handedly release Sarah Good from jail.

But I knew that no one had the power to do that.

Our feet trailed through the broken remnants of fall's leaves, which didn't even crunch under our shoes. When we reached a fork in the path, Joy's eyes darted to me. "I'm going home," she said. Before I could respond, she walked off down the path toward Salem Village.

I stayed at the fork until I couldn't see her any more.

No one was willing to risk their own safety to stop the trials. My throat tightened if I even imagined standing up in court to call Ann Putnam a liar. If I wouldn't risk my reputation, and my family's position, how could I expect anyone else to do the same?

All I could do now was wait.

NINETEEN

I didn't expect to face an angry mob in my own house.

My parents were furious when I finally walked in the door. I'd run off with Joy without saying anything and I'd been gone for hours. My mother was in a panic, wondering if I'd been caught up in the Village "problems," and my father had been ready to saddle his horse to go look for me.

I was grounded. Indefinitely.

Which suited me fine—I didn't want to go to the Village, anyway. At least out on my family's farm I could ignore the coming storm and throw myself into spring weeding. In a flash, the temperatures rose and every field and road turned into mud. The frozen ruts that had broken wagon axels turned to quicksand, ready to engulf a wheel and trap a wagon until summer.

No one came by our farm, at least not that I saw. My parents kept me busy with chores, and I pretended that I wasn't thinking about the witch trials every moment of the day.

Some days were easier than others. At times, I could almost ignore the accused witches sitting in jail. Weeks flew by, and I heard nothing about the trials. Sometimes I missed Joy, and in even rarer moments I missed the weeks I'd spent with the Glass Girls. The air always felt electric when we sat on that hill during lunch, drawing everyone's eyes.

Other days, a dark cloud descended. With barely any news from the Village, I was left to wonder if the number of women in jail was growing. If the furious Villagers had torn anyone apart because of a dark shadow or a black cat. If Ann had already been crowned Queen of the Afflicted.

When that happened, I threw myself into the work around the farm and tried to shut off my mind.

And the work was endless. We built a barn once the mud dried and we could finally bring in lumber on the road. We harvested an early crop of very small radishes. My dad finally bought a cow.

One evening, after I'd milked our new cow in the new barn, there was a knock at the door.

I hadn't spoken to anyone except for my parents—and the cow—in almost two months.

When the door swung open, Joy Titus stood before me. She looked the same in her black bonnet, but her eyes narrowed when she saw me.

A flash of guilt struck me. I'd completely ignored her, and the witch panic, because I was a coward. It was easier to avoid the crushing helplessness I felt every time I thought of Sarah Good sitting in prison.

And now, here was Joy. "Where have you been?" she demanded.

I glanced over my shoulder to make sure my parents couldn't hear. "I'm sorry. I was grounded. And I didn't think there was anything we could do."

"Well, the judge is here."

My stomach fell. "When?"

"He arrived earlier this afternoon. Maybe you've heard of him—William Stoughton. The king just appointed him lieutenant governor of the colony."

My head spun. The judge was the second-highest ranking official in the entire colony?

I guess this wasn't exactly the quiet agrarian community that my father had hoped to find when we moved north.

Joy's lips made a thin, bloodless line across her face. "I just thought you'd want to know that the trials start tomorrow."

"Tomorrow?" I echoed. I guess ignoring the trials hadn't made them go away. "But they haven't even ruled on spectral evidence yet. Is Joseph Porter still going to petition the judge?"

Joy shrugged. "No one wants to be caught talking about witches. You don't know what it's been like in the Village. Everyone watches everyone else and whispers behind their backs. And now Stoughton rides into town. I'm sure he'll try to wrap things up before people can ask too many questions." Her eyes flashed with anger—was she mad at me for avoiding the problem? Had I abandoned her to deal with the Villagers by herself?

"What do you mean, ask questions?"

Joy scowled. "All the witches executed in the English colonies have been from Massachusetts and Connecticut. Maybe there was one in Maryland a while back, but mostly it's been here." She paused as if she wanted to say more.

I shook my head. I didn't see her point.

Joy's frustration crested in her voice. "We're supposed to be Puritans. We're supposed to be this godly community, and yet we're the only ones dealing with witches?"

"Didn't Minister Parris say that the Devil doesn't want the Puritans to succeed?"

Joy slammed her palm down on the porch rail. "No, think about it. Witches only exist if people *choose* to turn their back on the community. Witches *choose* to make an alliance with Satan. If we're supposed to be good Puritans, why are so many eager to forsake that way of life?" Her voice cracked. "Dozens of people are in jail. And Tituba isn't the only one who's confessed, before the trial has even started. How many Villagers are there? Five hundred? Six hundred, maybe? Look how many have been caught up in this insanity already."

Joy's intensity shocked me into silence. Another wave of guilt washed over me—we were supposed to be friends, but I'd left her alone for two months, surrounded by angry, suspicious Villagers.

And *dozens* of accused witches.

But I could see Joy's point. I'd also had time to think during my self-imposed exile. The Puritan way of life wasn't very pleasant. It was so strict that any deviation could land you on a list of unredeemed sinners who were unlikely to be saved. If you didn't dress the right way, or pray the right way, you might be one of Satan's minions.

If they wanted to turn on each other and tear down the entire Village, I couldn't stop them.

Joy was on the verge of tears. I'd never seen her like this.

We fell into an awkward silence. Before, we'd been allies in the fight against Ann Putnam. But now, we both knew the struggle was much larger.

Instead of pulling us closer, the stress had driven a wedge between us. I'd fled from the watchful eyes of the Village, but she was stuck. Joy might hate the Glass Girls, and she might hate

Salem Village, but this was still her home. She couldn't run away as easily as I could.

Our bond had cracked under the pressure of witchcraft. But maybe it wasn't too late.

"Let's go to the trial tomorrow."

Joy's eyes rose to mine. "Really?"

"Ignoring it won't change anything," I said firmly.

Joy nodded and reached out a hand to grab mine for a second. She gave it a squeeze and then vanished up the road.

~ ~ ~

It took an hour to convince my parents to let me attend the trial. The entire Village would be there, I pleaded with them, so it would be safe. And I promised to do my chores before I left. Finally they relented.

The next morning I walked into the Village for the first time in well over a month. Everything looked different with the blush of spring in the air. The flowering trees had dropped their petals, leaving a pink blanket on the grass, and green buds were sprouting everywhere.

It didn't feel like the right atmosphere for a witch trial.

The road grew crowded as I drew closer to the meeting house. Suddenly I was surrounded by the whispered rumors I had avoided on the farm.

"Did you hear Stoughton was in the Village Square last night praying for the afflicted girls?"

"I heard he already visited Minister Parris to talk about Satan."

"He'll make short work of our witches, I promise you that."

I slipped into the meeting house and completely gave up on

the idea of finding Joy. The space was packed with people, even tighter than it had been during Hathorne's examinations of the witches back in March. The early summer heat was already rising, and the stifling weight of bodies made my throat tighten. I tried to get to the edge of the room, hoping that I might be able to inch forward and get a better view. From back here I couldn't see over the shoulders of the tall men packing the meeting house.

"Stoughton went to Harvard *and* Oxford," one woman sighed.

"The new king took our charter," another man muttered. "We aren't even the Massachusetts Bay Colony anymore."

I leaned in to hear more, but his voice was lost in the crowd.

Somehow I managed to find a pocket of space halfway up the meeting house on the right. I had to stand, but at least I could see the panel of judges at the front, the jurors, and the backs of the afflicted girls.

The perfectly arranged blonde hair hanging down from a starched bonnet had to be Ann Putnam. My chest tightened. What antics did she have planned for the actual trial?

There were even more girls sitting on that front row with the afflicted today. Ann's spell had spread. I craned my neck, but I couldn't tell if Mercy and Abigail were sitting with Ann.

Instead, I studied the faces of the three judges. One I recognized right away as Hathorne. Apparently he had been appointed to the court even though he'd done a terrible job questioning the accused witches. On his far side was a man I didn't recognize, perhaps in his forties or fifties, with gray hair and a solemn face. He watched the crowd with an irritated look on his face.

Sitting at the center of the row of judges was a tall, thin man who had to be Chief Justice William Stoughton. His narrow, pinched face and white hair gave him a dignified look. I wondered what he was thinking as he looked out over the rolling mass of Salem Villagers who had come to attend the trials. His face was blank and unreadable.

The whispers continued. "I heard Stoughton is friends with Cotton Mather."

"You can tell he never leaves the house without a Bible."

My entire body was on edge. I practically shook with nerves. Would Stoughton allow the spectral evidence? Had he, like Hathorne, already decided that the accused women were guilty?

Stoughton banged a gavel to call the proceedings to order. I jumped at the crash.

"I am Lieutenant Governor William Stoughton," he declared. A hush fell over the crowd. The Villagers were apparently impressed with his booming voice.

"This court will hear the case against Sarah Good and Sarah Osborne," he continued, reading the names off a sheet of paper. Unlike everyone else in the meeting house, Stoughton didn't know these women personally. "Before we begin, I will hear testimony against Tituba and rule on the use of spectral evidence."

I dared to take my eyes off Stoughton to scan the crowd. Would Joseph Porter finally speak out? I couldn't see him anywhere.

While my back was turned, Ann Putnam had taken a seat on the witness stand.

Why?

At least she looked paler than the last time I'd seen her. I silently hoped that the guilt was eating at her.

Ann's voice rang out in the silent room. "Tituba the West Indian attacked me many times with her specter, pinching me and trying to make me join with her in doing the Devil's work." She paused, tossing her hair over her shoulder. "But after she confessed in March, the torments stopped."

A voice in the crowd gasped.

Was it me?

Ann's declaration shook me. I caught a glimpse of movement in the front row—Abigail's face, framed by her bonnet as she searched the crowd over her shoulder. She locked eyes with me and gave a little nod.

Had she talked to Ann?

When I looked back at the witness stand, Ann was gone, replaced by Minister Parris himself.

"My slave Tituba tormented my daughter Betty and my niece Abigail," he began slowly. "She pinched them and gave them many pains. It did not stop until Tituba confessed." His words were almost identical to Ann's.

Anxiety churned in my belly.

Chief Justice Stoughton banged his gavel. "Based on this testimony I can only conclude that Tituba has repented and turned away from her previous sins. We should thank God that he has brought this woman's soul back from the brink. Her soul is in God's hands, now—he will judge her, rather than this court."

Murmurs broke out in the meeting house. Salem's first confessed witch would not stand trial.

I eyed Stoughton warily. Why would he set Tituba free while women who swore they had no dealings with Satan were put on trial?

And why would Ann and Minister Parris help him?

Stoughton quieted the room with another bang of his gavel, jolting me from my thoughts. "And now the matter of spectral evidence."

I leaned forward on the balls of my feet. My hands were damp with sweat.

Stoughton dramatically raised a sheet of paper. "I have received many comments on the admission of this sort of evidence in these trials, and I have evaluated them thoroughly. I hold a petition from a leading citizen of Salem Village—who asked to remain nameless—that claims spectral evidence is unreliable."

The paper was thirty feet away, much too far for me to read, and yet I strained my eyes, willing myself to find the name *Joseph Porter* on the sheet.

And then Stoughton's words sank in.

He'd *asked* to remain nameless. Even if Porter had written the document, the weight of his reputation would not be behind the petition.

He'd turned coward.

Stoughton's voice boomed through the room. "However, many believe spectral evidence is critical for this trial."

The door of the meeting house swung open with a squeak. The nearest Villagers began to shout in surprise. I twisted to see the new arrival, but I could only spot the very top of a powdered white wig bobbing up the center aisle of the meeting house.

"Is it really him?"

"I can't believe he came to Salem Village."

"Who is it?" I whispered to a nearby woman. Before she could answer, Stoughton solved the riddle.

"My good friend Cotton Mather has traveled all the way from Boston to argue in favor of spectral evidence."

My legs suddenly turned to water, too weak to hold me. I reached out to steady myself against the wooden wall of the meeting house. Cotton Mather? *Here?*

The wigged man stood next to the witness box, where he was nodding and smiling at the crowd like an actor in a play.

Of course, plays were banned in Salem.

"Thank you, Chief Justice Stoughton," Mather said in a reedy voice that didn't fit his densely powdered wig. His unlined face shone with youth, in spite of his attempts to appear older. Mather faced the jury. "Witchcraft is a very serious crime," he said gravely. "The most serious. It is a crime against God and community. And because of its unusual nature, sometimes the rules of judicial procedure must be *adapted*. Magic is a devious, hidden sin. You can't demand two eye witnesses to confirm a concealed sin."

The men of the jury were nodding along with Mather's words. Everyone in the meeting house was acting as though Jesus had risen and walked into the room.

I barely stopped myself from rolling my eyes.

Stoughton turned to Mather. "In your educated opinion, Minister, is spectral evidence reliable in the courtroom?"

Mather was already nodding so hard that powder cascaded from his wig. "Oh, yes, it is quite reliable. Especially if there is secondary proof to support the claims. But more importantly, it is *necessary* if you want to stamp out witchcraft. Witches are deceitful creatures who try to hide their evil works." His voice grew even more grave. "If you *don't* allow spectral evidence, these witches *will go free.*"

A low rumble rose in the meeting house. Even the jurors didn't try to hide their fear at Mather's words.

I ground my teeth together until my jaw hurt. Mather was practically arguing that an absence of evidence was proof itself of a crime.

Apparitions and ghost stories were not *proof.*

But no one else questioned Mather's theatrics. The minister had the entire Village so terrified of witches that if Queen Mary herself walked in, they'd toss her in prison.

"Thank you, Minister Mather," Stoughton droned. "We are in agreement. After a long, thoughtful process, this court has concluded that spectral evidence is *critical* to this case. The court will hear about the evil attacks on our innocent children." His eyes rested on Ann in the front row.

Bile rose in the back of my throat. I pictured Ann's angelic face gazing back at Stoughton. He didn't know her at all. He didn't know anything about her reputation, or her lies, and he wouldn't question her stories. Stoughton clearly didn't care about the truth, as long as he could play at Chief Justice and send innocent women to the gallows.

"These afflicted girls will testify in the coming trials," Stoughton continued. "I have personally encouraged them to speak up whenever the spirit moves them."

So it would be a circus, just like Hathorne's examination.

Stoughton directed his next words to the jury. "You should take this evidence quite seriously," he cautioned. "These innocent children are directly reporting what they see of the spiritual world. Their testimony is key to answering the central question of this case: are these women witches?"

I balled my fists so tightly that my palms ached. Stoughton was *telling* the jury how to rule. How could anyone get a fair trial?

A single bang of the gavel ended the day's work.

Was that it? No one would stand up to Stoughton?

Stoughton rose to speak with Cotton Mather, who was already heading toward the jury to sign pamphlets. A printer approached the Chief Justice, peppering him with questions for a

Boston newspaper. What happened in Salem Village was big news now, and Stoughton was sure to get his name in the papers.

I pressed my teeth together as tremors of rage shook my body. It was worse than I'd imagined. How could the jury possibly doubt Ann Putnam after Stoughton's proclamation?

I shuddered as a premonition came to me—Sarah Good and Sarah Osborne would be found guilty. How else could the jury rule?

And there was nothing I could do about it.

TWENTY

I was so caught up in my dark fears that I barely noticed Sarah Good being led into the meeting house.

So the trials would start right away.

Sarah looked thinner than the last time I'd seen her, and dirtier, too, after months locked up in prison. Her belly was the only part of her that had grown. She looked like she might give birth at any moment. How could anyone believe this penniless woman in rags was a witch? And yet as she walked past, several people in the room hissed in anger. Sarah ignored the sounds, her eyes trained on the jury. The expression on her face was unreadable.

And suddenly Stoughton was reading a list of names.

One by one Sarah Good's neighbors appeared to accuse her of all kinds of things—mostly social sins. A stout, ruddy woman said Sarah had spoken rudely to her years ago. Another went on and on about Sarah's sour expression and harsh voice. A sneering goodwife accused Sarah of begging—which wasn't illegal, exactly, but Sarah hadn't been sufficiently grateful when a neighbor offered her an old heel of bread.

The petty tales from years ago struck me deep in my chest. These were grown women, most old enough to have children of their own. But they'd leapt at the chance to tear Sarah apart.

Was the young goodwife who testified that Sarah didn't attend church the Ann Putnam in her class? And the dark haired woman who called Sarah a liar—had she been Abigail Williams a decade earlier?

There was no destroying the Glass Girls—they just replicated with each generation. And no one outgrew being a Glass Girl, either—they somehow became even more cruel with age.

The pain in my chest spread to my arms. These stories didn't make Sarah a witch. They made her a poor woman who had lost her house and had to rely on charity. But these women jeered and scowled at Sarah, as though asking for help was a clear sign of evil.

My eyes grew wider as the number of Villagers called to testify against Sarah went on and on. They gossiped about every minor infraction Sarah had ever committed. They made her sound like a threat to the community for a decade or more.

The woman next to me leaned over to whisper, "Her daughter's a witch, too, if you can believe it. Only four years old, and already sold her soul."

I shuddered and screwed my eyes closed. Their cruelty turned my blood to ice. I'd always assumed that we'd outgrow our petty grievances, but Sarah's trial was proof that grown women were no different.

Stoughton called out the next name. "Samuel Abbey."

A grizzled old farmer stepped forward. He took his place at the witness stand and began to speak. "Three years ago Sarah Good stayed at my house. She was destitute and had nowhere else to live, and being good Puritans, my wife and I welcomed Sarah into our home. But Sarah had a malicious spirit. She was always a spiteful woman. We had no peace in our home." He shook his head at Sarah. "I told her to leave."

He fell silent. The only sound was the scratching of a quill as one of the printers tried to take down Samuel's testimony.

"Sarah flew into a rage and called us vile names. And then our cattle began to fall ill. It was the strangest thing. They were struck with a drooping condition, but they'd eat like normal. No one could figure it out. Until my wife, Mary, overheard Sarah Good saying she didn't care if we lost all our cattle. We've had seventeen head of cattle die in the last two years, but the very day Good was arrested one of our calves stood and walked for the first time in months."

The jurors nodded and exchanged looks.

I gripped my apron to keep from shouting. Did they *believe* Abbey's tale? He'd kicked Sarah and her infant daughter out in the cold. Of course she was angry. That didn't mean she called up Satan to punish him.

Fury raced through my body, burning up my disgust like whale oil. Samuel Abbey must have been consumed with guilt for his ill treatment of Sarah. As he should—Minister Parris spoke all the time about Christian charity. But if Abbey called Sarah Good a witch, the farmer made himself blameless. His guilty conscience could rest easy, convinced that Sarah was the evil one.

And yet the Villagers believed everything. A man nearby was whispering loudly about his own cattle who'd died. He glared at the poor woman. "Was Sarah Good angry with me, too?"

Joseph Porter's petition wouldn't have changed anything, then.

Good's neighbors had already decided she was a witch.

But once Stoughton reached the end of his list, the real theatrics began. All the hairs on my arm stood up as a shriek cut through the meeting house.

Ann Putnam was having another attack.

"I see Sarah Good in the rafters," Ann wailed. Dozens of heads turned up, but no one else could see the specter that tormented Ann. "She's holding a yellow bird!"

One of the other afflicted girls moaned. "I see the bird! She calls it Coco and feeds it from her own blood."

A woman nearby screamed and a few Villagers actually fled from the meeting house.

Ann pointed to an empty spot in the rafters. "You go, Coco! Go away from here!"

Stoughton banged his gavel. After a moment, the hall fell silent. But instead of turning his ire on the disruptive girls, Stoughton scowled at Sarah, who cowered in her seat.

"You must stop your attack immediately, Sarah Good," he ordered sternly.

Good's mouth fell open, but no sound came out. How could she respond? Before Stoughton could say another word, a third girl fell to the floor, writhing in pain. I didn't even recognize her from school.

"She's stabbing me! She's stabbing me!" As one, the Villagers leapt to their feet and pressed toward the front of the room. I was the only one who pulled back, terror shooting through my body at what might happen next. Would the Villagers attack Good and tear her apart before the trial even ended?

Stoughton's bailiffs held back the tide, while the girl continued to thrash on the ground.

"Hathorne, check her for marks," Stoughton barked.

Hathorne leapt to his feet and rushed to the girl's side. "We'll protect you, Susannah," he vowed as he helped the girl to her feet.

Susannah's back faced the crowd when she pulled up the sleeve of her dress to show Hathorne her arm. I couldn't see what he saw, but I watched the blood drain from his face. Hathorne looked back at Stoughton.

"Show the court," Stoughton ordered.

Susannah swung her arm wide, first toward the jury and then at the assembled Villagers. Blood dripped from a row of marks on her forearm. My mouth fell open in a gasp as my eyes darted to Good. She was waving in her seat like a sail during a storm, but no one reached out to steady her. Both hands clutched at her heavy belly. Her eyes rolled back in her head as if she, too, had been afflicted.

My stomach turned at the sight of her. Was it possible—had I been wrong about Sarah? About the threat of witches? Susannah's arm was more proof than Ann had ever mustered that there were dangerous forces in our Village.

I'd wanted proof—and here it was.

Around me, Villagers were whispering prayers and clutching each other's hands as though Satan himself had entered the room.

As Susannah continued to hold out her arm, something small tumbled from her sleeve. It clattered to the floor, where Hathorne picked it up.

He held the sliver of metal up to the jury. "This must be the tool Sarah Good's specter used to assault Susannah Sheldon!"

My eyes never left Susannah, so I saw the panic flit across her face in the moment before Hathorne spoke.

The floor shook under my feet.

A voice in the back of the meeting house broke the silence. "Chief Justice!" My head whipped around to see a young man standing in the last row of benches, his raised hand clutching a knife. He pushed his way to the front of the room. "You have to see this."

Stoughton frowned at the boy. "Who are you?"

"Thomas Draper, your honor. I live in the Village."

"What do you want?"

"Yesterday evening I broke my knife in the Village Square. I searched for the missing piece but never found it. Susannah Sheldon was there when it happened." He held out a hand, and Hathorne reluctantly handed over the bit of metal. "See? It fits."

Susannah's face collapsed as she pulled her sleeve over the marks on her arm.

My legs nearly crumpled beneath me. I'd thrown Sarah to the crows so easily. Susannah's ploy was so thin, and yet I had believed her.

I leaned against the wall and tried to regain my footing.

I wasn't the only one shaken by Thomas's accusation. Angry mutterings filled the meeting house.

But Stoughton wasn't so easily deterred. "I don't see how this is relevant to the case," he growled at Thomas. "If you continue to interrupt our proceedings, I'll have the bailiffs escort you out."

Thomas's eyebrows pressed together. "I'm only trying to help," he pleaded.

Stoughton sneered at the boy. "If you're trying to help, tell me this, Mister Draper. Did you see the specter of Goodwife Good last night when your knife broke?"

Thomas blinked but didn't speak.

Stoughton leaned forward. "Did her *specter* cause your knife to break, so that she could force this innocent girl to pick up the piece? Just because young Susannah carried the weapon does not make Good innocent. Unless you can *swear* that Good was not in the Village Square yesterday—in her physical form *or* her spectral form."

Thomas finally shook his head.

"Then you have no proof at all," Stoughton concluded. "Leave us in peace so we can continue with the trial."

Thomas gaped for a moment and then returned to his seat.

My jaw hung slack, too. Stoughton had gone too far. The jurors would protest, surely. But as I scanned their faces, my hope was crushed. They weren't contorted with skepticism. Instead, they watched Susannah with pity in their eyes. None of them looked at Good. None of them showed an ounce of concern for the woman whose life rested in their hands.

These noble Puritan men were willing to bend over backward to protect the poor, tormented girls. They'd believe Stoughton's words over their own good sense.

Was I the only one who could see through the game Ann and her followers were playing?

The trial ended quickly.

Stoughton asked Good if she had any defense against the claims that she had assaulted Susannah Sheldon and used magic against her neighbors. Sarah's mumbled reply was so quiet that I couldn't even hear it.

Stoughton barely looked up from his desk before he turned to the jury.

"You have a serious responsibility today," he said. "You must evaluate the evidence of Sarah Good's guilt. You've heard from her neighbors, who have suffered after contact with

Goodwife Good, and you've seen the young girls here who say that Good is tormenting them. We all saw the marks on Susannah Sheldon's arms. Now you must decide the next step—will you reject Satan's influence?"

A cry died in my throat. What was the point of even having a jury? Stoughton had already decided Sarah Good's fate.

And the guilt wasn't his, alone. Sarah's neighbors lined up to tell tales of mysterious deaths and curses shouted in the past. Every single person in this room had probably spoken harsh words at some point in the past.

But only one might pay with her life.

He who is without sin should cast the first stone—I read that somewhere.

But in Salem Village everyone was lining up to grab stones and no one was innocent.

The jury deliberated for less than five minutes before they found Sarah Good guilty.

Stoughton took in their ruling with a faint smile. He promised the meeting house that Good would be executed—as soon as her child was born—to rid the Village of her terrible scourge.

I wanted to burst into tears.

TWENTY-ONE

I didn't stay to see Sarah Good carted back to prison.

After her guilty verdict, I ran home and threw myself in bed without talking to anyone. I refused to come downstairs for supper when my mom called me. Instead, I hid under the covers pretending that I lived somewhere—anywhere—besides Salem Village.

How could the Villagers be so *stupid*? Was I surrounded by idiots, or were they bloodthirsty lunatics just waiting for a chance to legally execute their neighbors?

And what if they *did* see through Ann's act, but they didn't care? Stoughton was the lieutenant governor—he wasn't a fool, and yet he barely blinked when Thomas uncovered Susannah's lies in the middle of the trial.

Of course, Stoughton didn't know Sarah Good. He saw her as a criminal disrupting the community. But what about Sarah's neighbors, who paraded in front of the court to trash her reputation?

I should have stayed on the farm. I never should have gone back to the Village.

I pulled the covers tighter until they blocked out all the light. Then I opened my eyes in the dark. Sarah was walking, talking proof that Salem's Puritans were not as charitable as they pretended. As soon as she turned to her neighbors for support, they accused her of witchcraft.

Sarah was an inconvenient reminder of all the ways Salem fell short of its lofty goals. And so she had to be eliminated.

How else could I explain their desire to believe the afflicted girls? The jurors might recognize the lies, but they were still willing to burn their neighbors to save themselves.

They were sheep, and worse, they were eager to follow a wolf.

I screwed my eyes shut as tears flooded them. I cursed the day Ann had started talking about magic, and I cursed Cotton Mather's book that filled Salem with ideas about Satan. I cursed the Villagers who sentenced Sarah Good to a certain death, and I cursed William Stoughton for leading ignorant people astray.

And then I cursed all Puritans everywhere.

I cursed their names one by one as the sun set, until my lips settled on one name: Ann Putnam.

Yet my hollow words changed nothing.

And so I stayed in bed.

Later that night, long after the sun had set, there was a muffled knock on my door. "Cavie?" It was my mother's worried voice. I didn't respond. "Are you feeling okay?"

I rolled over and faced the wall. A few seconds later, the door squeaked open. The floorboards creaked as my mom walked across the room and sat next to me on the bed.

I felt the comforting brush of her hand along my back, and in a flash I remembered falling ill as a little girl back when we lived in London. She'd sat at my bed for hours. When I was young, my mother's touch was enough to reassure me, but things were different now. A comforting hand couldn't undo what was ailing Salem Village.

"Are you ill, Cavie?" my mother whispered.

The hot flush of guilt rose in my chest. I didn't want to worry my mom, but how could I put my feelings into words? I was powerless against the crushing hatred of witches that had gripped Salem Village.

And if I tried to explain, I'd have to tell my mom about the role I'd played in the witch trials.

As much as I wanted to deny it, I was partly responsible. I had gone along with the Glass Girls, playing at magic in the woods. I hadn't spoken out against Ann when it might have made a difference. And today, I'd watched in the meeting house, a silent spectator, as the court condemned an innocent woman. Stoughton might have shot Thomas down, but at least he'd stood up and said something.

All I could do was lie in bed and cry.

Finally, my mom stood and quietly left the room. I listened as her footsteps down the stairs grew fainter.

Some part of me had childishly hoped she could fix everything, but I was old enough to realize that grown-ups usually had no idea what they were doing. And what did I expect? If my parents were afraid and wanted to ignore the trial, who was I to contradict them? I was afraid, too. I didn't want to see my mother—or myself—thrown in jail, accused of witchcraft.

We were all trapped.

I wasn't willing to risk myself to save the accused women. The risk terrified me more than being labeled a coward.

Which meant that I *was* a coward.

It felt like hours before I finally fell into a restless sleep.

I dreamed that I was on trial for being a witch. The jurors glared down at me from their box and Stoughton scowled from behind his judge's desk. My limbs were heavy and I couldn't stand, couldn't run from the meeting house. I twisted and turned in my seat, pleading silently with the rows of Villagers who sat as spectators. But no one stood up for me.

Then Ann Putnam rose before me, her arm outstretched toward me. "She's the witch, she's the witch," Ann cried.

My tongue was thick in my mouth, but I struggled to speak. "I'm innocent," I bleated. "I did nothing wrong!"

The jurors began to laugh and the corners of Ann's mouth tilted upward.

"She's lying, she's lying," I wailed, but no one would listen.

Ann slowly moved closer and closer, like a viper stalking its prey, until she leaned over and whispered in my ear, "They'll *never* believe you."

I sat up, suddenly awake and coated in sweat, as if I had a fever. I raised a hand to my forehead. It was clammy.

Ann's words echoed in my head. She was right. No one would believe me if I called Ann Putnam a liar. She was *Ann Putnam*. The Villagers worshipped her—and not just the teenagers. To the adults, she was perfect Puritan Ann, a model daughter and future goodwife. To the kids, she was like a celebrity, unimaginably cool. That gave her power.

But what if she lost her power?

I threw back the covers and dressed quickly in the dark.

Why hadn't I thought of it sooner?

Today would be different.

Today I'd start my plan to destroy Ann Putnam and save the Villagers from her reign of terror.

I ran downstairs and snuck away before my mom and dad were awake. The sky was just light enough to avoid the deep ruts in the road. I could hear my breath pounding in my ears as my mind raced. It might work. I might be able to stop the trials.

By the time I reached Joy's house, the sun had peeked above the trees. I snuck around the back and tapped on her window. Joy's groggy face popped up and she scowled at me. I signaled that she should meet me in the glade and slipped away.

I waited on the rock for a long time before Joy showed up. She was still scowling. "What's so important?" she grumbled.

"We're going to stop Ann Putnam."

Joy rolled her eyes as she sat on the stump across from me. "We've tried before and it never worked."

"This time will be different. This time we'll convince everyone that Ann Putnam is a *liar*." I tried to pour confidence into my voice and ignore the nagging doubts at the back of my mind. If I wasn't fully behind the plan, it wouldn't work.

"How?"

"We can't attack her head-on. Everyone loves her. But what if she wasn't so popular?"

Joy looked at me like I was speaking in tongues. "She's always been popular. She's *Ann Putnam*."

"But what if she *wasn't*?" I let the question hang in the air between us for a minute. "Ann's just a person. If we figure out why people like her, we can take those things away from her. We can destroy her."

I reached into my bag and pulled out a notebook and a pencil. It was time to get to the center of Ann's popularity.

Joy was staring at my hand. "Wow, you have a pencil?"

Sometimes I forgot how far Salem Village was from the civilized world. Practically everyone in London had a pencil.

"I got it a few years ago for Christmas. It's German." I handed over the pencil and Joy inspected it.

"All I get for Christmas is socks. Puritans aren't big on holidays." She reluctantly handed back the pencil.

"We need to focus. Why is Ann so popular?" I poised the pencil over a blank sheet of paper.

Joy scratched her head. "She's been popular as long as I can remember. I guess she was born popular."

I shook my head. "No, she was born a *Putnam*. That's part of her appeal, right? If she was Ann No-Last-Name, the daughter of a poor farmer, would anyone pay attention to her?"

"I doubt it," Joy said.

I wrote "Putnam" on the blank paper.

"But how do we make her not a Putnam?" Frustration leaked from Joy's voice.

"We have to make the Putnams look undesirable. And the best way to do that is to get the support of the Porter family. Maybe we can get a group of people to oppose the Putnams and . . . sign a petition or something. Maybe if more people came out against the trials."

"But it's not just that she's a Putnam," Joy sighed. "It's that she's beautiful, and smart, and she knows all the latest fashions from Europe, and . . . well, she's just *popular*."

I had never been popular—except for the short weeks when the Glass Girls had invited me to sit with them.

But that meant I had spent my life watching popular people.

All that experience taught me something about popularity, and now it was time to put it to use.

"We can take those things away from her," I said, locking eyes with Joy. "We can make her seem stupid and ignorant and ugly."

Joy bit her lower lip. "Wait. Ann uses this French face cream. She talks about it all the time, because it's imported from Paris. What if we messed with it? We could put horse dung in the cream, or fish oil. Something to make her smell terrible."

"That's perfect." I grinned. "And she won't look so beautiful once she's covered in fish."

"But that's just one thing."

"Don't you see? That's how we'll take her down. One thing at a time. Like, where does Ann get her fashion trends? I don't think she really knows what's fashionable in Europe."

Joy's eyebrows popped up. "She subscribes to a monthly journal from London. That's where she hears what's popular."

I leaned over my paper. "Well, what if we sent her a fake one? We could make her do all kinds of crazy things. Like . . . put rouge on her forehead."

Joy shook her head. "Ann's careful about wearing cosmetics in public. Puritan rules."

"Then we'll think of something else." I thought back to Ann's house, to all the beautiful things in her room. And then I remembered something else. "That's it. You know how Ann loves fancy foods?"

"Yeah, she always has crazy expensive imported foods, like coconuts and oranges."

"Don't you see? That's one of the reasons she's popular. Her hair is shiny from all that imported olive oil, and her skin is perfect because she eats so much fruit. But what if she looked ragged and starved like the poorest people in the Village?"

"You want us to sneak into her house and steal her oranges?"

"No, I want to convince her to eat something gross. Like, we send her a magazine that says everyone in Europe is chewing wheat stems. If she only chews wheat, she'll start to look sickly and sallow. When she's a skinny husk of herself she won't look so fashionable."

Joy started nodding. "She'll look like a poor farmer's daughter instead of a rich girl."

"Once she's ugly and smelly no one will want to hang out with her."

"Even the Glass Girls won't want to be around Ann."

"That's exactly what we want. If Abigail and Mercy reject Ann, the other afflicted girls might follow. And if they recant their testimony . . ."

Joy sucked in a breath of air. "Cavie, what about Edmund Hale?"

His name sent a sharp twinge through my body. I hadn't seen him in weeks, but apparently I still wasn't over Edmund Hale. "We have to break them up." I knew they were still together. Ann was obviously just using him for his popularity. At least that's what I told myself. "If Edmund dumps Ann, she'll flip out."

Joy's eyes widened. "No one dumps Ann Putnam."

I smiled. "Once she's hideous and reeks of fish, Edmund will."

"So first we make Ann gross, and then we drive away her friends. Do you really think that will destroy her credibility?"

"It's our best shot," I said. "Plus, imagine Ann, friendless and dumped—imagine how angry she'll be. Once she starts screaming and cursing, the Villagers won't think she's the perfect Puritan." I looked down at the sheet of paper. I had scratched notes across the page during our conversation. At the top of the sheet, I penciled, "Plan to Destroy Ann Putnam." I looked back at Joy. "The younger girls won't want to follow Ann and make up lies about witches once they realize Ann is toxic. And if she goes crazy, the adults won't like her either."

"Cavie, you're a genius." Joy leaned back. Her scowl had vanished.

I plastered a smile on my face, but in the pit of my stomach, I wondered if I was still acting like a coward. Was plotting behind Ann's back enough to lift the guilt that had settled into my mind? Had I waited too long to put the plan into motion?

I hadn't said anything to Joy, but I knew the plan wouldn't work unless Ann's supporters had a new queen bee to follow.

And I knew the perfect person.

TWENTY-TWO

Everything started out perfectly.

The next day the Village was empty—everyone was at church. Attendance had skyrocketed since the trials began. I guess people hoped it would protect them from being accused of witchcraft.

With Joy as my lookout, I snuck into the Putnam house. It was dead silent and black as pitch. I didn't linger. I avoided the windows and took the back stairs up to Ann's room. Here, light sparkled from the lush colors and expensive decorations. I wanted to lie on her bed just for a minute to see how soft it was—I'm sure it was nothing like the straw-filled mattress in my room—but I stopped myself.

If anyone caught me in Ann Putnam's room, I'd be in huge trouble.

The jar of face cream was on top of her table, next to her expensive brush. I lifted the small container and studied the label. It was just called milk cream in French, but it must have been worth a fortune if Ann made her parents import it from Europe. I snuck a jar from my bag and upended the contents into the cream. For a minute, the fish oil sat on top, a greasy blemish on the milk-white surface. I stared at it, not wanting to stick my finger into the pungent oil. Then I grabbed the brush and stirred the cream with the handle. I wiped it off on the underside of Ann's bed.

Blood pounded in my ears. Was that a noise from downstairs?

I rushed to the door and stopped to look back at the room.

Was Ann's Burning Book hidden somewhere inside?

There was no time to look for it. I ran down the stairs and burst out the back door, my chest heaving.

Joy reassured me that no one had seen us, but I couldn't stop looking over my shoulder.

The next day we spent hours writing a letter supposedly from the duchess of Cornwall that said raw wheat was all the rage in Europe that spring. Joy and I couldn't stop laughing as we pretended to read the letter in terrible aristocratic accents.

"Take note: all the fashionable ladies at court have turned to a new tonic, guaranteed to make you look comely. Her Royal Highness Queen Mary II imported the magical food herself from the Low Countries. It's called the farmer's secret. Don't tell your rivals, but nothing makes a woman more attractive than chewing on a stalk of raw wheat! But remember—eat *only* raw wheat on this diet, or you'll surely ruin your complexion."

I copied out the message three times with a quill before it looked perfect. Then we packed it up to look like an insert in Ann's European journal. We dropped a few coins in a boy's hand to deliver it to the Putnam house.

Later that week I saw Ann walking through the Village Square chewing on a stalk of wheat.

I almost shrieked when I saw her. I couldn't believe the plan was working.

And as she walked past, a boy twisted his face in disgust and hollered, "What *died?*" Before his mother could shush him, she smelled it too, and dragged her son away from the square.

A few days later I made sure to run into Abigail and Mercy. It was time to see how the Glass Girls were responding to the new Ann Putnam. Plus, I hadn't spoken with Abigail in weeks. Did she still doubt Ann's stories? Abigail still sat next to Ann every day during the trials, but I had no idea what she really thought about the trials.

Abigail didn't say anything when I asked to eat lunch with them, but Mercy patted the bench next to her. "Where have you been?" Mercy asked.

"It's been really busy on my parent's farm."

"You were *working?*"

I nodded. "Plus, I figured you were busy with the trials."

Mercy rolled her eyes. "The trials are *so boring.* I wish they'd end."

Abigail stared at the ground and didn't say anything.

I looked over until I caught her eye. "Did you see what Ann was wearing yesterday?"

Abigail's eyes flashed. "I can't believe she cut a hole in the back of her bonnet. Everyone saw her hair. *Everyone.*"

I shook my head and suppressed a smile. That had been Joy's idea. "It seems like she's dying for attention."

Mercy frowned. "I kind of liked it. You could pull your pony tail through the bonnet hole."

Abigail gasped. "That's not how you wear a bonnet," she scolded. "My uncle said he's going to talk to her about modesty." Abigail leaned in and lowered her voice. "And did you smell her?"

Mercy plugged her nose. "It's disgusting! I can barely stand to be in the same room with her."

"But you sit next to her every day during the trials," I pointed out. "And I bet some people wonder if you're the smelly one."

Mercy's mouth fell open. "I never thought of that."

Abigail rolled her eyes. "Why do you think I stopped sitting next to her?"

Mercy slapped her playfully. "You should have told me!"

Just then, I saw Ann walking toward us. She already looked pale from her new diet and she'd tucked her long hair up under her bonnet so it was completely hidden. I wondered what her hair must look like after week of only eating raw wheat.

When Ann saw me sitting with her friends, she nearly tripped. Worry flashed in her eyes as her gaze darted between Abigail and Mercy. "I waited for you on the hill. Why didn't you come?"

Abigail looked at the ground again.

"Well? Come on!" Ann ordered.

Neither of them stood.

Ann's hands were on her hips—she had already lost weight, I saw, and she looked ill—but neither Abigail nor Mercy jumped at Ann's command. "Is this about my face cream? It's *French*!"

Still none of us spoke. Ann spun around and stomped off. I saw her pull more wheat from her apron.

Before she'd even left the square, Mercy was giggling. "Did you see that?"

"She looks terrible," Abigail murmured.

Mercy stifled her laughter. "That wheat diet is making her crazy. Yesterday she asked me if there's wheat in *butter*. I mean, of course there's wheat in butter. What does she think goes in the butter churn?"

I held my tongue. If Abigail and Mercy were already avoiding Ann, the plan was going even better than I'd hoped. And now, it was time to pull Abigail and Mercy to my side. I started by telling them stories about the summer I'd spent in Paris. Abigail couldn't stop asking questions.

Inside, I was singing.

It took a week to turn Ann into a hollow shell of what she'd once been.

But as I plotted, the trials continued. I wasn't fast enough. After Sarah Good was found guilty, the next five trials also ended with convictions.

The jail in Salem Village was so full of accused witches that they started housing some of the suspects in neighboring cities.

During the height of paranoia, as summer's heat crushed New England, someone even accused the former minister, George Burroughs, of witchcraft. Burroughs didn't even live in the Village anymore. He'd been arrested a decade earlier and driven out of town. He spent ten years in the wilds of Maine, where he tried to forget Salem Village—until he was dragged back to stand trial, the first male witch in the Village.

Stoughton loudly proclaimed that Burroughs was the leader of the witches' coven, so I took a break from the plot against Ann to attend his trial. Accused witches, eager to curry favor with the Chief Justice and terrified after Sarah's conviction, gleefully testified to all of Burroughs's depraved actions.

"He led me to a witches' sabbath!"

"He showed me his Devil's mark!"

"He made me kiss Satan's hoof!"

Burroughs had to be the most hated man in Salem Village. Dozens of people appeared to testify against their former minister. One spun stories of Burroughs's superhuman strength. "He carried a barrel of molasses on his shoulder as if it weighed nothing. But when I tried to lift it, I couldn't even get it above my knees. He surely had the Devil's strength."

Burroughs sputtered that other men had lifted the barrel—he'd been with an Indian friend who'd also carried it.

Stoughton loudly muttered, "Or maybe it wasn't an Indian—it was the Devil himself!"

Another man testified that Burroughs could run faster than a horse—no, wait, that Burroughs rode horses with the Devil.

The Villagers soaked up the stories like manna from heaven.

Ann, apparently jealous of the attention such stories garnered, began to spin even more fantastical tales. She looked thin and weak after a steady diet of raw wheat, and the stench of fish followed her everywhere. But the Villagers managed to look past her deteriorating appearance when she cried out during Burroughs's trial.

"I see them," she yelled, interrupting the testimony of a rare Burroughs supporter.

Stoughton eagerly turned to his star witness. "What do you see?"

"I see the ghosts of Burroughs's wives."

A gasp shot through the meeting house. The Villagers had never seen such entertainment.

"Do they speak to you?" Hathorne demanded from the bench.

"They do."

I rolled my eyes. Of course the ghostly wives would speak to Ann.

"What do they say?" Stoughton leaned so far forward that it looked as though he might tip over the bench and tumble on his head.

He would no doubt blame a witch.

"They say—" Ann trailed off, her eyes focused on the rafters as if she was actually communicating with spirits. "They say that George Burroughs was a terrible husband."

Another gasp. Another eye roll from me. Not very original material.

"There's more," Ann promised. "But I cannot speak. The specter has turned against me!" She fainted.

While a concerned group fanned her limp body, Stoughton glared at Burroughs. "Is that true?"

"Of course not."

"And you expect us to believe an accused witch over the heavenly spirits of your deceased spouses?"

Burroughs stammered.

"Mark down that he did not respond," Hathorne directed the court recorder.

It was farcical, except the court seemed to buy everything.

And of course Burroughs was found guilty.

After that, I vowed not to let the trials distract me. I had a goal: I had to take down Ann Putnam. If I could undermine her, the whole panic might evaporate.

The guilt of avoiding the meeting house weighed on me, but I convinced myself it was for a noble cause. I tried to push down the uneasy feeling that I was happier not watching innocent people convicted of witchcraft.

Once I knew that the Glass Girls were turning on Ann, I went after Edmund. He was still courting Ann, but since she was busy at the trials they barely saw each other. I asked around about Edmund and learned that he spent most of his time out at the farm.

During one of the trials, I retraced my steps to his house. I wanted to catch Edmund alone, when there was no chance of Ann showing up.

Edmund was in the field, pulling weeds. The mud might have dried, but the hot and damp weather was perfect for weeds. If it was this bad in June, I didn't want to see what it would be like in July or August.

I hadn't spoken a word to Edmund yet, but this wasn't the time to be afraid.

I had to stop Ann.

I donned a sweet grin and waved to Edmund.

"Cavie, right?" He stood up and brushed a hand across his forehead, leaving an adorable trail of dirt.

I had to stay focused.

"Sorry to interrupt you like this," I said, twirling my hair around a finger. I tried to imitate Ann when she spoke with boys. "Ann asked me to send you a message."

"She did?"

"She's so busy with the trials that she couldn't get away."

"Oh." His face was unreadable, but I caught a hint of coldness in his voice.

His eyes were so blue.

"Anyway, you know she's being attacked by witches."

"Yeah."

I wondered for a minute what Edmund thought about Ann's fame. He seemed so committed to his farm. Why did he like Ann, anyway? She was totally wrong for him.

I paused before my next line. "The doctors think it might be causing *permanent damage*."

"Really?" Suddenly there was more emotion in his voice. He even took a step closer.

I leaned in as though he were a warm fire on a winter day. I had to remember why I was here. "Haven't you seen her lately?"

Edmund frowned and mumbled something.

"She doesn't look healthy," I continued. "She's so thin. And the smell. Maybe a witch cursed her. But you know what Cotton Mather said. Even if the witch dies, the curse might *never* end."

I studied Edmund. His eyebrows folded down at the ends and he wasn't looking me in the eye anymore. But he hadn't turned against Ann yet.

I'd have to go even further.

I sighed loudly. "And I probably shouldn't be telling you this, but she might never be able to have children. What a shame, right? What farmer would marry a woman whose fields are barren? She'll probably end up an old maid." I gave an exaggerated gasp and threw a hand over my mouth. My other hand shot out touch Edmund's forearm.

How did his *forearm* have muscles?

"Oh, I shouldn't have said anything. You and Ann are still together."

Edmund's eyes flicked to the house. I'd heard he had built part of it himself. He was probably planning to live there once he got married. And what Puritan man didn't want to fill a house with little children? It was God's highest wish, after all, for men to create more souls for heaven.

I waited for Edmund to speak. Finally his eyes dropped to the field. "No children?" His voice was low and hollow.

"It's a terrible curse," I agreed. "But take heart, Edmund. She's not the only girl in Salem Village." I gave his arm a squeeze. His eyes jumped to mine.

It was more forward than I'd ever been, but it was working. I could practically see thoughts of Ann vanishing from Edmund's mind.

And it only took a few well-placed lies.

"Cavie?" he said, and my heart jumped. "Thanks."

He wasn't the most talkative guy, but those words warmed me more than a Shakespearean sonnet. I lowered my eyes, making sure he could see the blush in my cheeks. "Of course, Edmund. I just want to help." I let my hand linger on his arm before I pulled away.

I risked one last look at him before I turned to walk back to the Village. I could feel his eyes following me as I left.

Mission accomplished. Edmund wouldn't be thinking about Ann Putnam any more. I couldn't believe how easy it was to distract him from his girlfriend.

Or, should I say, his *ex*-girlfriend.

Everything was going according to plan: Ann had lost her luster in the eyes of many Villagers, the Glass Girls were rejecting Ann, and Edmund started visiting my house every afternoon.

Suddenly I was the most popular girl in the Village. Every time I walked through the square, Ann's former followers would trail in my wake, whispering about me.

I made sure to catch Ann's eye when Edmund escorted me through the Village Square. Her face contorted with rage, but I only smiled back. She knew she was losing, and I loved it.

But that still didn't stop the first execution.

TWENTY-THREE

They killed Bridget Bishop on the tenth of June.

I had been too busy running around the Village trying to destroy Ann Putnam's reputation to pay much attention to her trial. It pains me to admit it, but at some point the trials became a constant background noise in our lives. There was always something happening at the meeting house—some new accused witch, or an old woman set free after she confessed. It was exhausting to watch the constant deluge of accusations and denials, false attacks and confessions. And terrifying.

While I had been off with Edmund, giggling at some joke, Bridget had been examined by Stoughton. She denied everything. She tried to pass herself off as a healer, a wise woman, but in Salem, they only saw her as a witch.

Bridget had a bad reputation—which meant everything in Salem Village. People whispered that she was immoral, she visited taverns, she removed her bonnet in church. She swore in front of children. She couldn't recite the Lord's Prayer. A yowling cat was stationed in front of her house, surely marking her as Satan's minion.

And she had been married *three times*.

Even before the witchcraft accusation, Bridget Bishop was no model Puritan.

While I was off playing childish games, Ann was working even harder to convince the Village that she was the victim of invisible attacks. She must have felt her power slipping away. Like a crone desperately clinging to her youth, Ann viciously directed the afflicted girls just like she'd once ruled the Glass Girls. She orchestrated new spectral attacks and timed them perfectly for dull moments in the trials.

That's what happened to Bridget.

When Bridget refused to confess, Ann fell into a fit and cried out that Bridget prayed to Satan instead of God. Moments later, as if they'd coordinated it, another girl declared that Bridget's specter attacked her with a knife and only her brother's intervention had saved her life. Stoughton ordered the bailiff to examine the girl's coat. When he swung it wide in front of the jury, they saw a long, jagged tear in the lining. Even after Susannah's antics, the jury found it convincing.

Right after they hanged Bridget at the newly built Village gallows, before Bridget's body was even cold, Joy ran to my family's farm. She told me in breathless gasps about Bridget's trial and her testimony. She narrated Bridget's attempts to clear her name and her confrontation with Hathorne, who was convinced she was a witch.

Bridget had vowed, "I am no witch."

Hathorne had pressed. "Have you signed your soul over to the spirits?"

"I have no familiarity with the Devil."

"Then how does your specter attack Ann Putnam?"

"I am innocent."

"Then why do the afflicted girls fall down, here in court, right before our eyes?"

"I don't know. I am innocent. I don't even know what a witch is."

"How do you *know* then that you are not a witch?"

"What?"

"How can you know that you are not a witch, but you don't what a witch is?"

"If I were a witch, you'd know it."

"Is that a *threat*?"

"I am innocent."

Joy was blinking back tears as she spoke each part.

How did they expect a woman to argue against that logic? It's no surprise the jury found her guilty. They had decided she was guilty long before the trial even began, long before Ann Putnam cried that witches were tormenting her. Salem had declared Bridget a bad Puritan, and in 1692 that was a capital offense.

The tenth of June. That's the day they hanged Bridget Bishop just outside the Village Square. Hundreds of people gathered to watch her last moments of life.

I didn't even realize she was dead until Joy found me in the fields.

That's the day I finally admitted that the problem was much bigger than Ann Putnam and the Glass Girls.

~ ~ ~

I'd like to say that I stood up for the accused witches.

But that would be a lie.

Bridget's death sent a chill over the Village. She'd been

executed merely on the word of her neighbors, and no one knew who might be next. No one wanted to draw attention to themselves.

We all saw what was happening—the prison was overflowing with accused witches and nearly all of them were women. The wives of Salem stopped coming to the meeting house to watch the trials, unless they were among the afflicted.

No one could predict who might be the next victim of the witch hunt.

And so I didn't stand up in the meeting house to condemn Stoughton's terrible behavior, or Ann's lies.

I was a coward.

But I wasn't the only coward in Salem.

The execution hung over Salem like a black cloud. While the women of Salem ran for cover, some of the men became more vocal about their doubts. For a brief moment it looked like the tide would turn. Hunting witches was God's work, Stoughton tried to remind everyone, but to the Villagers, killing your neighbors was a different matter.

With the dirt still fresh on Bridget Bishop's grave, the next trial began.

But this trial was different.

Bridget's death changed the jurors' calculations in some invisible way. Suddenly they were wary about sending more women to the gallows.

Especially Rebecca Nurse.

In a wave of disreputable women, old widows, and poor beggars, Rebecca Nurse stood out.

Goodwife Nurse was in her seventies and as far from Bridget Bishop as you could get in Salem Village. Everyone agreed she was a good Puritan woman and everyone respected her.

Except for the Putnams.

Joy explained to me that Rebecca had fought with the Putnams over some land on the edge of town. It had been years earlier. Most people in the Village had probably forgotten, but the Putnams remembered. They saw Rebecca Nurse as an obstacle to their goal of expanding their power in Salem. If she were gone, Thomas Putnam could finally seize her land.

Ann probably didn't care about Rebecca Nurse—why would Ann Putnam care about a seventy year old woman?

But her mother cared.

Ann was a perfect copy of her mother, just younger and more popular. They were so similar that they shared a name: both were Ann Putnam. And Ann Senior wanted to recapture the glory days of her youth, in the 1670s, when she had been the queen bee of Salem Village.

It started slowly. Every time Ann cried out at a trial, drawing all eyes for one of her fits, Ann's mom would make a noise. A little louder each time, until a fair share of Villagers looked to Ann Senior during the trials. Soon, Ann's mom was having fits of her own, crying out that witches were attacking her.

Accusing witches became a mother-daughter bonding activity.

It turned my stomach. She was a *goodwife*, but she wanted everyone to know she was still cool. I kept remembering the day we'd spoken in Ann's house, the day Ann told me that Salem needed a witch trial. Ann Senior's voice was as bubbly as champagne when she declared that she and her daughter were more like sisters.

If Ann Putnam got attention for being persecuted by witches, her mother would, too.

And it all came to a head during the trial of Rebecca Nurse.

Ann Senior accused Goodwife Nurse of witchcraft, and Stoughton's tribunal leapt into action. In no time, old Rebecca had been arrested and thrown into the crowded jail.

But this time, something was different. Rebecca Nurse didn't fit anyone's stereotype of a witch. She wasn't cranky, she never cursed anyone, and she always attended church.

No one wanted to testify against her.

Even Hathorne, who usually drooled at the chance to interrogate an accused witch, shook his head. In a doleful voice, he proclaimed, "It is a sad thing to see good church members accused."

Villagers whispered that maybe the afflicted girls were wrong just this one time. Maybe Satan was tricking them into accusing an innocent woman—he was the master of deception, after all. Rebecca Nurse couldn't be a witch. It just wasn't possible.

Right before her trial began, Joseph Porter appeared in the meeting house with another petition. This time, he had gathered the signatures of forty men of standing in the Village, who all claimed Rebecca was a woman of good character.

And this time, they weren't anonymous.

Stoughton's face drained of blood when Porter slapped the paper onto his desk.

And when the trial began, people stood up to testify on Rebecca's behalf.

My heart pounded as one by one, Villagers rose to defend an accused witch. It was the first time I'd seen anyone publicly declare that the hysteria had gone too far.

The Putnams raged against Rebecca Nurse, writhing on the floor and proclaiming her Satan's handmaiden, but the spell had somehow been broken. The jurors didn't look at Ann Senior with pity when she cried out that Rebecca's specter was pinching her. One even threw up a hand to cover a laugh at her performance.

I was in the meeting house when the jury returned their verdict.

"Not guilty."

I gasped, and I wasn't the only one. My eyes jumped to Ann Putnam. Were her shoulders slumping slightly? Did she realize what had just happened? The jurors didn't believe Ann's fits. They didn't believe that Goodwife Nurse was really a witch. They drew a line: a woman with a good reputation couldn't possibly be one of the Devil's minions.

If only I could see Ann's face.

A shriek broke the silence. Ann's mother had fallen to the floor as though struck by another fit. "Satan is rejoicing!" she cried. "You've let his witch go free!"

The meeting house was dead silent. Not even the creak of someone adjusting their position on the hard wooden benches broke the quiet.

I wanted to pull my bonnet over my face. It was too embarrassing.

Ann Senior rolled and rolled, but no one came to her side.

"Rebecca Nurse has the Devil's book, filled with the names of witches!" Ann Senior howled.

At that, Stoughton stepped in. He wasn't from the Village, so he didn't care about Rebecca's longstanding reputation. To him, she was just another witch. In between Ann Senior's cries, Stoughton eyed the jury and spoke to them in a voice almost too low for the rest of us to hear.

"You must reconsider your verdict."

My jaw dropped. The jury had ruled. How could the Chief

Justice tell them to change their verdict?

Stoughton raised his voice. "I would remind the jury that Rebecca Nurse confessed in this very room."

At that, Goodwife Nurse cried out. "I am a Godly woman. I never confessed to witchcraft."

Stoughton ignored her and kept his attention on the jury. "She confessed. Did you not hear Nurse call George Burroughs 'one of us'? George Burroughs, who this very tribunal convicted of witchcraft just last week?"

Joseph Porter stood up. "Now wait a minute, Stoughton."

"That's Chief Justice Stoughton."

"You're twisting Goodwife Nurse's words."

"Twisting them like Satan twists good women away from the Godly path?"

Porter shook his head. "I'm sure Goodwife Nurse meant that Burroughs is another prisoner, like her." Murmurs of agreement echoed through the meeting house.

Stoughton ignored Porter and looked to the jury. "If that is so, why was Nurse silent when I asked what she meant?"

"Maybe because she's deaf?" Those were the first words I spoke during the trial, and I'm proud of them. I might be a coward, but the trial record will show that I was not silent.

But it didn't matter. Stoughton ordered silence in the meeting house and railed on about Nurse's guilt. He pointed at Ann Senior, still on the floor, as proof that Rebecca was a witch. He ranted on and on until the jurors agreed to reconsider.

This time, they returned with a guilty verdict.

Stoughton slammed his gavel into the bench dozens of times, but nothing would quiet the turmoil in the meeting house. Joseph Porter stormed out, followed by a large group of Villagers. Others shook their heads and lamented the verdict.

Nurse's family surrounded her. The woman's mournful prayers rose above the angry voices filling the meeting house.

Ann Senior sat back and watched everything with a faint smile on her face.

How many times would I think the trials might be over, only to have my hopes dashed? How many heads of this hydra had to be destroyed before the hysteria would end?

I hid away on my farm, rage burning through my thoughts.

I didn't go back to the Village until the hot day in the middle of summer when five women went to the gallows. There were tears in the crowd that day, though most of them were for Rebecca Nurse. Her supporters still refused to believe she might be a witch.

I shed tears for Rebecca Nurse, yes, but also for Sarah Good. She had given birth in prison. The baby had died, so the court could finally execute Sarah.

I lowered my eyes before their bodies began to swing in a row. I tried to ignore the sounds from the women whose necks hadn't broken in the fall. I wanted to be anywhere but this bare, dry patch of ground in Salem Village, but I owed it to these women to watch.

I was a coward, but I wouldn't run today.

When the bodies hung limp, I looked around at the faces of the Villagers crowded around me. Many were pale and shaken, undone in some way by what they'd seen. I tried to find solace in the Villagers who stood up for Rebecca Nurse. The jury had found her innocent at first, after all. Wasn't that a good sign?

But Rebecca was still dead.

To my left, the Putnam clan watched the swaying bodies. Thomas Putnam grinned and joked with one of his cousins. I'd heard he'd taken control of Rebecca Nurse's land the same day she was found guilty. Ann Senior also preened as if she were royalty. Between them, Ann looked like a pale, shrunken version of herself. She wasn't smiling.

I might have taken Ann down, but that hadn't stopped the executions. There were still dozens of afflicted in the Village—and not just girls. Ann Senior had been joined by other grown women who said witches were attacking them.

I saw a figure standing behind the gallows, barely watching the bodies. It was Stoughton.

I tasted copper in my mouth. I'd bitten my lip so hard that it bled.

Ann Putnam hadn't killed Rebecca Nurse. Stoughton had.

He forced the jury to find her guilty.

Not even a verdict of innocent could protect an accused witch in Salem.

The Village was trapped in a mania for finding witches. It showed no signs of burning out or slowing down. There were still dozens and dozens of innocent people in the jails, and convicted witches waiting to see if they'd be next on the gallows.

And I could only think of one thing that might stop it.

I had to accuse Ann Putnam of witchcraft.

TWENTY-FOUR

But I wasn't ready to accuse Ann. Not yet.

Ann's hair had lost its luster. Her skin was sallow and the fire in her eyes had vanished. In the Village, I heard whispers that the witches had taken their toll on the former golden girl.

But I knew better.

The halo of popularity that had surrounded Ann was gone. Abigail and Mercy never ate with Ann any more. They didn't want to be tainted by association. And Ann's gaggle of younger girls abandoned her, too.

After all, they had a new queen bee.

I walked through the Village with my mahogany hair streaming down my back, just like Ann had once done. I'd whip off my bonnet the minute the adults were gone. I made sure everyone saw me in the Village Square with Edmund. Abigail asked me about what the girls wore back in London and Mercy spent days trying to imitate the soft wave in my hair, even though her stick-straight locks refused to comply.

I was popular.

But I wasn't popular enough to accuse Ann of witchcraft.

Not yet.

I had won over all the teenagers in the Village—or, at least, everyone not related to the Putnams. But I needed the support of Salem's adults, too.

I didn't dare confide my new plans in anyone, not even Edmund or Joy. In truth, I was so busy with Abigail and Mercy that I didn't see Joy very often. I had to maintain my reputation in order to challenge Ann, so I walked the other way when I saw Joy in the Village Square.

She'd understand.

Instead, I stayed up late, burning precious candles. I ran over my plan again and again.

The Villagers had finally fought back when Rebecca Nurse was accused. Her execution had lit a fire under the silent doubters. Many of them whispered loudly that maybe George Burroughs was innocent, too. No one spoke out against Stoughton, but the Villagers were noticeably cold when his name came up in conversation.

In the heat of summer, the passion for hunting witches was burning out.

And I knew something that could douse that fire.

But first, I had to look like a model Puritan.

I asked Edmund to take me for a walk every afternoon, so that the Villagers would see me with a hard-working young farmer. I prayed loudly with Abigail and Mercy in the Village Square. I offered to help the older Villagers without being asked. In short, I acted like the perfect Puritan.

I stepped into Ann Putnam's role seamlessly.

And I started attending church twice a week. Minister Parris's eyes widened the first day I appeared at his services, but I only nodded and kept my own eyes on the ground. I'd been in

Salem long enough to play the part.

That day, Minister Parris railed about the dangers of worshipping Satan. Fire and brimstone, sulfur and hellfire. He praised the Villagers for rejecting the Devil's advances and staying on the Godly path.

By the end of most sermons, girls were in tears, or at least shaking in terror.

But after a few weeks in the pews I noticed a change in the minister. His descriptions of Hell lost their vivid terror. The sermons barely mentioned witches.

The day after they hanged George Burroughs, the minister looked pale. He spoke about forgiveness and charity. Thomas Putnam, sitting in the front row, frowned and shook his head. I could almost hear him thinking, where had the fire and brimstone preacher gone?

Parris wasn't the only one in the Village who was changing. Joseph Porter rarely appeared in the Village until midsummer, when he suddenly became a permanent fixture in the Village Square. Almost every day he stood with the same group of Villagers. I tried to overhear their conversations, but they fell silent whenever I drew near.

In my heart, I hoped they were also plotting to resist the trials.

Then, at the end of summer, not long after Rebecca Nurse and George Burroughs were buried in unconsecrated ground, I was ready.

Ann Putnam had the Burning Book. She had started the witch craze.

And now I would take her down.

It was during another trial. Where else?

Everyone in the Village still gathered in the meeting house

religiously to learn of Satan's attacks. Even Joseph Porter, who had become the loudest critic of the trials, attended.

This time, the Coreys were on trial. Or, I should say, Martha Corey was on trial. Her husband, Giles, refused to enter a plea. This put the Chief Justice in a bind. Giles Corey's trial couldn't move forward if he refused to plead innocent or guilty. With Stoughton fuming about Giles, he put Martha on trial to pressure the recalcitrant man.

By now, we were all familiar with the pattern. Martha proclaimed her innocence. A few of her neighbors dug up ancient grievances to parade in front of the jury. Everyone was waiting for Ann to cry out that she was being attacked by Martha. We all knew that Ann hated Martha. The older woman had been spotted with Joseph Porter in the weeks before she was accused. She'd even loudly muttered that Ann Putnam exaggerated her attacks.

Martha was one of the doubters who'd become more vocal in recent weeks.

Until she was accused of witchcraft.

Ann had to be planning a performance that would send Martha to the gallows. But before she could cry out, I threw a hand to my forehead.

"Ah," I whimpered.

No one looked.

"AY!" I cried, louder. The people nearby turned toward me. I heard whispers. Now I had their attention. "I'm being attacked!"

A hush fell over the court, as it always did when someone claimed a spectral attack. Stoughton glared at me. I wasn't sitting in the front row like his star afflicted girls. For a moment, my heart stopped beating. Would Stoughton ignore my interruption, like he'd dismissed Thomas Draper?

But Minister Parris stood up and pointed at me. "Young Margaret Lucas is a good Puritan. Listen to her."

My time attending church had paid off.

The minister's seal of approval won Stoughton over, but I could see that his patience was limited. The Chief Justice looked at me expectantly.

I took a deep breath. I knew the script. I'd seen Ann act it out a thousand times.

But this time, the ending would surprise her.

"A specter is pinching me," I wailed.

"Is it Martha Corey?" Stoughton demanded.

I glanced at the lonely old woman and saw the terror in her eyes.

"No," I whispered.

"What?"

"She said no!"

"Then who is it?"

I let out another pitiful wail. I knew how to pay the game.

"She's being tormented!"

"Someone help her!"

"Only God can help her."

The Villagers were whipping themselves up into a frenzy over the newest afflicted girl.

"Please, stop her!" I cried. "The specter. She plagues me!" I ripped back my sleeve to reveal a row of red marks, which I had carefully created earlier that day, ignoring the pain as I pricked myself.

The woman next to me gasped and clutched her heart.

"Do something! Save her!" a girl wailed. I recognized Mercy's voice.

"Margaret Lucas, I command you to reveal the specter's name," Stoughton ordered.

I raised a delicate hand to my brow, pantomiming weakness, and made sure everyone could see the red marks on my arm. "She is draining my spirit," I moaned.

Then, with all eyes on me, I went stiff as a board. I shot out an arm, pointing an accusing finger.

"It's *Ann Putnam*!"

Pandemonium broke out in the meeting house. Voices howled and cried. Over it all I could hear Ann wailing her innocence.

I continued to writhe as though tormented by invisible forces, but I snuck another glance at Martha Corey and saw the faintest glimmer of a smile on her lips.

Then across the meeting house I saw Thomas Putnam, Ann's father, shoving people aside as he strode toward me. His face was contorted with rage.

I scrambled back, slamming into the wall behind me.

"What farce is this?" Putnam demanded, turning read. He shoved a finger in my face. "She lies!"

I was cornered, pressed against the wall with no way to escape. A wave of dizziness crashed over me. It felt like my lungs were in a vice. But I couldn't stop now. I moaned, "I see Ann Putnam holding a yellow bird."

Putnam roughly grabbed my shoulders, shaking me as he spoke. "Recant your lies, witch!"

Pain shot through my body and my blood turned to ice. I threw up my arms to protect myself. How far would Putnam go to protect his daughter? She'd sent innocent people to the gallows for him, so surely he wouldn't hesitate at the thought of violence to protect his family.

The meeting house had fallen silent, all eyes trained on us.

Finally, Hathorne pushed his way through the crowd. "Stop right there, Putnam," he commanded.

Thomas Putnam released his grip and I collapsed onto the bench, my terror no longer an act. My shoulders ached where he had held me.

Hathorne stepped between us to block me with his body.

"She's lying," Putnam insisted.

"If she's lying, then Ann Putnam lies, too!" Martha Corey yelled from her corner of the meeting house.

Shouts once again erupted. I kept a wary eye on Thomas Putnam. He stood still, but his eyes flashed with fury.

"The court has agreed to accept spectral evidence," Hathorne reminded Putnam. "Your own friend Cotton Mather recommended that course of action."

Putnam shook his head, his narrow eyes still trained on me. "She's lying," he repeated. "It must be a trick of the Devil."

Stoughton gaveled for attention. "What evidence do you have for that accusation?" he demanded of Putnam with a frown.

Putnam finally turned to Stoughton. I could almost feel the room cool. "Satan is the prince of deception. Everyone knows he can take multiple forms," Putnam said.

Another of Ann's relatives called out from the crowded rows of benches. "That's right. The Devil is pretending to be Ann Putnam to cast doubt on her claims." Murmurs of agreement shot up from the Putnam corner of the meeting house.

"Then Satan must have taken my form to torment Ann Putnam," Martha Corey insisted. "It wasn't me."

Stoughton glared out at the meeting house, the sheer power of his will silencing the Villagers. Then he turned his gaze on Thomas Putnam. "You are on dangerous ground. Such claims threaten to undermine confidence in this court."

"But—"

Stoughton interrupted. "Satan cannot take the form of an innocent person," he declared. "The court has ruled on that matter."

I lifted my head to sneak a glance at the Villagers. A dozen Putnam family members surrounded Ann. Her mother was crying, and one of her uncles was baring his teeth at Stoughton. Thomas Putnam shook with anger. I was glad that Hathorne still stood between us.

Hathorne raised a hand to support Stoughton. "The Chief Justice is correct. Either Margaret Lucas is lying, or Ann Putnam is a witch."

I swallowed hard and dug my fingernails into my palms. I had no idea how Puritans punished liars. It couldn't be good.

But I wouldn't recant.

As terrified as I felt, I knew I was doing the right thing. The rage in Thomas Putnam's eyes was proof that I had rattled the system. I had stopped running from the trials.

I might be a liar, but I wasn't a coward anymore.

"I'm Godly," Ann cried. "And I can prove it!" She leapt to her feet and pushed past her relatives.

My eyes were still wide with shock when she vanished from the meeting house. I'd expected her to fight back, but I thought she'd attack my reputation. Or, even better, take back her lies.

What was Ann doing?

I wasn't the only person who was stunned. Ann's unexpected exit left everyone shaken and uncertain how to proceed. Thomas Putnam gave me one last glare and returned to his wife's side. Hathorne took his place at the front of the meeting house. Even Stoughton looked unsure how to handle his star witness running out of the meeting house. He seemed on the verge of recommencing the trial when Ann burst back into the room, a book clutched under her arm.

"Look!" Ann commanded. But she already had our full attention. She raised the book into the air. "It's the Burning Book!"

A woman at the back of the meeting house fainted.

"The what?" Stoughton demanded, trying in vain to keep order.

"The Burning Book!" Ann marched to the front of the meeting house, the Villagers parting in front of her. No one wanted to get too close to the mysterious book.

Blood pounded in my ears. What was she *thinking*?

Ann reached the front of the room and opened the book. She thrust it in front of Stoughton. "See?" she said, pointing. "This page is about *me*. It lists the names of the witches who've attacked me."

Stoughton leaned over the page. His expression revealed nothing.

A note of pleading entered Ann's voice. "This proves I'm not a witch."

The Chief Justice glanced up and locked eyes with Ann. Her back was to me, but I saw his expression. Terror flashed across his face, as though he'd seen a ghost.

The moment passed so quickly I wondered if I'd imagined it.

A second later Stoughton was scooping up the book and stalking out of the meeting house. "We will reconvene tomorrow," he declared as he reached the door. And then he was gone.

The meeting house was silent for a lingering minute, until every Villager began to speak at once. Hathorne ordered everyone to leave the building. The bailiff asked what to do with Martha Corey. A crowd of Putnams was muttering and glaring in my direction.

And over everything, I heard my name.

Ann Putnam was walking toward me, her jaw clenched. She stopped a few steps in front of me and raised the corners of her mouth into a grin that didn't touch her eyes.

"You'll pay for this."

TWENTY-FIVE

Noise buzzed in my ears.

I didn't stay in the meeting house to see if Thomas Putnam would confront me again. Instead, I slipped out into the Village Square where I was instantly surrounded by Villagers who wanted to ask me about the attack. I pretended to feel faint until they stopped peppering me with questions.

And then I listened to what the Villagers were saying.

Ann's Burning Book had lit a fire in Salem Village. Everyone was talking about it and trying to guess what it might contain. That day, and the next day, and the next, Villagers congregated in the square as if it were church and spent all day praying to the gods of gossip.

Stoughton had vanished back to Boston, presumably taking the book with him. Ann shut herself up in the Putnam house, refusing any visitors. Not a single member of the Putnam clan was spotted in the Village Square.

In their absence, rumors flew.

"I heard the book had hoof marks from the Devil himself," Anna Wilkins whispered to Isaiah Porter.

"It's Satan's yearbook, I guarantee it," Sarah Holton vowed.

"Ann Putnam found the book in a puddle of sulphur," Rebekah Preston claimed. "I saw the pages steaming when Stoughton opened it in the meeting house."

I sat in the Village Square every day, listening to the words of frightened Villagers. The book was evil, all agreed. It was the Devil's own work.

"But, then, how did Ann Putnam get the book?" James Kittel asked. I heard a similar sentiment voiced by others, though not by any Putnams.

Ann thought the book would prove her innocence. But in the Village, it only convinced people that she was guilty.

That's why I'd never expected Ann to reveal the Burning Book. She had to know the book made her look bad. What reason could she possibly give for owning a satanic book that recorded the names of witches?

But Ann couldn't stand someone else becoming the center of attention. I had seen the glint in her eyes when she confronted me in the meeting house. Ann wouldn't let me tarnish her reputation.

She would rather destroy us both.

This time, I refused to run back to my house and shut myself up like Ann had. I made sure to position myself in the square where everyone could see me.

No one cared about the truth in Salem. The girl who ran and hid was guilty. The girl who smiled in public was innocent.

And just as I'd hoped, the Villagers began to fawn over me. Abigail and Mercy posted themselves at my sides and shooed off younger girls who wanted to ask about my affliction. Dr. Griggs offered to examine me to make sure the spectral attacks hadn't caused permanent damage. Mary Sibley whispered in my ear that she knew a protection charm. Even my old teacher Mr. Green asked after my spiritual health.

I was suddenly the most popular person in Salem Village.

And I was now firmly the leader of the Glass Girls. Ann was out, and I was in.

It was intoxicating, sitting on the throne and commanding my adoring followers.

But it wasn't over yet.

The days dragged on and the Village waited. The trials were suspended until Stoughton's return. No one knew when he'd be back, and he hadn't written with any instructions about how to proceed in his absence.

As the Village waited for news from Stoughton, I spent every day in the Village Square with Abigail and Mercy. It was almost like the trials had never happened, except for the dozens of people in jail waiting to learn if they'd be found guilty. Mercy prattled on about eligible men and Abigail insisted that I show her the special way I wore my bonnet.

Neither of them spoke a word about Ann Putnam, except one time when Abigail mentioned her.

"My uncle's working on a big sermon," she told us.

"Isn't he always working on a sermon?" Mercy asked.

"Not like this." Abigail shook her head. "He barely sleeps anymore. He's using up all our candles."

I had only half-listened to their chatter. In the back of my mind, I was daydreaming about Edmund. A few days earlier we'd snuck away and shared our first kiss in the woods.

But then Abigail caught my attention.

"It has something to do with Ann."

"What?" My head jerked up. "Ann Putnam?"

"What other Ann?" Mercy asked.

"There are a lot of Anns in the Village," I pointed out. "Ann's mom is also named Ann."

"Wait, her mom is Ann Putnam, too?"

Abigail rolled her eyes. "You just put that together?"

Mercy frowned. "My mom's name isn't Mercy."

I sighed and spoke to Abigail. "What did Minister Parris say about Ann?"

"He's worried about her soul or something. Last night he kept babbling on about how *the Village has lost its way.*"

I chewed on the inside of my cheek. "Do you think it's about the trials?"

"What else could it be about?"

And then Mercy got distracted by a black cat. I meant to ask Abigail more questions, but we were so busy talking about the schoolhouse, which was set to reopen in two weeks, and about Edmund, and a new bonnet shop in Salem Town.

But Ann was always in the back of my mind.

She had vanished, but I couldn't forget that I had accused Ann Putnam of witchcraft just last week. I'd spent months plotting against her in secret, but now everything was out in the open.

I knew we were enemies. She had to hate me for destroying her reputation. Every time I thought about Ann Putnam, a wave of dizziness flooded me.

I started to wonder if Ann really *was* trying to attack me with magic. She'd already shown an interest in the dark arts and she hated me more than anyone. She'd lost her Burning Book, but that would never stop Ann Putnam.

Hathorne's words in the meeting house rattled through my mind: either I was lying, or Ann was a witch. I tried to put myself in her shoes. We both knew Ann wasn't a witch, so she'd try to prove I was a liar.

How would she attack me? Would it be out in the open, in the middle of the Village Square, or would she send her uncles to steal me away in the middle of the night?

I barely slept wondering what would happen next.

Ann had to be planning something. *But what?*

I tried to shake off my worries about Ann and concentrate on my new status as head of the Glass Girls. So far, my rise had halted the trials. I wanted to keep it that way.

But my position wasn't secure. I had to stay popular with all the afflicted girls, who had stopped accusing new people of witchcraft under my direction, and maintain a good reputation with Minister Parris, Hathorne, and Joseph Porter. I had to be the model Puritan girl for a minister, a supporter of the trials, and an opponent of the trials.

It was exhausting.

And it was a dangerous game.

I realized just how dangerous one afternoon when Joy tried to approach me as I sat with Abigail. I was telling Betty the story of my spectral attack for the hundredth time.

As I finished the tale, Betty looked at me with wide eyes. "You don't think Ann made the whole thing up, do you?" she whispered.

Joy interrupted me before I could respond. I silently cursed the missed opportunity to undermine the trials.

"Cavie?" Joy said, her hands balled at her sides.

"Excuse me?" I said, looking up.

Abigail frowned. "You're bothering us," she said as she waved Joy away.

"Cavie, we need to talk."

Joy was putting everything at risk.

"Why would I talk to you?" I pressed my lips into a thin line. I was walking a narrow path, trying to hold back Parris and Stoughton while protecting myself from the Putnams. I had to treat Joy just like Ann would, or the entire plot could fall apart.

Her open-mouthed hurt expression only stoked my anger. Joy should be smart enough to give me space. "You look like a fish," I told her. I turned back to Abigail.

Joy stood in front of us for an awkward minute and finally left.

"I can't believe Joy Titus talked to you like that," Abigail said.

"I know, right?" I watched Joy's slumped shoulders as she crossed the Village Square. Maybe I could try to pass her a note. But really, she should know better than to approach me in the middle of the Village Square when Abigail was right next to me.

Abigail's eyes lit up. "You don't think *she* might be a witch, do you?"

Betty's head swung up in the direction Joy was heading. "Really?" she squeaked.

A cold sweat broke out on my forehead. Why had Joy put me in this position? I didn't want to accuse her of witchcraft. She was my friend. Or at least, she *had been* my friend before I became popular.

But in Salem Village, anyone could be a suspect. At least a hundred names had been brought up at trial, and nearly a dozen had been executed for witchcraft already.

Plus, I knew the Putnams thought I was a witch. I had to watch every word that came out of my mouth to make sure I wasn't giving them fresh ammunition. If Ann was plotting to get back at me for accusing her, she might try to brand me a witch.

I didn't want to hurt Joy, but I had to protect myself. I

clenched my jaw and wished Joy hadn't been so stupid. "I'm sure she just wanted to ask about the yellow bird," I muttered. "Everyone wants to hear about Ann Putnam's bird."

"Maybe," Abigail said. She bit her lip. "Joy's such a freak."

"Yeah." I frowned as Joy disappeared into the crowd. "She's the worst."

I looked down at my hands, rough from a summer helping my father in the fields. Before I moved to Salem Village, I'd always thought I was a good person. I listened to my mother and father. I studied hard. I tried to do the right thing.

I barely recognized the person I'd become, this stranger who cursed her friend and cared more about popularity than people's lives.

We had been in Salem Village for nine months, enough time for a new life to grow and begin. But instead of building a new life, I had just stolen someone else's.

I had spent months trying to stop Ann Putnam. But instead, had I become her?

TWENTY-SIX

Everything came to a head a week later.

As usual, I was sitting in the Village Square with Mercy and Abigail. We were chatting about fall fashions—a narrower style of bonnet was all the rage and we were planning a trip to Boston to buy some. Weeks had passed since the last trial and I started to believe that the mania had finally faded. Ann was still in hiding and Stoughton hadn't been spotted since Martha Corey's interrupted interrogation.

And then Minister Parris appeared in the Village Square, carrying a worn Bible.

I didn't notice him at first. He positioned himself at one end of the square and drew a crowd immediately. Sermons couldn't wait for Sundays in Salem Village.

Abigail and I exchanged a glance. Could this be the sermon Parris had been working on for weeks? What message did he have for his witch-obsessed congregation?

Mercy scrambled off the wooden bench where we sat. "You have to stand for a sermon," she whispered. Abigail shook her head and we remained sitting.

Before Parris began speaking, I saw a movement from the corner of my eye. I craned my neck and saw Ann Putnam slip outside her front door. I hadn't seen Ann in over three weeks. She wore Puritan black with a white bonnet, and she looked thinner. Unhealthy. Dark circles had formed around the hollows of her eyes.

It didn't seem like she was ready to launch an attack against me. In fact, she looked defeated.

I swallowed at the sight of her, a husk of what she'd once been. Because of me.

Ann stayed on the porch, not drawing any attention to herself. Her eyes were fixed on Parris.

As if Ann's arrival was a signal, Parris began to speak. His voice, loud and clear, rang out through the Village Square.

"My congregation. Today I speak to you as a minister, yes, but also as a resident of Salem Village. I bring you a message— nay, a plea. We must examine ourselves. We must ask who we are. Who *are* we, as church members?"

I glanced back at Ann. She looked so small and meek on that porch. Had my accusation torn her apart?

I shrugged off my guilt. Ann Putnam didn't deserve it.

Parris raised his voice. The charismatic preacher held all eyes. "Make no mistake: we are either saints or devils. Saints or devils. Scripture permits us nothing in between."

Ann shrank back at those words as if they burned.

She had to know that she was no saint.

She'd sent innocent women to their deaths, whether to show her power or to aid her family. Neither motive forgave her sin.

And if she wasn't a saint, that left only one alternative.

But I also felt an uncomfortable itching between my shoulder blades. I'd acted in the best interests of the community,

I told myself. It was true that I relished my newfound popularity, but what did that matter in comparison with the lives I'd saved? Still, Ann's hollow presence was a totem of my guilt.

I had not acted like a saint, either. Did that make me a devil, too?

"For too long, Salem Villagers have turned against one another," Parris continued. "For too long, we have torn each other down rather than hold each other up. That ends today."

"What's he talking about?" Mercy whispered.

Abigail responded. "I don't know." Abigail lived with Minister Parris. And she knew *every* secret. If she was admitting ignorance, it must be serious.

"The Devil has been among us here in Salem Village," Parris declared. I heard a woman gasp in shock. "But the Devil takes many forms. His fuel is deception. Satan lives to turn saints into demons, and we have given him much ammunition."

My hands started shaking. Parris had been an early instigator of the trials, stoking fears of witchcraft in his sermons. He had insisted that Abigail and Betty's strange disease had a supernatural cause. But something had changed.

Was Parris admitting the Villagers were wrong?

"The Devil commands the powers of darkness. His delusions can strike even those of the strongest faith. Was not Anthony plagued in the desert? Was not Christ himself tormented? None among us is completely innocent or blameless. We are all sinners. And as humans, we make errors." He paused, scanning the crowd with his eyes. My own followed. I saw all the town's most prominent families represented: the Porters, Hathorne, and even a few Putnams. "I invite each of you to stand before the community and admit to your errors. *Confess*, so that we can cast off Satan's spell and return to the Godly path."

Silence descended in the square. No one stepped forward.

Then Sarah Holton spoke in a low, shaking voice. "I have spread gossip. I am a sinner."

Joseph Porter called out next. "I took the Lord's name in vain. I am a sinner."

And then Isaiah Wilkins. "I had impure thoughts. I am a sinner."

From there, it was an avalanche of voices, the air ringing with sins.

"I wished ill on my first husband."

"I was disobedient to my father."

"I never returned Goody Putnam's porcelain bowl."

"I celebrated Christmas!"

And then I saw Joy, standing only a few yards away from me. Her head hung low. During a break in the confessions, she spoke in a voice so quiet that I could barely hear it. "I have harbored hatred in my heart."

I screwed my eyes shut. What sins had I committed in Salem? From the beginning, I plotted to destroy Ann Putnam. I stole her friends. I falsely accused her of witchcraft.

My throat was tight.

Abigail rose to her feet. "I tried to predict the future," she confessed. "I knew it was a sin, but I still did it."

Mercy raised her hand, and when no one called on her, she spoke. "My breasts can tell when it's raining!" Everyone turned to stare at her. "Oh, and I said 'breasts' in the Village Square." She sank back onto the bench.

Minister Parris broke in. "We are all sinners. But Satan's attack has gone further in Salem Village. Satan has sent hallucinations. He has used his powers to turn us against each other. The Prince of Air has used false witches to turn neighbor against neighbor."

The Villagers murmured, unsure what to make of Parris's declaration.

Was Parris really saying that there were no witches?

My eyes darted back to Ann. She had turned as white as her bonnet.

Parris eyed the crowd. "Who will confess that their afflictions were sent by Satan, not witches?"

It was so quiet in the square that I could hear the creak of wood coming from the Putnam porch. Ann was trying to sneak back into the door.

"Ann Putnam, stop!" Minister Parris pointed a finger at her. "Stop right there."

"I have nothing to confess," she said, her chin jutting forward.

"Everyone has something to confess." The entire Village watched Ann. Parris lowered his voice to a gravely breath. "Will you confess that your afflictions did not come from witches?"

"I saw their specters!" Ann folded her arms tightly around her waist. "I saw them attack me."

"Those were not specters," Parris said. "That was Satan himself. He wanted to turn you against your neighbors."

The younger Booth sister jumped in. "Minister Parris is right! I thought I saw the specter of Sarah Good, but it was Satan."

Her older sister nodded. "Satan tormented us at Bridget Bishop's trial. It wasn't Bridget at all."

Other afflicted girls who had participated in the trials began to call out that they had been fooled by Satan.

My eyes stayed on Ann. Her mouth opened, but no sound emerged. Suddenly, her shoulders slumped. She looked out at the crowd of Villagers. "I—"

I leaned forward, eager to hear her confession.

But at that moment, young John Wilkins ran up, shouting at Minister Parris. "Stoughton's back! They're all at the gallows!"

Panic gripped my chest. Ann was forgotten in the chaos that followed John's words. Villagers began to run toward the gallows, led by Parris. The minister rallied the Villagers, shouting, "Satan won't win today!"

When I looked back at the Putnam porch, Ann had vanished.

I leapt to my feet and followed the crowd to the gallows.

When I burst into the clearing where the summer's executions had taken place, a sob choked my throat.

The gallows were not empty.

Instead, eight women trembled on the platform, nooses already around their necks. Next to them, Stoughton stood with the glimmer of a smile on his face. Three strong men stood beside him.

"Stoughton, this must stop!" Minister Parris stood at the base of the gallows. "Salem Village will kill no more witches!"

"Have you forgotten your Bible, Parris? Exodus 22:18. *'Thou shalt not suffer a witch to live.'*"

"Satan has been active in Salem Village, Stoughton, I grant you that. But the afflicted girls have recanted their testimony. There is no reason to continue these needless executions."

Stoughton frowned. He stepped closer to the woman shaking at the end of the gallows. Her name was Alice Parker. Her trial had been so quick that I had missed it.

"This woman was convicted by a jury. She is guilty of witchcraft, a capital offense. Are you saying we should simply *let her go?*"

Parris raised a hand. "Stoughton, juries are not always correct. I have prayed on this for weeks and God had shown me the error of our ways. We cannot continue this witch hunt."

Stoughton's eyes flickered away from Parris. He gave a nod to the men standing beside him, who stepped forward. In an instant, before anyone could object, his men had shoved three women off the platform. The women did not even have time to cry out before their necks had snapped.

A cry went up from the crowd of Villagers standing before the gallows. A few people were sobbing. In truth, I could be counted among their number.

"These witches cannot be allowed to live," Stoughton proclaimed. A second nod sent his men to execute the next three convicted witches before anyone could intervene. And suddenly six bodies swung from the gallows, their ropes emitting eerie noises as they twisted and pulled. None had survived the drop.

Shock froze my feet in place. Six women had just perished before my eyes, in a flash. Some combination of lies, self-interest, and puritanical fever had led us to this field, to witness these executions that might be lawful, but were certainly unjust.

The last two women standing were Martha Corey and Mary Eastey. Before Stoughton could order their deaths, Mary cried out. "I am innocent, I swear it! I am innocent, just as my sister Rebecca Nurse was innocent!"

Mary began to recite the Lord's Prayer. Her voice shook, but the words rang out across the clearing.

A chill came over the field. In the moment of silence after Mary's recitation, Minister Parris spoke. His voice was low, but it carried a hint of warning. "A witch cannot speak the Lord's Prayer, Stoughton. We all know that's true. This woman is *innocent*. Satan has led us down a dangerous path, but these

Villagers renounce his influence."

The crowd rustled with assent.

"You all believe Mary Eastey is innocent?" Stoughton turned his glare on the Villagers. "You do not trust the court to render a just verdict?"

Joseph Porter stepped forward. "She is innocent," he said. A dozen voices rose to call out their agreement.

Stoughton shook his head, his eyes narrowing. "Then you are all guilty, too." He leaned over and shoved Mary Eastey off the platform.

I screwed my eyes closed. I couldn't watch.

My conscience was heavy with guilt. I hadn't stopped Ann Putnam at the beginning, when it might have made a difference. I should have done more. Instead, the mania for hunting witches had infected Salem Village. And Stoughton was still feeding off that mania.

When I opened my eyes, I saw Martha Corey, standing alone on the platform. Her face was tilted up toward the sky, where she could not see the seven dead bodies that surrounded her on the gallows.

Her lips were moving, but no sound came from her mouth.

"Stop!" I called out without thinking. But once I began to speak, I found that I couldn't stop. "This is madness! Justice Stoughton, you will surely be judged harshly for your actions this day." I pushed through the Villagers until I stood in front of the scaffold. I turned my back on the gallows and addressed my neighbors. "I have a confession to make. I lied. I did not see Ann Putnam's specter. I lied to *stop* these executions. I hoped that if you doubted Ann, you might doubt the entire witch hunt."

My eyes scanned the crowd and landed on one person. Ann.

She'd followed us after all.

I blinked back tears. I had been too late to help the seven bodies swinging from the gallows, but maybe we could save Martha. Maybe there was still a small chance for redemption. "I'm sorry, Ann." My voice cracked. "I shouldn't have lied. But you have to stop this. Tell Stoughton that you made it up. Tell him that Martha Corey is innocent."

The Villagers standing near Ann stepped back, as if she carried a stench. Ann's lips were pressed together in a grimace.

Stoughton turned his icy glare on Ann. "Is this true, Miss Putnam? Did you *lie* to a court of law?"

Ann's eyes darted around and her mouth hung open. I could sense her rising terror, like a cornered animal.

Stoughton did not wait for her to speak. "That is a serious crime, Miss Putnam. You could easily find yourself on these very gallows if you lied."

Ann closed her mouth.

No, no, I thought, *backing her into a corner will never work.* Ann couldn't stand to lose face in front of her entire social world.

I balled my fists so tight that my nails dug into my palms. I stepped forward, blocking Ann's view of Stoughton. I kept my voice low. "Ann, you cannot let anyone else die. You *know* Martha Corey is innocent. Her death will be on your conscience."

Ann's face contorted, guilt mixing with anxiety and shame. She looked at Mercy and Abigail, standing together, and then back at me.

I tasted the tang of blood in my mouth again—Ann had to stop this, *now.*

"I . . ." Ann's voice quivered. "I lied." Her eyes dropped to the ground and I could see her shoulders shaking. "No one attacked me. I made the whole thing up."

Stoughton snorted. "This is pointless. Martha Corey is a witch." And as casually as if he was pushing open a door, he shoved Martha off the ledge.

"No!" I howled as I ran forward. I caught Martha's legs and tried to lift her. I tried to save her. But I felt her go slack as life left her body.

I stumbled back. My vision flashed black and my entire body boiled with rage. I spun toward Stoughton, ready to leap onto the platform to attack him. He deserved to feel the pain he had inflicted on so many innocent women. He tried to hang the courtroom around his shoulders like a protective cloak, but there was no justice in his executions.

But Minister Parris's voice stopped me in place. "You were Satan's instrument," Minister Parris told Stoughton. The words came out in a deep rumble. "Just as all of us fell for his delusions."

Stoughton shook his head. He looked at the bodies hanging around him and took a step back. "No. Those women were witches. They were all guilty." His eyes flashed with anger and he gestured to one of his men. "I can prove they were guilty."

The man handed Stoughton a thick book. I recognized it right away.

"This book proves that the witches were real." Stoughton flipped open the pages. "Right here, it says that Rebecca Nurse turned into a cat and tormented her neighbors." He flipped to another page. "It says that George Burroughs was leader of the witches. It says that Martha Corey pinched innocent girls."

"It's all lies," Ann said, her voice cracking. "I wrote the book, not Satan."

Stoughton recoiled and almost dropped the Burning Book, as if it had turned hot in his hand. "No. You're lying. Cotton

Mather warned us that Satan would take many forms." His eyes darted erratically, seeking allies in the crowd. "Ann Putnam must be a witch!"

But the Villagers had no appetite for Stoughton's claim. All around us men shook their heads. They might have believed his accusation a few week earlier, but not today.

The Villagers had chosen sides, and they did not stand with Stoughton.

The Chief Justice must have sensed the change. His face turned ashen and he quickly checked that his men were still standing beside him. He spared a single glance for the hanging bodies before turning his attention back to the Villagers. "Everyone in Boston is right. Salem Village is surely cursed." He shook his head and hurried from the scaffold to leap on his horse. "The governor will hear of this," Stoughton vowed as he kicked his mount.

The Villagers began to whisper to each other. The sounds grew louder until Minister Parris mounted the scaffold.

"Neighbors," he called out. "We must bury our dead."

No one had saved these eight victims from Stoughton's fury, but we could at least give them a proper burial. A dozen men stepped forward to lower the bodies from their ropes.

I turned away. I couldn't stand to watch them, wondering if I could have saved them.

Abigail and Mercy stood nearby but they kept their backs turned to me.

"I can't believe Ann confessed."

"She didn't write the Burning Book alone."

"Are we going to be in trouble?"

"Only if we stay here too long."

Without speaking a word to me, they vanished into the

woods.

I searched the crowd for Ann, but she was gone.

TWENTY-SEVEN

The witch craze had claimed its last victims in Salem.

I didn't stay to watch them bury Martha Corey and the others. I couldn't stand the looks Villagers cast my way, as if they were trying to decide whether I was a saint or a devil.

So I ran home and buried myself under a pile of blankets. My thoughts raced. I had managed to stop the trials, but not before they'd taken nineteen victims.

What if I had accused Ann earlier?

What if I had realized sooner that Minister Parris was turning against the trials?

What if I had stood up in court for Sarah Good, and Bridget Bishop, and Rebecca Nurse, and Martha Corey?

I had come to Salem Village hoping to make friends. I never expected it would be so deadly.

I groaned when I thought of Joy Titus and the way I'd rejected her the last time we'd spoken. She had been my friend, the only person I could trust, and then I discarded her just like Ann had years earlier.

Joy must hate me.

How could I make up for all the harm that I'd done?

I stayed in bed until the next day. I just didn't have the energy to face my parents, or the Villagers, or the Glass Girls. Another day passed. I barely picked at the soup my mom set next to my bed.

And then, on the third day, my mom knocked on my door. "Cavie? Someone is here to see you."

Who could it be? Abigail and Mercy had acted like I didn't exist after the showdown with Stoughton. Joy wouldn't visit. And I couldn't picture Ann walking all the way out to my house. "Tell whoever it is to go away."

"I don't think that's a good idea."

I threw off the blankets and stomped downstairs.

My eyes widened when I saw Ann Putnam standing in our doorway.

Her cheeks weren't hollow any more. Her skin glowed and the circles under her eyes had vanished. And her signature vanity, her long blonde mane, was back to its former fierceness. It was like looking at a portrait painted six months ago.

I blinked. This was the Ann Putnam who had ruled Salem Village when I arrived last year.

"You look beautiful." It just slipped out.

"Don't act so surprised. You almost killed me with that ridiculous raw wheat diet."

"I'm sorry about that."

Once my mind wrapped itself around her appearance, I wondered why Ann Putnam would possibly visit me. Was she here to make good on her promise to ruin me? Had she hidden a mob in the trees across the road, ready to haul me off to jail at her signal? Or would she attack me herself?

Her green eyes held no clues about her intentions.

She raised an eyebrow in a move so familiar that it made me shiver. "You know what? I sort of wish you'd never moved to Salem Village."

Was she serious?

"Me, too," I shot back.

A guilty look flashed across her face. That knocked me off balance. Ann Putnam never looked guilty. "I just mean, you showed up looking all *perfect* with your stories about London and Paris . . . And Edmund always liked you, even when I was his *girlfriend* he kept talking about you. I just . . ." She trailed off.

My eyes widened. Was Ann Putnam jealous of *me*? That made no sense. From the minute I'd met the Glass Girls, she'd laughed at how I dressed and my bracelet and . . . And she'd fallen apart when she found out I liked Edmund. And also when everyone paid attention to Abigail during her illness.

She hadn't just faked the witch attacks for attention. She invented the whole thing so that people would like her. And look what happened—once she started accusing people, all the adults in the Village fell over themselves to protect her.

I shook my head. Ann was guilty, of course she was, but she'd also been a pawn. Hadn't she accused Rebecca Nurse to please her father? He'd jumped at the chance to enrich himself by seizing the innocent woman's lands. Minister Parris wrote sermons based on Ann's tales. And Stoughton treated her like his star witness for months, defending her and sheltering her.

They all saw what they wanted to see when they looked at Ann Putnam. She knew how to be all things to all people. They believed her because they *wanted* to believe Salem was assaulted by witches.

Fear, self-interest. It all ended in the same place.

And now she stood before me, a glimmer of worry in her

eyes. "Anyway," she continued. "I just wanted to say . . . I'm sorry, or whatever."

It wouldn't bring them back. But it was something.

~ ~ ~

And that was the end of the witch trials.

Stoughton's court was disbanded and he never set foot in the Village again. He was too busy as lieutenant governor. Apparently his turn as an executioner hadn't hurt his political prospects. I heard from Joy that Minister Parris wrote to the governor about Stoughton's behavior, but apparently only accused witches paid the price in the Massachusetts Bay Colony.

Parris wasn't the only one who atoned for the Village's sins. A group of jurors wrote a letter to the governor apologizing for the court's "errors." They mainly blamed Satan for leading them off the Godly path. I couldn't tell if they were trying to alleviate their guilt or if they were truly remorseful.

Minister Parris and Joseph Porter led the efforts to release all the imprisoned women from jail. Some had been found guilty but missed the noose by chance. Others were still awaiting their trials, which thankfully would never come.

I was there on the day they released Dorcas Good, Sarah's four year old daughter. Her mother was dead, and her father had accused her mother of witchcraft. I heard young Dorcas was being shipped off to live with relatives somewhere. As I watched her wide-eyed expression, I wondered if she could ever live an ordinary life.

Or if *any* of us would ever feel normal again.

There were a lot of people in Salem Village who *should* feel guilty. In a community of six hundred souls, nearly two hundred had been accused of witchcraft. Fifty had confessed to making pacts with the Devil. Ann might have been the catalyst, but the Villagers were happy to go along on the witch hunt.

What dark part of human nature had made it so easy to execute our neighbors? Our petty grievances, our selfish desires, clouded our reason.

And I shared that guilt. I had seen Ann for what she was, and yet I'd allowed myself to *become* her. I had felt the tug of popularity, the way it made everything seem brighter. I knew why Ann had gotten caught up in her lies, because I'd felt the rush when I accused her of witchcraft.

I never wanted to feel that way again.

It was also the end of the Glass Girls.

Ann and I never talked again about what had happened. But when she reappeared in the Village Square later that fall, she had transformed. Her blonde hair was tucked under her bonnet and she kept her head down. She didn't whisper about people as they walked past. Instead of surrounding herself with Abigail and Mercy, she was usually by herself, or walking with girls that she'd declared terminally unpopular a year ago.

And she never pulled off her bonnet whenever the adults weren't watching.

Abigail and Mercy didn't seem to be friends anymore, either. Abigail started hanging out with the godly kids, who usually congregated outside the church. With her eyes screwed shut as prayers tickled her lips, she looked completely different from the striving, insecure girl she'd been when I moved to Salem Village.

And Mercy married some farmer from Ipswich. He had a side business making coffins.

Joy and I made up, too. That was harder. One warm afternoon in early October, I think it was October third, I made the long walk to her house. She was sitting outside, and when she first saw me, a sneer passed across her face.

I'd treated her almost as badly as Ann had, and that guilt gnawed at me.

"Joy—" The words caught in my throat. "I was terrible. I'm sorry. Can you forgive me?"

She rolled her eyes as a huge grin broke across her face. "Well, you *did* destroy the Glass Girls. So I can get over it."

I couldn't stop myself from laughing.

Somehow, sitting in the shady glen with Joy, watching the leaves burn in shades of yellow, orange, and red, I felt better.

Still, I would never forget what Salem Village had done—or the part I'd played in the witch hunt.

It would take the Village a long time to heal. If it ever did.

But I wasn't going to be around to watch. My dad decided that farm life wasn't for him, and I convinced him that we should move back to London. Back to civilization.

It meant I had to break up with Edmund, but let's be honest—I was never meant to be a farmer's wife.

And when I told Joy I was moving back to London, she grinned and pulled off her bonnet. "Can I come with you?"

Of course I said yes.

The End

AUTHOR'S NOTE

Salem witch trials meets *Mean Girls*—the idea first hit me when I was teaching a college class on the history of witch trials. The story of Salem, dominated by young women accusing their neighbors of witchcraft, sounded like a high school drama. My students kept asking why the afflicted girls sent so many people to the gallows. Was it temporary insanity? A psychedelic poison? No, I tried to explain, it was something even darker—human nature.

One day, I jumped to using *Mean Girls*—everyone can understand the craving for popularity, right? And it clicked. Peer pressure. Conformity. The anxiety of the moment before adulthood. Suddenly, Ann Putnam's behavior didn't seem so old and dusty.

With time, I saw more and more connections between Salem and *Mean Girls*, from the group mentality of the afflicted girls to Ann Putnam's mother horning in to claim *she* was also afflicted.

The two seemed to melt together in my mind, the perfect marriage between history and pop culture.

And thus, *Salem Mean Girls* was born.

You're probably wondering what's real and what's fictional in this story. First—almost all of the history is true, even though I took some liberties with the language. I added quotes from the trial records, incorporated theories from leading scholars on witchcraft, and blended it into this fictional retelling.

In order to tell the story, I invented Cavie Lucas and Joy Titus, along with Cavie's parents and Edmund Hale. Everyone else in *Salem Mean Girls* lived—or died—in Salem Village.

All of the Glass Girls were prominent figures in the trials. Ann Putnam was the star witness in the trials, and Abigail Williams and Mercy Lewis also testified that their neighbors were witches. I did change a few details, including their ages. Ann Putnam was only thirteen when she accused over sixty people of witchcraft. Abigail Williams was twelve. Mercy Lewis was closer to sixteen, though her exact age is unknown. The pressures of conforming with Puritan society, especially for women, were felt at a very young age in colonial America.

Among the Villagers, Minister Parris did stoke the flames of panic by preaching that the Devil walked through the village, and men like Hathorne did take up the call to eliminate the witches. The disputes described between the Putnams and Porters, including the many problems of Salem's ministers, did create rifts in the village community and made Salem notorious for its quarreling. And Stoughton was the Chief Justice of the trials as well as the lieutenant governor of the Massachusetts Bay Colony, though in reality he didn't personally execute anyone (as far as we know).

My retelling of the accused witches' examinations and trials sticks closely to historical documents about the Salem witch trials. Dialogue from Tituba's examination, as well as those of Sarah Good, Bridget Bishop, Rebecca Nurse, and others, comes straight from the court record—updated, in some cases, to clarify the language. Some of the more dramatic moments in the trial—when an afflicted girl accidentally dropped the knife piece she'd used to cut her own arm, and when Stoughton ordered a jury to reconsider their verdict against Rebecca Nurse—actually did occur during the trials in 1692.

The accused witches named in *Salem Mean Girls* were all executed in Salem, along with a number of others. Nineteen in total were executed, and another, Giles Corey (husband to Martha Corey) was pressed to death with stones for refusing to stand trial. Four others died in prison. Eventually over forty people in Salem claimed to be under attack by demonic forces, and they accused nearly two hundred people of being witches. The trials grew so out of control that the afflicted eventually accused the governor's own wife of witchcraft.

As dramatic as the Salem witch trials were, they were one of the smaller trials in the movement to execute witches that swept through Europe and its colonies, peaking in the late sixteenth and early seventeenth centuries. Historians estimate that as many as 200,000 people were accused of witchcraft, and half of that number were executed. The majority of accused witches were women—around 75%—though thousands of men were killed for the crime of witchcraft as well.

Why were witches almost always women? In England and its colonies, over 90% of executed witches were women. Men across Europe agreed that women were the weaker sex—and that made them vulnerable to demonic seduction. Women couldn't resist Satan's charms, and sold their souls for a pittance of power. In truth, witches were people who didn't conform to societal rules. Older women, unmarried women, or childless women were socially dangerous because they were not under patriarchal authority. Women who cursed or complained, drawing unwanted attention, might find themselves branded witches.

Europeans executed women who frightened them. Women who resisted power structures. Women who claimed their own powers, sometimes magical, sometimes not. And women who persisted in the face of warnings. A witch trial was a disciplining mechanism. It was a warning to follow society's rules, or face the ultimate penalty. And tens of thousands of women were executed for a crime that does not exist.

Why did Europeans believe witchcraft was real? Well—you don't have to believe in magic to believe in witches. Witchcraft was defined as a religious crime: the sin was making a pact with the Devil, even if the accused witch never caused harm. The accused were often tortured until they confessed to maniacal dancing orgies, cross-trampling parties, roasting babies, and other fantastical crimes. And even in places where torture wasn't used—Salem, for example—the conditions of being imprisoned for months with little hope of release could easily drive people to confession. Tituba, for example, did voluntarily confess (her conversation with Minister Parris, represented here, is fictional), whether because of social pressures or fear.

In a time of turmoil and upheaval, it was all too easy to believe that society was under attack by dark forces. During the witch trials, Europe was experiencing famines, wars, religious upheaval, and devastating plagues. Blaming witches was a coping mechanism.

Salem was one of the last major witch trials, decades after England and France had nearly halted witch trials. But Salem followed a recognizable pattern in large-scale witch hunts. The first accused witches most strongly matched the stereotypes:

older, female, unmarried or widowed, and "socially disruptive." But as trials snowballed, they pulled in people who didn't fit the witch stereotype, like Rebecca Nurse and George Burroughs. At this point, most witch crazes collapsed as people began to doubt the accusations. In *Salem Mean Girls*, Ann Putnam is probably the last person anyone would accuse of witchcraft: a seemingly model Puritan, the perfect daughter, and popular. Cavie was right, then, that accusing Ann might unravel the entire witch craze.

In seventeenth-century Salem, the hysteria died down nearly as fast as it began, and less than a year after the last execution many of the jurors publicly apologized for the error of believing witches were attacking their community. During the high anxiety of 1692, when Puritans feared their community would crumble, it had been plausible for residents of Salem to believe that the Devil was assaulting their village. The jurors thought God was testing them, and the only response was to exterminate the witches. This dangerous combination of hysteria and righteousness cost many lives.

It ruined others, too. Ann Putnam never recovered from her guilt. After her parents died in 1699, Ann devoted her life to raising her eight younger siblings. She never married. In 1706, she publicly apologized for her role in the trials, proclaiming, "I desire to lie in the dust, and earnestly beg forgiveness of God."

She also said she was a deluded by Satan.

Salem Mean Girls, like the witch trials and the movie *Mean Girls*, is a story of how easily people fall into a mob mentality, and how easily we can lose our humanity. It is also a story of how people justify their cruel choices, transforming themselves into victims instead of villains in their own minds.

These stories also remind us of the dangers of social

expectations and the pressure to conform. The witch trials might be a thing of the past, but today we still struggle with the need to fit in, and the urge to blame someone else for our problems. Searching for a scapegoat is easier than facing our misfortunes.

Today, just like in seventeenth-century Salem, it is too easy to demonize our enemies—and become demons ourselves. The solution is the simplest thing, and also incredibly challenging: empathy.

ACKNOWLEDGEMENTS

Thank you for reading *Salem Mean Girls*. I started this book in 2013, so it is an amazing privilege to finally share it with readers. Special thanks to my support system—Emma Prince, Mama Prince, and Mr. Sylvia Prince—and to the students in my witchcraft classes (you know who you are!).

And thank you in advance to all the readers willing to share their opinions by writing a review—reviews from people like you help other readers find *Salem Mean Girls*.

For more, visit http://www.sylviaprincebooks.com

email: SylviaPrinceBooks@gmail.com
Twitter: @SPrinceBooks
Facebook: facebook.com/SylviaPrinceBooks

ALSO BY SYLVIA PRINCE

THE LION AND THE FOX

When a mysterious letter sends Niccolo Machiavelli to investigate the murder of a Medici, he stumbles into a dangerous world of rich young patricians, mysterious prostitutes, and shocking violence. Niccolo thinks he can play the fox to outwit his enemies—but has he underestimated the lion?

THE ZORZI AFFAIR

In the rich world of Renaissance Venice, daughters are valuable commodities. But Zaneta Lucia refuses to be bartered away in the marriage market. Instead, she flees to Padua disguised as a boy so that she can study science. Her new life seems perfect—but it can't last forever.

PALAZZO GALILEO MYSTERIES

Can you trust your senses?
When your landlord is Galileo, you should question everything.

A MATTER OF GLASS
(Book One of the Palazzo Galileo Mysteries)

When Paolo Serravalle travels to Venice to pick up a mysterious package for his landlord Galileo, he quickly realizes that the man harbors dark secrets. Is it really worth risking his life just for a discount on rent?

COMING SOON

STOLEN CROWN TRILOGY

Can Caterina de Medici unravel the secret behind her mysterious Highland guard before it destroys them both?

A BLOOD-RED SEAL
(Book Two of the Palazzo Galileo Mysteries)

The scrappy stableboy isn't what he seems—and neither is the beautiful woman who chased off papal assassins in Venice. Paolo unravels the mystery of Fonso and Rosa in Book 2 of the Palazzo Galileo Mysteries.

ABOUT THE AUTHOR

Sylvia Prince writes intense, page-turning novels that bring the past to life. She specializes in historical fiction and young adult. Sylvia holds a PhD in history—and loves the bizarre but true stories she has encountered over the years working as a historian. Did you know, for example, that in 1492 the pope received a blood transfusion by literally drinking the blood of three young boys? (It didn't work—the pope and the boys all died.) Sylvia lives in the Pacific Northwest with her husband and two daughters. She and her sister, bestselling author of historical romance Emma Prince, love comparing notes and picking each other's brains about all things historical.

For more, and to sign up for Sylvia Prince's newsletter, visit http://www.sylviaprincebooks.com.

email: SylviaPrinceBooks@gmail.com
Twitter: @SPrinceBooks
Facebook: facebook.com/SylviaPrinceBooks

Made in the USA
Monee, IL
13 November 2019

16735594R00185